Under a

Shifter's
Moon

Under a
Shifter's Moon

Kari Thomas

Black Lyon Publishing, LLC

UNDER A SHIFTER'S MOON
Copyright © 2009 by KARI THOMAS

Our books may be ordered through your local bookstore or by visiting the publisher:

www.BlackLyonPublishing.com

Black Lyon Publishing, LLC
PO Box 567
Baker City, OR 97814

This is a work of fiction. All of the characters, names, events, organizations and conversations in this novel are either the products of the author's vivid imagination or are used in a fictitious way for the purposes of this story.

ISBN-10:   1-934912-21-2
ISBN-13:   978-1-934912-21-8
Library of Congress Control Number: 2009936058

Written, published and printed in
the United States of America.

Black Lyon Paranormal Romance

To LoAnna Janz and Mary Corrales who fell in love with Kitlene and Lyon as much as I did, and kept pushing me to write their story. Also, to my support team: Teresa Berg, Amanda Peters, and Callie Seifert; you're the best!
And to Dad, as always, for being so proud of my books!

Chapter One

"*W*hy the hell do we have to do this again?"

Lyon Savage stared down his best friend, Mason Trent. "We keep at it until one of us either kills the other or one concedes."

Mason snorted. "He's not going to concede."

Lyon shrugged, keeping his tone even. "There're only two choices."

"You're one cold bastard, my friend," Mason told him. "Even if you're supposed to be the good twin."

Lyon frowned at him. He was getting tired of hearing that expression every time someone spoke about him or his brother, Bryce. They differed in many ways, especially in the way they conducted their business and personal lives, but it didn't necessarily mean that one was the good guy and the other was the bad. Hell, he'd been accused of being a cold bastard more times than he could remember. His people and associates readily acknowledged his take-no-prisoners personality was sometimes harsh and when necessary—deadly. But he was fair, and no one could accuse him of being unnecessarily ruthless. As for him and Bryce, they just had different ways of handling things. And they couldn't agree on certain issues.

Like which of them would rule as Alpha over their divided Jaguar Clans.

Or … which side of the preternatural world they should join once they finally became a unified Pride.

Born Alpha meant you ruled, no matter the situation. But being born twin Alphas meant that one would have to eventually back down and let the other be sole ruler. Yet, Alphas never backed down. Therein lay the problem. Lyon and Bryce had ruled side by side since the death of their elderly father but their reign had been full of strife and competition between them. Half the Clan members followed Lyon, the other half followed Bryce. A divided Pride was a dangerous state of affairs. It left them vulnerable, easy prey to enemies.

And Lyon knew those enemies were just waiting, silent and ominous, to strike at the first sign of complete weakness. What the hell was Bryce thinking, wanting to join with the other races rebelling against the human populace? Shifters and other preternatural beings had lived with humans since the beginning of time. Why should now be any different?

Because a Battle was coming. Rumors among Shifters of all races, and other Beings, hinted that something was stirring among the supernatural world - something that wouldn't tolerate humans being the dominant race much longer. Bryce insisted that the Jaguar Clans should follow the other Cat Shifter races that were joining the side preparing for an eventual war.

That was the main conflict between the two brothers. Bryce wanted his Shifters to be part of a unified force—"us against them"—joining with others he considered more powerful and who believed the humans shouldn't be the dominant race. Lyon wanted his people to stay neutral, their Pride a unified race, remaining primal and free. Like they had always been. He saw the need for the Clan to be amalgamated and strong, but there was no need for any dominance in the human world. He enjoyed living in the human world. There were times when his jaguar counterpart demanded the open freedom of the wild, but living alongside humans, being a part of their world, was a necessity for Shifters whose species were getting smaller and smaller. Interacting with humans, even marrying them, was the only way they could survive extinction. He didn't have to like the idea that his people depended on the human world that much, especially when Shifters married humans and weakened the bloodlines, but he accepted the reality of it.

His nightclub Primal Beat, in the deepest part of downtown Los Angeles, was his Clan's main income source. It was a large two-story building, and a popular spot for both humans and Otherworldly Beings. Bryce ran the ranch compound, outside L.A. city limits, but the property wasn't as productive. The jaguar Shifters who followed him lived on the one thousand acre set-up, but the ones who followed Lyon lived in the city. Lyon, Mason, and

Mason's nephew Caleb, lived with a few security-bodyguards at the nightclub. The top second floor had been converted into private living arrangements and each man had his own suite.

Lyon and Mason exited the back entrance of the club and got in Lyon's Jaguar parked just a few feet from the exit doors. He'd been ribbed enough about the sports car bearing the jaguar emblem, but he didn't care. He liked the sleek, smooth driving car, relished the "fast freedom on wheels" power under him. When things got too claustrophobic in his life, he took the car out for long hours of fast driving just to help clear his mind and his never-ending conflicting thoughts about the unsteady state of the Pride. It was one of the rare times he actually felt at peace. The only other time was when he ran free as a jaguar.

Mason grumbled about not taking his jeep. "Bryce's lazy Shifters haven't repaired that dirt road after all the rains," he muttered a little louder. "You're going to regret taking this show-off can of metal."

Lyon smiled for the first time that morning. "You're just jealous because I found it ironic enough –first –to buy a Jaguar."

"Ha ha. Then don't start cussing up a blue streak when your tires hit the first rut in the road."

 Lyon shook his head. Okay, so he was well known for his foul temper and just-as-bad language. He grinned again. And they called him the 'good' twin!

Mason grinned back, but quickly sobered. "Do you think this is going to be another meeting where nothing gets decided, or is it possible Bryce is ready to concede?"

Lyon mulled over the chances. His brother had ulterior motives, he was sure of it. His plans didn't center on anything more than gaining complete control as Alpha. If circumstances made him ruler of the Pride, then he wouldn't stop there. He was going to lead the Jaguars straight into a war. Lyon couldn't allow that to happen.

"Whatever happens today," he said, hearing the final truth in his own words, "I'm going to have to make a decision. Bryce and I are going to have to accept the only way to settle this is to do it the old fashion way."

He glanced at Mason and saw him nod his head.

He would have to fight his brother for the position of reigning Alpha. Fight him to the death.

He didn't want to kill his brother. But it was their way, their Law. The two divided Clans needed unification under one Alpha. Primal rage surfaced for one brief moment just thinking about the inevitable Challenge, and Lyon relished the hot surging emotion. He sure as hell wasn't going to be the one defeated. This was his birthright, his people. He had ruthlessly protected the Clan, keeping them safe from discovery in a human world, making the rules up when necessary, and even killing when he had to. He'd be damned if he'd allow his brother to lead them to their extinction in a needless war. He'd fight that alternative with his last dying breath.

An hour later Lyon drove up the long winding driveway of the main ranch house and stopped in front of the wide set of entry steps. He automatically scanned the area and then around the main house, his instincts always on alert whenever he was in his brother's territory. It didn't pay to be off guard around a Shifter who was in every aspect your potential enemy for the time being.

He noted the three-story ranch house was showing its age. The whitewashed wood boards were fading with several spots needing repairs. The paint was dull and cracking in noticeable places. If he didn't know that the interior was dressed up like a palatial castle, he'd wonder at his brother's lack of attention. Bryce liked his comforts, but he made extra effort to hide that fact from the outside world.

Lyon glanced at the row of vehicles parked off to the side of the house. There were more Shifters here today than the norm. The hair on the back of his neck rose. Damn. What was his brother up to now? Had he talked more of the clan members into joining him? Lyon wasn't aware of the desertion of some of his own men, but lately things had been so unsettled, the inner battle between the divided group constantly tense, he didn't doubt the possibility. An edgy sensation settled in the pit of his stomach. Not good. The clan members had the choice of which Alpha to follow, but the idea that some of his people would go behind his back and join his brother ignited the slowly simmering jaguar fury that was always present deep inside him. He growled under his breath. If there were deserters, he'd deal with them. The only way an Alpha would.

He and Mason got out of the car, made a quick scan of the area one more time and then casually climbed the outside entry stairs. Mason pushed open the wide, unlocked doors and they slowly entered the large foyer, finding it empty. From there they walked directly to the huge circular meeting room in the back of the house. The shouting coming from the room could be heard all the way down the long hall. Bryce had obviously started his "join me" speech early.

When Lyon entered the chaos immediately stopped. Dead silence reigned. He carefully, deliberately looked around the room and met each man's gaze, one at a time. He recognized some of them from his own group. As soon as his hard stare landed on them they respectfully lowered their own gazes. No one met an Alpha's direct stare when he demanded complete attention and subservience. Behind him, he heard Mason choke on a covered-up snicker. It almost made him forget his ire and grin. He really needed to talk to him about respect. Sometimes his friend forgot his place.

Bryce Savage slowly stood up from his chair at the head of the long table. As twins, both men had the same six-two, hard-muscled body frames. Bryce was more bulky than Lyon because of his lifestyle as a rancher. Lyon's jaguar counterpart was very apparent in the sleek, sensual flow of his toned muscles, his body a contradictory combination of grace and restrained power.

Though twins, the brothers weren't identical. Bryce's light tawny hair was cut short, the lion's mane texture spiky and thick. Lyon wore his thick hair longer, shoulder length. The darker tawny color was naturally streaked with black strands and more resembled the unique color of a jaguar's gold and black Rosetta-patterned fur.

Bryce's large, round cat eyes were a pale shade of turquoise, always gleaming with some inner rage that never seem to dissipate no matter the circumstances. Lyon's turquoise eyes were narrower, darker in intensity and brilliance. His roughly chiseled handsome face closely resembled his brother's, but Bryce's features were sharper, almost harsh.

The shared genes were the only similarity between the two men and Bryce used every opportunity to make that known.

"You're late, brother," he stated.

Lyon stared at him and purposely let the moments tick by. It was a constant show of dominance between them, and lately he had to force himself to keep his jaguar self under control instead of doing what he instinctively wanted to do. The time to challenge Bryce wasn't right. Not here. Not yet.

"I took the time to look over the ranch on the way in," Lyon drawled. "It needs upkeep, Bryce. Especially the road."

Bryce growled low at the intended admonishment. "The road doesn't have to be so accessible. Keeps unwelcome guests out."

A cough from the other end of the long table interrupted before Lyon could respond. He looked at the three Elders sitting at one end, their expressions stern. That bad feeling sitting in his gut clenched his insides into a knot again. *What the hell are they doing here?*

The divided Jaguar pack had three Elders whose sole purpose was to make sure the clan members obeyed the Pride Law to its fullest. Each generation of jaguar and every Pride were guided by a Chosen Three. The Alpha's word was always the final say, but no one was allowed to go against the Elder's decision should one of them decide to interfere in any situation. They rarely interfered, were seldom present in any meeting, and to have them here now when things were starting to heat up between the two Alphas, wasn't a good sign. Lyon glanced at his brother. Had Bryce brought them into this, hoping they would be swayed to declare him the reigning Alpha? *Think again, brother.*

One of the Elders spoke, his voice raspy with age. "Sit down, Alpha Lyon. There is much to decide here today."

Lyon's dominant nature rebelled at the command but he respectfully nodded his head and moved to the position at the opposite end of the table. He sat down and casually leaned back in his chair crossing his arms over his chest. He kept his features neutral. His instincts were telling him that whatever was about to be decided here today didn't bode well. Everything that was primal cat inside him warned him that he was in for the fight of his life. Finally, he thought with satisfaction. He was long past the time of being ready for the fated event.

Elder Zachary cleared his throat as he looked from Lyon to Bryce. He was a tall man not yet stooped with the ninety years of life he boasted of, and he still managed to command an audience by his natural 'elder air' attitude. "Since the death of Alpha Ryan, we Elders have waited in neutral patience for one of his sons to declare his right to be reigning Alpha. It has come to our attention that this strife between the brothers has completely divided the Pride, making it dangerously vulnerable, and unsettled. This is not acceptable.

"In times past, when there was competition for the right to be Alpha, the dispute was settled by a Challenge. To the death."

Bryce straightened in his chair, but Lyon kept a tight reign on his iron control and didn't move a muscle. It had finally come to this. He'd known all along it would be the only way. There wasn't much love loss between him and his brother, but he had harbored the slim hope that he wouldn't have to kill him.

A rumble of aggression moved around the table at Elder Zachary's words. Most of the Shifters there were Bryce's men with the exception of Mason and a few others. Lyon could feel their feral desire for the Challenge. They foolishly thought his brother would win. He had no doubt that he would be the victor. There could be no other outcome. His people needed him if they were to survive.

Elder Zachary raised his hand and glared hard at the rumbling men. "Silence. There will be no Challenge." He paused to let that sink in. "Yet."

He stared again at Lyon and Bryce for a long moment. Lyon tried, but couldn't read the old man's expression. There was a wealth of wisdom and countless secrets in those eyes. Not for the first time, he wondered about the elusive Elders that came and went in the lives of the jaguars. Who were they, really?

"Your father was one of the strongest Alphas this Pride has ever known," Zachary stated. "He fought three Alphas in one day to win the Challenge. He killed all three. He ruled the Pride for decades with an iron will and strength that was undefeatable. I have no doubt that his sons have inherited that same indomitable power. When you were born he foresaw the power struggle that would one day come from having twin Alphas. He took measures to safeguard the Pride and his sons' futures. We, the Elders, were to expose this … secret Law as a last effort when there was no other choice but to have the Challenge between you both."

Secret Law? Hell. Lyon didn't like the sound of that. He was ready for the Challenge. And he knew his brother was too. His jaguar soul slowly rumbled awake. The tenseness in his muscles, the jaguar fury simmering in his blood, had him making the mental effort to hold back the Change. He remained silent as he waited with a patience he didn't feel...and hadn't felt in a long time.

"Our Pride, though divided, is over one hundred strong." They were the only Jaguar clan in the United States, and one of the few Jaguar Prides left in the world. "Though we are few and can not afford to lose any of our people, anyone who does not live by the dictates of his or her ruling Alpha and does not abide by a unified Law is considered a rogue and is banned from the Pride."

He straightened, and his voice became hard and cold. "And a banned rogue is marked for death. He cannot be allowed to live."

It was their Law, had been since the beginning of time. It was the only thing that kept them safe as Shifters in a human world. Rogue shapeshifters risked exposure, and that left every Shifter vulnerable to the same fate. Lyon had been forced to kill a couple of times when rogue Shifters had rebelled against Pride Law. He didn't doubt he would have to do so again.

"This is why there can be no division among our Pride. Any one who rebels against this Decree will be considered rogue and destroyed."

"Get to the point, Elder." Lyon heard the jaguar rumble in his voice, despite wanting to appear neutral until the long-winded Elder said his peace. "Why are we just now hearing about a Decree?"

"Because the time for the Challenge can no longer be delayed."

Zachary raised his hand in warning as the rumblings among the men started up again.

"The Decree is thus: Every fifty to one hundred years, for one full night, the moon aligns into what the preternatural world has named a 'Shifter's Moon.' Our shifting abilities are enhanced beyond comprehension and we are near indestructible. An Alpha is at his most powerful during that twelve-hour period."

Lyon knew about the event; every Shifter child was told about it and left to hope that they would be alive during one of its phases. But what did that have to do with this situation? A Challenge could be executed at any given time.

"It was decided and put into Prophecy Law by the late Alpha Ryan that his sons' fate as to which would be ruling Alpha would be decided on the Shifter's Moon phase. Because that event will occur on their thirty-first birthday. In one month's time."

"The Shifter's Moon is also the most powerful time for our women to be fertile, and an Alpha's mate to become pregnant with an Alpha heir. A child born from this event would be destined to be a Ruler unsurpassed. We have not had such an Alpha born in centuries."

Elder Zachary's gaze glowed with unearthly power as he stared at Lyon and Bryce. "Twin Alphas have never happened either. Your mother was one of the precious and rare humans that carry our Jaguar genes but have no shifting abilities. There are but a few women like this left in the world. Although they are human, the jaguars have diligently protected these women. Only a few privileged and those that protect them know who these women are and where they live."

"Why haven't we heard of these women before now?" Bryce demanded. "Our people are becoming extinct, despite intermarrying with humans, and you're just now telling us that there are women out there who can bear pure jaguar children?"

Lyon had heard more behind the words than Bryce, and he wasn't happy with the direction of his thoughts. "These women," he drawled, resolutely holding back his anger, "They're full human?"

Zachary nodded. "They were blessed centuries ago to carry the jaguar genes so that if needed they could one day help us avoid extinction. They can be mated to any jaguar, but we have only needed them in the past to help create strong lines of Alphas."

"You used them like a breeding tool?" Lyon slowly stood up. It took every ounce of willpower he had in him to keep from changing right then. That ever-present, simmering jaguar fury rose up, hot and fast. "The Jaguar do not use women," he stated, his voice gravelly yet still controlled. "We cherish them, protect them. We do not harm them. I could kill you for suggesting less, Elder."

"As ruling Alpha, you could do just that." Zachary's eyebrows rose. "But you are not yet ruling Alpha, Lyon. And until then, my word as Elder is Law."

Lyon growled, his hands clenching into fists. He'd been taught from birth to respect and to obey the Elders. It took more discipline than he believed he possessed but he managed to nod his head in acknowledgement of the old man's statement. He'd let him finish his announcement. Then, he would Challenge Bryce. Killing an Elder was forbidden; but damn if he didn't contemplate that as next on his list. Human women as breeding mates! What had the threat of extinction done to them as a once proud species?

Zachary waited until he sat back down. Then continued, "Our history as Shapeshifters in a world mostly human has been filled with danger, strife, and the inevitable threat of extinction. Throughout the centuries we have had need of more than the normal Shifter strength to win battles that might otherwise destroy us all. At those times, our Alphas have needed help.

"A child born of one of these special women and an Alpha, as a result of a sanctified mating on the night of a Shifter's Moon, will become a rare Alpha possessing enhanced powers and incredible strength. He will have a longer than normal lifespan. His rule will be iron clad. Undefeatable."

"Say it, old man," Bryce growled out the words. "You know as well as we do that a war is coming. An Alpha like that just might be our only salvation." He stood up, throwing back his shoulders, standing aggressively. "But we don't need a new born babe to lead us. We have the power to defeat our enemies. Now. With me as Alpha."

Lyon came slowly to his feet, muscles tightening and his hands already changing into clawed paws. "Then we have the Challenge now, brother. I will take great delight in proving you wrong." His body started the shifting process before he even finished speaking. His jaguar counterpart pushed forward, primal instinct surfacing in a hot rush of adrenaline.

"Stand down!" Zachary roared the command. "The first man to strike will be the first to die at my hands."

Primal, ferocious growls filled the room. Mason abruptly stood next to Lyon and began his own shift. Lyon knew if they had to fight, with only the two of them, they would kill a lot of the men here … but most likely wouldn't come out of this alive. He didn't want to take the chance that Bryce might live if he died. He swallowed down the primal fury, and then forced back his change, the restraint painful in its intensity. Then, he clasped Mason's arm. "Hold," he told him. He looked first at Bryce, then to Zachary.

"Finish your words, Elder." *Then, I'll decide if any of you deserve to live.*

Lyon could have sworn he saw a glowing spark of admiration in the Elder's eyes as their gazes locked. It didn't matter. What ever else was said, nothing was going to change the fact that he was going to challenge Bryce and end this once and for all.

"As I stated, Alpha Ryan's mate was one of these special women. As it turned out, she was also his Truemate. Their union was during peaceful times for the Jaguar so there was no need for a Shifter's Moon or for the birth of a 'special' Alpha male child. Still, she gave birth to Alpha twins—an unheard of event in all our history. That alone makes you both incredible men.

"It has been prophesized that one of you will be the father of the special Alpha that will one day lead our people to victory over the enemies that wish to eradicate us completely. Even though the date for this predestined war is yet unknown, the Alpha child must be born this year.

"We have chosen the two women who will be mated to you, in the sanctified ceremony on the night of the Shifter's Moon.

"Your vows will be consummated in a blessed union when the Shifter's Moon first rises.

"The child born from this union, bearing the 'moon-and-jaguar' birthmark will be the future ruling Alpha.

"The father of that child will become the ruling Alpha now."

Lyon placed both his hands, palm down, on the table in front of him; purposely showing that he was in control of his jaguar. In a voice deep and deadly he simply stated,

"No way in hell."

The proverbial "you-could-hear-a-pin-drop" was very evident in the silence that followed. Rage blurred his vision, but he kept his deadly stare locked with the Elder's. Mason was his Beta, he would protect him from any side attack he might not see coming while his sights were set on prey. Every primal jaguar instinct in him was shouting *attack now* to regain the control he suddenly felt irrevocably slipping from his grasp.

The two other Elders pushed back their chairs and stood beside Zachary. Their combined auras were powerful in an odd, visible intensity. The room suddenly felt smaller. Colder. Every Shifter there held his tongue, not daring a sound. Lyon gritted his teeth together, a nerve clenched in his jaw.

"Our Law states that all Elder Decrees must be obeyed or the refusal is grounds for punishment. Death." Zachary's voice was colder than the temperature in the room. "If either of you decide to take matters in your own hands and Challenge the other, then you will be deemed a rogue and sentenced to death. Should you fight each other, there will not be a victor. I will personally kill the man who survives. Elders have ruled the Prides in the past, and we can do so now without an Alpha."

"What stops us from mating our chosen one before the Shifter's Moon and getting her pregnant so that we can finally determine the outcome of this damned fiasco?" Bryce's voice was harsh, his sneer evident. Lyon growled low. His brother was determined to win, no matter what he had to do. *I won't let you hurt an innocent woman, brother. No matter what the consequences are.*

"These special women can mate with another Shifter not Alpha, and bear pure jaguar children. Some have done so. But ... only the sacred ceremony and blessed union on the night of the Shifter's Moon will result in the special Alpha child's birth."

•

The warning words echoed in his head for the rest of the day and night and Lyon fought an inner battle with his conscience that finally resulted in an unhappy conclusion. If he wanted to protect his Pride, then he had to do whatever it would take. He didn't doubt he could win a Challenge against his brother. But he couldn't risk a war within the divided clans if the Elders proclaimed his death as punishment. Mason, as Beta, wasn't strong enough to lead, and Lyon had already seen the hidden power the Elders possessed. He'd felt it in an invisible restraint when he tried to change earlier. He'd known that control had come from all three Elders. These men were beyond just powerful, and he didn't like the idea of allowing them reign should something happen to him.

Everything Jaguar and male in him balked at the idea of mating for the purpose of an heir. He'd always known that to be a full Alpha he would need a mate at his side, and eventually heirs. But he never thought that choice, of who she would be, would be taken from him.

Hell, he was only thirty years old. He'd dated his share of women, Shifters as well as humans, but had yet to meet the one woman he'd willingly share his life with. Casual sex was one thing. Marrying was another. And he didn't think for one minute that a mate would turn out to be a Truemate. They were rare among all preternatural races, and his father had been one of the few lucky men to find his.

He and Bryce would be thirty-one on the day of the Shifter's

Moon. Never in a million years had Lyon thought he'd be spending his birthday consummating marriage vows instead of celebrating being named Alpha.

"Damn it all to hell!" really didn't eloquently express his emotions. He had a bad feeling deep in his gut he'd be thinking far worse thoughts before the end of the month.

Chapter Two

"This is cruel beyond words," Ariel Skye proclaimed in a high-pitched voice. Her light blue-grey eyes flooded with tears. She tossed her long sun-gold hair back over her shoulders and then ran her fingers through the elbow length strands in agitation. Her pretty, sharp features were set in pre-mutiny lines. "I can't believe Grandfather would demand this. It's like some kind of weird nightmare that a fantasy writer would make up."

Her aunt, Kitlene Skye, sat on the sofa opposite of where Ariel was theatrically pacing the living room floor of their condo. She sighed. "Calm down, Ariel," she commanded softly. "You know Grandfather does only what's best for us."

Kitlene wished she felt as convinced as she tried to make Ariel. Truth was she was feeling the same shock as her niece. Granted, they had both grown up knowing that this might happen one day, but neither of them had really prepared for it. Ariel was right; the reality of it was like something out of the mind of a fantasy writer. What normal human woman could comprehend being chosen to marry a ... Shapeshifter of all things, and in the process have everything in her entire life change?

"Stop being dramatic, sweetie, and come sit down. We'll think this through and make some sense of it." *I hope.* Kitlene patted the spot beside her on the couch. Her niece had always been a hyper, dramatic woman and Kitlene was the only one, ever, who managed to keep her grounded.

Woman! She's only eighteen. What made Grandfather choose her? The most obvious answer slammed into her mind before she could habitually push it back into the dark recesses of her thoughts. Now wasn't the time to think about it. She had to figure out a way to help Ariel.

She loved her niece, had raised her since the death of Ariel's father and mother. She was her legal guardian, surely that would hold some sway in changing her grandfather's decision. If she refused to allow Ariel to be married so young, wouldn't that make him choose another?

Where there any others left? *You*, a taunting voice whispered in her mind. *Worthless you. The old Elder loved you enough to not risk the chance with you.*

Kitlene rubbed at her aching temples. The sudden announcement from Grandfather and then Ariel's explosive tantrum had brought back the headache she'd suffered through during last night's thunderstorm. And the cutting words of her conscience were beating out in perfect rhythm with each pound of pain. *It's your fault he chose Ariel instead.*

"You can tell him no, right, Aunty? I'm still under age and he can't force me if you refuse to allow it."

If only it was that easy. "Grandfather told us a long time ago that there were less than twenty of us left in the world. You were eleven then and I was only eighteen. It was right after your parents passed." She had to reiterate, say it out loud, for both of them; maybe it would help them to finally accept the inevitable. "Remember when he sat us down and explained that as the years passed and more of us were taken from the list, the remaining women became even more precious to them? There are only a few Jaguar Prides left in the world, and only one here in the U.S. and that narrows down the field—sort of. We could be their only salvation, Ariel, in the end." The words sounded hollow even to her ears. Where was the justice in it all?

"But we're humans! Just because we were cursed to carry those freaky jaguar genes doesn't mean it was our choice." Ariel lunged to her feet again and re-started her pacing. "We're humans! We have our own lives, our own plans for our future. Why are we forced to obey the decree of some old men who call themselves Elders? They're not our elders, or whatever! They didn't raise us, share our lives, and they shouldn't have any say over us now."

It was a matter of honor and destiny. Kitlene frowned at her own nonsense. Ariel was right, they shouldn't have to obey the decree of a race they didn't belong to. Being a 'special breeding mate' wasn't exactly a privilege. But even as the rebellious thoughts reared, the part of her that was imbedded deep, deep in her soul knew that it really was Destiny. She and Ariel couldn't deny it or refuse it. No matter the circumstances. None of the others had.

Even you. No matter the circumstances. She resisted the urge to join her niece in the frantic pacing. Panic slowly simmered to life, increasing the tempo of pounding in her head. Her grandfather would protect her to the very last because he loved her. But what would happen when the time came and she was the only choice left?

She would die.

Because those incredibly rare, cursed jaguar genes in her body had one major glitch. None of the women in her direct line of ancestry—right to her mother—had ever survived the childbirth process. Every one of the women since the very beginning of time, had died moments after the birth of their first child.

She was twenty-five years old and still a virgin. And the sad thing was, she would also die one. Not exactly a choice there, either, she thought dismally.

Ariel called her a coward. She didn't think Kitlene had to remain a virgin simply because she couldn't have children. But she couldn't bring herself to get involved with anyone knowing that she couldn't follow through with a permanent relationship. For one thing, her virginity belonged to the fated destiny, but for another, she wasn't willing to risk falling in love with a man and then having to deny him her body—and her heart and soul. Because she didn't want to die giving him a child …

There were times when she'd almost chosen to go on the Pill or some other form of birth control. But no matter the temporary solution, it was always just that. Temporary.

The pre-determined providence of her life was a deeply painful, immensely heavy burden she had to bear.

She glanced at Ariel as the young girl became more and more agitated. She had to bear the burden but she didn't have to let Ariel face it if there was anything she could do. Anything. Her niece was going to start college in the Fall, and she had her entire life ahead of her. Surely their grandfather could choose one of the remaining women.

Kitlene rubbed her forehead again with that thought. Therein lay one major problem. Zachary Alban wasn't *really* their grandfather.

The seemingly ancient Latin man had been in their lives since the time of their births. Both Kitlene and Ariel had been raised knowing their destinies and having Zachary there to guide them and teach them. They learned early to simply call him grandfather; he was loving and kind to them, and was always there when circumstances called for any interference or protection in their lives. He was the one ruling disciplinary in their lives, even over the parents, and neither girl ever realized how odd that was in the normalcy of other children's lives.

Kitlene's father had willingly given up the raising of his daughter after the death of his beloved wife during childbirth. An archaeologist, he chose to leave her in the care of his brother and wife and travel the world. He'd died at a dig when a cave-in trapped him and several men almost a half-mile underground. Kitlene hadn't grieved; she'd never had the chance to get to know or love the man. Then the death of her aunt and uncle, along with Ariel's parents, in a car crash, had left a too-young Kitlene now the surrogate parent for her niece. Ariel's father was actually a stepbrother to Kitlene. Her father's son from a previous marriage, he was already grown and in college before Kitlene's birth. She'd love him dearly, even though she hadn't had the chance to grow up with him, so when he died she was more than willing to take his daughter under her wings. Incredibly naïve at eighteen she was nonetheless determined that she could take care of eleven year old Ariel.

And now seven years later she was failing in that duty. How could she force Ariel to accept a destiny that would change her life forever, a choice that wasn't even hers?

Ariel interrupted her frustrated thoughts. "We can make it on our own, Aunty. I can put off going to college until next year. I'll get a job and save up the money. We don't have to accept Grandfather's imperious decree."

Zachary's generous trust fund was the only thing that kept them from being broke. Kitlene had tried various jobs over the years, barely making enough to keep a roof over their heads and food on the table. She'd graduated high school a year early, despite protests from Ariel and friends, but she couldn't afford to go on to college since she then had Ariel to take care of. Discovering the situation a few years later, Zachary had stepped in and set up the trust fund.

She had no doubt that if she or Ariel refused the command, that life-saving money would no longer be there for them. Granted, she knew they could make it on their own, but so many plans would have to be put on hold. Some might not even see fruition. Ariel going full time to college and getting her medical degree was one that couldn't be compromised.

There was no rule saying Ariel couldn't continue her education plans once she was married. The Jaguar people were Shapeshifters in a human world that didn't know they existed, but that didn't make the way they lived their lives much different from other humans. Shifters lived among and even married humans. Looking at them, having them work side by side with you in every day life, you wouldn't even know their secret. Ariel's chosen mate was an Alpha and he owned a business, a nightclub, in downtown Los Angeles. Her niece's life would be a little different—but surely not as drastically different as they both feared.

As for herself, Kitlene was sure that even after Ariel was married and no longer under her guardianship, her life would go on the same. She didn't have a career but she had a steady job. And that gave her the desperately needed stability in moments when she would feel the always-hovering panic rise to remind her that her destiny was still yet to be decided by an uncompromising fate.

For now, she had a steady job working at a local nightclub in downtown Stuart, Florida. She and Ariel had been born in Stuart and had lived there all their lives. She was comfortable with her life for now—and living in their hometown was a security she was thankful to have. Locals knew her, and she had life-long friends. The pay from the nightclub wasn't enough to keep them from not having to use the Trust Fund, so she put away as much as she could manage to save for Ariel's future.

"We could always run away," Ariel muttered. Her statement brought Kitlene out of her dismal thoughts immediately. How many times had she been guilty of thinking that same thing too?

"It has never been an option, honey. You know that." *Never. No matter how many times I did it in my dreams.*

Ariel frowned at her, anger mixing with her tearful voice, "You sound like it's a done deal. Don't you care that I'm being forced to do something so outrageous as this?"

"You know the answer to that," Kitlene chided her gently. "I would do anything to spare you this. But running away wouldn't solve anything. We have been protected from the rest of the preternatural world all our lives, and one of the main reasons for that was to keep us safe from being prey to Others, races that would want to use us for their own purposes. If we tried to run away, tried to disappear, we would be hunted down. We've never seen our 'protectors', Ariel, and there's a reason for that. Those same protectors would become our hunters, and we their prey." She cringed at the suddenly tearful sound in her own voice, knowing it didn't help to steady Ariel any. "And there is no place on the face of this earth we could hide where they wouldn't find us."

Believe me, I've thought about it a million times over the years...

The doorbell rang. Kitlene got up and went to the door. She already knew it was Jade Tempest because she had called earlier after Zachary had left. Her best friend wore a ferocious frown on her lovely exotic face. And just like her last name, she was a potential tempest ready to erupt. Jade was also one of the few rare women who carried the jaguar breeding genes. They were the only three left in North America—the only three they knew about—so they had stuck together all their lives with the secret that bound them, heart and soul, and in deepest, unfailing friendship.

Jade was a year older than Kitlene and already a practicing physician. Her special field was in women's natural health. She had chosen it because of her own unique genes that she shared with Kitlene and Ariel. She had spent her entire teenage and adult years determined to find a cure for them and finally be able to release them from the cursed fate.

And she worked tirelessly now to find a cure for Kitlene. She refused to accept the possibility that she couldn't do something to prevent Kitlene's death should she ever give birth.

Her exotic beauty was a head-turner in a small city like Stuart. Her Greek heritage was very prominent in her sharp features, dark amber-gold eyes with large black pupils, and dark, richly vibrant, sable colored hair. She was the tallest of the three women but her frame was willowy-slender.

She stepped into the foyer and waved a small bag in Kitlene's face. "Time for another injection. Then, you and I—and Ariel can figure a way out of this mess."

Kitlene followed her into the living room. She loved her friend for the relentless pursuit to help her, but she hadn't believed –hadn't dared believed that one day there might be a way to fix that glitch in her genes. Truth was, she couldn't allow herself to hope. She was too afraid of the soul-destroying pain should it all prove futile.

Nevertheless, she obediently sat, pulled up her blouse and let Jade inject the special serum into her stomach. Darn, but she hated needles. "Can't you figure out a way to make this into a pill or even liquid?"

"Stop grumbling," Jade admonished with a smile. "The needles are the tiniest made, so it can't even hurt."

"Said by someone who doesn't have countless needle pricks in her navel."

"You can't even see them, Kit. What a baby."

She knew Jade teased to keep her from thinking about the possibility that the injections weren't working. So far, tests hadn't been conclusive either way.

"I wish you had a serum to get rid of our curse," Ariel muttered as she finally settled down beside Kitlene.

"I'm working on it, honey," Jade said, her tone hard. "I swear I won't fail us."

Kitlene held back her sigh. Even if by some miracle Jade succeeded, it still wouldn't be in time. For Ariel. Possibly not for Jade. And definitely never for her ...

•

Kitlene tried to contact Zachary for three days with no success. The man had retreated to wherever it was the three Elders lived somewhere in the wild uninhabited jungles of South America—and she couldn't get him to answer his cell phone.

Ariel had gone into a deep depression after a long night with the three women trying to figure out a solution to her problem and having no success. She stayed in her room, refusing to eat, refusing to talk to Kitlene.

Kitlene paced, hearing her niece cry herself to sleep every night, and felt more helpless than she'd ever felt in her life. Most of the time she raged silently at the cruelty of fate. Other times, she prayed harder than she'd ever prayed that something would happen to save Ariel from this unwanted fate. Three days later she was no closer to a solution than before.

Except for one. The only solution.

It had taken a lot of soul searching. A lot of facing the deeply rooted fear sleeping in her soul. A lot of choking back the panic attacks that threatened to make her run screaming in never ending fear. She'd lived with that fear from the time she'd been old enough to understand the horrible fate that awaited her should she ever get pregnant. All the heart-breaking nightmares over the years, the never ending heartache, the isolation and forced aloneness, was so deep in her soul, she could easily visualize the countless invisible scars that had to be deep inside her.

But, still, there was one solution that might save Ariel. The only thing she could think of. She loved her niece, had raised her, and had always been willing to sacrifice anything for her happiness. Had the time ever come that she would have to forfeit her own life for Ariel's, she'd always known she'd do it willingly.

And that time had finally come.

She would go to the Alpha male intended to be Ariel's husband. And she would offer herself as a replacement.

Chapter Three

The plane ride to Los Angeles was filled with strained tension between the three women.

Jade was furious that Kitlene would even think of doing "something so stupid and not even completely thought out. Honestly, Kitlene, I should have you committed or something!" She'd raged at her for hours but Kitlene had resolutely ignored her. She knew her best friend was actually scared to death at the plan. Kitlene had assured her that she was just as scared...but she couldn't let Ariel see that.

Ariel had been horrified at Kitlene's plan. She'd cried in bitterness, exclaiming that she couldn't let her aunt sacrifice her life for her. In calmer moments she would admit she couldn't help but hope that maybe in going to the Alpha and explaining things like Kitlene told her that she would do first, might actually bring about a solution for them all.

Kitlene didn't hold out for any hope that things would go as she planned. Ariel had been chosen and the Elders weren't going to allow their Decree to be changed. If Zachary discovered what she was up to before she could convince the Alpha it was the best solution, then he'd make sure he punished her by isolating her in some far-away place; and chances were that she would never see Ariel or Jade again. She'd never harbored any doubts about his strict rules or the extraordinary powers he had as an Elder of an ancient shapeshifting race. Her only chance in this was if Lyon Savage agreed to marry her instead of Ariel.

She'd gone over the upcoming conversation a thousand times in her mind, all the arguments she could come up, all the logical reasons to convince him. But she knew it would all depend on what Lyon decided.

Once again, our lives are being controlled and our fate decided by men who care only about the outcome.

Kitlene swallowed the rise of hot bile in her throat. For one long rebellious minute she hated. She hated fate. She hated her mother for passing those cursed jaguar genes to her. She hated Lyon Savage for agreeing to such an outrageous Decree.

And most of all she hated Zachary for loving her so much that he chose Ariel in order to save Kitlene.

•

They landed in Los Angeles late afternoon and went straight to the hotel. Now that they were here, Ariel was an absolute mess. She cried constantly. Kitlene knew she was going to make herself sick and asked Jade to give her a sedative. Her niece finally drifted to sleep, hiccupping the tearful plea, "Don't do it, aunty. I've changed my mind. Don't go to him."

Kitlene's heart was racing as she changed clothes and then called a cab to take her to the Primal Beat nightclub. She almost asked Jade for a sedative too. The panic rising in her was enough to make her lightheaded. At the door, Jade laid a restraining hand on her arm but Kitlene shook free. She hugged her, and asked her to keep watch over Ariel while she was gone. It took every ounce of courage and strength she had in her to finally walk out.

The cab ride through downtown Los Angeles would have been an exciting experience for her if she'd been able to enjoy the newness of it all. She'd never traveled anywhere outside Florida, much less to a place this huge and wild.

'Wild' seemed to be the perfect description. No wonder the jaguar pride had chosen to live here. The city was full of all kinds of people, all different races, and she had no doubt, many different species. Zachary had taught her and Ariel at the earliest age about the preternatural world and the many countless beings that inhabited the world alongside humans. Los Angeles was so huge it was no doubt easier for 'Others' to blend in without fear of exposure.

The ride to the nightclub was the longest and the shortest ride she'd ever taken. On one hand, she wanted to get this over with while she still had the courage to follow through. But on the other hand, she dreaded the coming confrontation.

Zachary had told them a little about the man chosen for Ariel.

Born a twin Alpha, he was an undeniable force of strength and power. Though he ruled over only half of the Pride until a permanent Alpha was chosen, his men were more like warriors than the other half ruled by his brother. He kept them trained on a weekly basis, and was a warrior himself of unsurpassed strength. He never let his people forget that they were jaguars living in the human world—not the other way around. He demanded their loyalty, their trust, and their respect. And he got it. Unconditionally.

He owned and ran the Primal Beat, and lived on the premises. His Beta, Mason Trent, worked alongside him to keep their clan safe and united, and lived at the nightclub too. Zachary had told her that most of Lyon's clan lived in L.A. but he preferred the nightclub. The entire top floor had been turned into huge, private suites. She wondered, not for the first time, if Lyon would insist they live there after the marriage.

That's if there is a marriage ...

Once again she reminded herself to breathe. Holding your breath, then passing out, certainly wasn't going to make a good first impression.

She wished she knew more about him. Would he be open to her plan? Would he actually care, considering he wasn't marrying for love but for the means to finally claim his leadership as an Alpha of one united Pride? That thought alone made her dislike him. What kind of man—okay, a shapeshifter—would marry for that reason? What did he expect of Ariel once they were married? Had he planned to send her off to some home in the country and then spend his time taking over uniting the Pride?

There were too many questions, and she had to admit she was a little afraid of the answers.

The cab pulled up to a large, two-story, stone building. She knew from Zachary that the stone exterior and interior was fireproof, and the entire place was secured to the maximum. Lyon didn't take any chances; he made sure it was safe in every way possible. Above the wide, double, oak doors in front was a sign that flashed P*rimal Beat*. Along the sidewalk, for almost a block long, a line of people stood waiting to get past three large bouncers standing guard. It was almost eight in the evening and already the place promised a full house. She'd heard that the club was incredibly popular for the area, and was mostly frequented by otherworldly races as a place to fit in and remain safe while enjoying the benefits the luxurious nightclub offered. The crowd and the noise were almost too intense to tolerate, and she hadn't even stepped out of the cab yet. Kitlene shook her head, took a deep inhale, released it with a shaky sigh, and reached for the door handle.

•

Lyon slammed the phone receiver down so hard it bounced off his desk and clattered to the floor. "Damn! What kind of idiots did he have watching over them all this time? It's a wonder they've remained safe this long."

He was ready to kill someone. Preferably the Elder Zachary, and the six—six men, for hell's sake—supposed to be protecting the two Skye women and the Tempest woman. Zachary had told them the women had been watched over and protected their entire lives. Not one of them had ever made a move that wasn't checked out, followed, and reported to the Elders. Lyon was still pissed that he'd never even known women like these three existed and were so essential to the jaguar race. If he'd known about Ariel, he would have been protecting her and the other two all along. Not because she was to play a major role in his future, but for the reason alone that they were precious females. Jaguars protected their women above all else. There were so few of them left.

"Have they told Zachary that their charges slipped past their guard?" Mason asked, his tone hard.

Lyon spat out a few more cuss words. "Damn idiots didn't even have the guts to come tell me to my face. I doubt they've told Zachary yet. They're on the women's trail now." He rubbed at the back of his neck. "One of them said they've actually traced them to the airport in Tallahassee. He says it's just a matter of minutes before he can confirm their destination." He suddenly grinned; the idea that three innocent women had managed to slip past the constant protection surrounding them was interesting. "He wasn't too eager to admit that they were smart enough to use fake names."

So his intended bride, Ariel Skye, had spunk. He liked that in a woman. His natural animal instincts made him overly protective of the female species, wanting to coddle them, protect them, keep them safe from all adversity. But the man in him liked a woman to have fire in her. It made things … more than just interesting.

On the other hand, his bride-to-be had now caused a serious

situation he didn't have time for. She was obviously on the run. From him. But where was she heading? He'd have to get a few of his own men tracking them down. Now. Mason's nephew Caleb was their best. If anyone could locate the three women, he could.

And time wasn't on his side. His thirty-first birthday and the night of the Shifter's Moon was less than twenty-seven days away. The thought of those women out there on their own, and without any protection, didn't sit well with him. If Zachary was wrong and others did know about their existence, they had just made themselves easy prey. He didn't want to dwell on the idea that even Bryce would be a danger to them. If his brother thought that he could keep Ariel from him before the Shifter's Moon, then he'd become her most dangerous enemy right now.

A hard pounding on his office door had Lyon sitting up straighter in his chair. "Enter."

Beau, one of the bodyguards who lived at the club, rushed in. Lyon took one look at his face and immediately came to his feet.

"Lyon, we've got a situation downstairs. I don't know how the hell they got past the bouncers, but there are five Shifters—coyote pack–grouped together and looking like they're about to let loose with a mess of trouble. The bouncers should have stopped them at the door; they had to have smelled the danger on them, it's so stinking obvious."

Lyon frowned, running his hand through his hair. They hadn't had trouble with the coyote pack living outside L.A. in a long time. Why now? Rumors were rampant that the pack's alpha was leaning toward joining with the other Shifter clans planning to unite for war. Because of that, Lyon had limited their access to the club whenever they were in town. His bouncers had strict rules to keep out any otherworldly being that even showed—or smelled—the least aggressive.

It was poor timing for the coyotes downstairs. He was itching for a fight after that phone call. Throwing a couple of Shifters out on their asses was just what he needed to calm some of his rage. He threw Mason a grin of pure malice. "Let's go have some fun."

On his way out the door he told Beau to call Caleb in from his watch on the ranch. He'd set several watchers on the perimeters after it was reported that suspicious-looking men—most definitely otherworldly beings by their smell—were coming and going. He knew Bryce was up to something. Something he probably planned to put into effect before the Shifter's Moon. Caleb's job was to follow a few of the strangers, and track them when they left the ranch. He'd have to put someone else on the job. Finding Ariel Skye and the other two women was priority for the moment. Their lives depended on him being one step ahead of whatever danger the women were now facing.

Leaving the long hallway that led to the stairs, Lyon and Mason were stopped by another of the bodyguards.

"What the hell now?"

"You've got a—uh, a visitor, Lyon."

"Whoever it is can wait." Lyon didn't have the time for business right now. His muscles were already tightening in anticipation of the coming fight. His jaguar fury bubbling, his other self ready to break free. He hadn't had a good fight in too long. He'd have to remember to thank the coyotes before he beat them senseless.

"I think you'll want to see her."

Her? "Spit it out, man. Who is it?"

"She gave the name 'Ms. Skye.'"

Ariel? His earlier assessment that she had spunk made him grin again. Instead of running from him she'd come straight here. His grin disappeared just as quick. He'd have to have a talk with her about her impulsiveness. He wouldn't tolerate her placing herself in danger like that again.

Beau spoke up from behind him. "Trouble again, Lyon. I've got Caleb on the cell. He says two limousines just arrived at the ranch. He was close enough to get a sniff of the four men who got out. They're African Lions. He's coming in now and has to talk to you about more information he's discovered."

Lyon groaned. This was turning out to be a hell of a night. First off, six incompetent men had lost track of his fiancée. Then, he was being stopped from a good fight because that missing fiancée was now within his reach. And now the news from Caleb. He turned to Mason. He was sure his own expression of disbelief mirrored that of his Beta's.

"You handle the coyote jackasses, and I'll meet my fianceé."

Mason chuckled and slapped him on the back. "Bet I'll have more fun than you."

"Wise ass."

They stood at the top of the large, doublewide stairs leading down to the main floor of the nightclub. Lyon's sharp gaze quickly scanned the crowd and he sniffed the air in order to distinguish the coyotes separate from the other patrons. He located them in a dark corner at a large table, nursing drinks and looking around with intense glares. Definitely trouble.

He continued perusing the crowd. Where was Ariel Skye? The club was full tonight, countless women moving around. His preternatural senses picked up the strange tension slowly building, as though it physically moved among the crowd. He didn't think that all of what he was suddenly sensing was coming from the antagonistic coyote Shifters. There was a bad feel in the air. The hair on the back of his neck rose and he held back a growl of aggression.

"I don't like this, Lyon," Mason muttered. "Something is off tonight."

"Take Beau with you to confront the coyotes. They could have backup waiting somewhere else in the room." The club was always full of different Shifter races, along with other beings. Now days it was hard to tell who was foe or friend. Rumors lately had suggested that a lot of the different species were actually banding together in fights. "Get them out in the alley—if you can—before fighting."

Mason nodded and mock-casually descended the stairs, Beau right behind him. Lyon quickly glanced over the floor again. Where the hell was Ariel? Had she been left alone while his man came up to announce her? Damn fool. He'd be punished for that mistake.

The bright light from the strobe that circled periodically over the main floor lit momentarily on a lone woman standing close to the front entrance. Lyon's senses went on instant alert. His sharp sight narrowed in on her. From his vantage point above the crowd he had a good look at her, and he let his thorough gaze take in every thing about her. It was Ariel; he knew it. The certainty startled him for a poignant moment, feeling as though someone had just sucker punched him. Countless women in the club and he'd zeroed in on her immediately?

His eyesight was sharper than most Shifters and he took advantage of it now to study his fiancée. She was nicely curvy yet slender, about five three if he was guessing right. Her long, thick hair was a deep rich auburn that caught the lights of the room, making it look like a soft red-gold cloud around her shoulders.

She was facing the direction of the stairs so he could see her face clearly. His breath caught. She was incredibly beautiful; an oval face, softly pink-tinged complexion, cupid-bow mouth, small nose. Her long-lashed eyes were large and round. For some reason, her eyes made him instantly think of a Persian cat's eyes. He grinned at the contradiction; he had the odd thought that her obvious spunk would keep her from being as sweet natured as the Persian breed.

Even from his distance he could see the soft, dove-grey color. They were the most fascinating eyes he'd ever seen on a woman. A man could easily—willingly drown in their mysterious, sultry depths. He could. He frowned at the disturbing thought. He let his gaze roam over her one more time before coming back to rest on her ethereal face. She wasn't wearing makeup—or she was an expert at making it appear that way—and the look was as much innocence as it was sensual. The odd combination was fascinating and it intrigued him like nothing else had in a long time. He watched her gaze around the room. Her expression was neutral, but even from this distance he could see her eyes mirror her nervous thoughts. What would those expressive, lovely eyes reveal when her gaze first met his? He was suddenly anxious to find out.

Lyon found his feet moving before he even had the actual thought. He bounded down the stairs, sending a glance toward the corner where Mason and Beau were talking to the coyote group. His body was tight, his muscles tense and ready to allow his jaguar self to emerge. But this time it wasn't because of the anticipation of a fight.

No, his jaguar soul had sighted prey. His prey. *His.*

That soul-felt confirmation only proved he was right. This woman was Ariel. Somehow his jaguar self already recognized her.

Whoa. That shocked him. Realization hit him like a hard, breath-stealing punch to the gut and then arrowed straight to his soul. He came to an abrupt standstill yards away from her. He inhaled roughly, taking her sweet, oddly familiar scent deep into him. His entire body immediately went into hard sensual overload. Stark, possessive instincts rose in him for the first time in his life. He'd never felt anything like it. His jaguar self pushed forward. Primal. Domineering. He clenched his muscles and forced the change to stop.

The truth slammed him so hard he nearly went to his knees, and he had to grip the counter next to him. Now he knew why Zachary had chosen Ariel for him. The Elder's potent mystic powers had allowed him to know all along. Why the hell hadn't he been told?

Ariel Skye was not only his future.

She was his Truemate.

•

Kitlene tried to keep from shaking so much that it was noticeable. The man who had left her to wait by the inside entrance was even now telling Lyon that she was here. She so wanted this to be over with. *Whatever the outcome is.*

She slowly perused the huge main floor of the club. Elegance was apparent in the décor. Although she'd never been in a nightclub other than the small one in Stuart, she was sure this one was different than others. It felt different from what she'd expected, despite knowing that Lyon Savage was a wealthy man and his club would naturally show that. It was crowded and she wasn't a fan of crowds. She backed away from a jostling group passing her, unease suddenly settling deep. She looked around again, trying to calm her nerves. She felt something off. It was as though the entire room was waiting for something to happen. Her gaze landed on the dark corner where a group of men where arguing with two other men facing them. If their body language was anything to go by, a fight was about to erupt any minute.

Great. Where is Lyon? She wondered if she should follow the man that had left her standing here. He had disappeared up the long staircase that led to the second floor. She turned in that direction.

And bit back a startled gasp. *Oh God.* The man standing a few feet from her took her breath away. She'd never felt such an incredibly stark reaction to any man in her entire life. Their eyes met and Kitlene felt suddenly, oddly lost. Instantly. Irrevocably. The stark feelings ferociously swamping her were as foreign to her as the piercing, overwhelmingly sensual reaction her body was having. She felt flushed. Shivery. Alive.

She had to breathe. Her hand flew to her heart; it was beating so hard and fast she was sure he could hear it from where he stood.

She tried to speak but couldn't. She forced air in through her parted lips, opening them on a slight gasp. Her heart nearly stopped when his expression turned oddly savage at her movement. His utterly dark, sensual look lasted only a moment but it thoroughly scorched her. From head to toes.

In a few breathless seconds she noted everything about him. He was tall, with a lean body muscled and powerfully strong. His dark jeans molded to long legs and slim hips. His dark green shirt was open to the waist, giving her a perfect view of a wide, slightly hairy chest. The color of the shirt matched the dark turquoise of his eyes. His face was chiseled handsomeness, high cheekbones, strong square jaw, and wide sensuous lips. His dark brows matched the odd color of his shoulder length hair; a mix of several shades of dark tawny, streaked with blacker strands. She felt the sudden urge to run her hands through that thick, unusual, beautiful hair.

Kitlene gasped. What was she thinking!

At her slight gasp, his eyes darkened again, the turquoise turning almost black. His cat eyes narrowed, his sensuous lips moved into a slight smile.

Cat eyes! Her heart stuttered. *He can't be.* She was in so much trouble.

He slowly advanced, looking too much like a large cat stalking his prey. She was definitely in trouble. Because that shiver barreling through her again had nothing to do with fear.

He stopped less than a foot from her. She had to remind herself to breathe again. *Heaven help me.* This wasn't supposed to happen. *What's wrong with me?*

"Ms. Skye, welcome to my home. I'm Lyon Savage."

If she'd had any sense left in her she would have turned and ran as fast and as far as she could. His dark, deep voice instantly captivated her. It slipped over and into her like the heated feel of molten honey pouring over her skin. *Why don't I just melt into a puddle now and get the embarrassment over with?*

Better to plunge in while she could still think straight. "I'm here because we need to talk, Mr. Savage." There, at least her voice sounded firm enough.

His tawny brows lifted in question. Then that hovering, sexy smile disappeared and his lips thinned into a slight grimace. She had the odd thought that he could be a very hard man when pushed. Great. She was about to do just that.

"There's a lot to talk about, Ms. Skye," he said in a low voice edged with anger, but nonetheless ultra-sexy in its tone, "The first, being your explanation on why you purposely ditched your watchers and came all the way here without protection." His turquoise gaze roamed over her face again. "What was going on in that pretty head of yours? Don't you realize how foolish and dangerous that was?"

Kitlene blinked in surprise. She couldn't believe he had the nerve to lecture her before she even had the chance to explain. She straightened her shoulders, a habit she did whenever she was about to get angry. "Those watchers would have stopped us from coming this soon," she told him, "And this is too important. I couldn't reach Zachary, and you were the only one I could think of to try and—"

"And what?" he drawled low, "Try to change the Decree?"

"Yes." There was no sense in denying it. He was already one step ahead of her. How was she going to convince him of her plan?

Lyon slowly shook his head, a nerve in his jaw muscle jumping as he stared at her. She watched in fascination as his eyes raked slowly over her, once again, from head to toes. Usually, she was able to figure out what someone was thinking just by facial expressions or the look in their eyes. It was a small talent that came in handy a lot of times. But now, this enigmatic man was a complete mystery to her, and she really wasn't sure she wanted to know what he was thinking at that very moment. That look was too—too sexual.

Or maybe … She had a moment to hope that if his very intense appraisal were any indication, maybe it wouldn't be so hard to convince him to consent to her as a replacement for Ariel after all.

"You're right. We really should talk." He rubbed a hand over his eyes, and that possessive look was back on his face again. It made her heart race alarmingly. "There's a lot to be discussed. But, you might as well accept the fact that the Decree can't be changed. There's too much at stake. Not just yours, or my, future, but the entire Pride's. I know Zachary explained all that to you."

"He did." She had to look away from his piercing gaze for a moment. His expression was keeping her off balanced. "But he didn't allow for freedom of choice. That's not right."

Lyon stared so long at her that she was starting to get that shivery feeling again. This strange attraction to him didn't bode well. If he didn't accept her …

"Right or wrong, it's going to happen."

Well, that was a domineering command if ever I heard one.

Kitlene released a pent up breath of frustration. "Are you really the type of man who would marry without being in love?" That wasn't the way she'd planned to approach this, but the question slipped out before she could sensor her thoughts. For some reason, love suddenly seemed like the topic that had to be brought out.

With his mesmerizing gaze holding hers captive, he reached out and touched her cheek. The two-finger caress was amazingly soft but she felt the strange heat of the touch. She had to remind herself to breathe again. In all her imagined scenarios of this meeting she never for one moment thought it would be like this.

"You're destined to be mine," he murmured finally. Kitlene's knees nearly buckled from that statement. She couldn't pull her gaze from his and watched as his eyes darkened to sharp brilliance. "Something tells me that love won't be a factor we'll have to worry about."

"What?" Love? He thought that a forced marriage would allow love to come later? She blinked, breaking his hold. *Oh no.* Common sense pushed forward and she suddenly realized he thought she was Ariel! She had given her last name only, and Lyon assumed she was the Ms. Skye he was to marry. That was the only reason he was acting this way, as though he already owned her. Could things be any more complicated? "Oh. You don't understand. I'm not here because of—"

She never got the chance to finish. A loud commotion across the room interrupted her and she and Lyon both swung to face that direction. Kitlene stared in horror when a group of five men suddenly lunged to their feet and, as one, attacked the two men standing in front of their table. Fists flying, deafening shouts and roars, tables and chairs flying in all directions, the fight instantly became one huge mess of bodies converging as one.

Lyon swung back to face Kitlene. He grabbed her by the arm in a tight grip. "Go up the stairs and into one of the rooms there." His voice was harsh, strained. "Stay there until I come." He didn't give her a chance to argue. He gave her a little push in the direction of the stairs and then released her with a deep growl rumbling from his lips. He strode across the room with preternatural speed, and then plowed right into the fight.

Kitlene stared in shock. As she watched, more men joined into the brawl, until it looked like every man in the place was tangled up in the large mass of fighting. Women were screaming. Some were cheering. She'd never seen anything like it. The sound of pounding feet coming down the stairs made her look in that direction. More men. They raced across the room and jumped into the battle.

She leaned back against the wall behind her, trying to stay as calm as possible. She'd seen fights before, after working in the club at home for several years, but this was different. There was an undeniable, smothering air of feral danger in the room. Instinct told her most of the men fighting were Shifters. *This can't be good.* The onlookers were crowding around the fight, and she was being shoved farther back into the corner. She looked for an escape, glancing at the stairs, but she wasn't sure she could make it now; the crowd was already blocking her way.

Suddenly two hands clamped down on her shoulders in a painful grip. She screamed and looked up into the hard, craggy face of a stranger. One look into the gleaming, dark glare in his eyes and she knew he wasn't trying to help her. She started struggling instantly. Two more men appeared at her side, reaching for her. Terrified, she struggled harder. The first man suddenly released her shoulders and then quickly bent. One moment she was trying to kick out at her assailants and the next moment she was upside down as he threw her over his shoulder.

Kitlene screamed as loud as she could. The three men headed for the entrance just yards behind them. Shocked truth hit her, hard. She was being kidnapped! She lifted her head and frantically searched the area of the fight. With what little strength of voice she had left in her, she screamed out his name in hopes that somehow he would hear her. "Lyon, help!"

Just as she was being carried out the doors she saw him erupt from the brawling mass and stare in her direction. The look on his face was deadly. He shouted out a primal, savage roar and started toward her.

It was the last thing she saw. One man had decided her struggles were a nuisance. He slapped a rag over her mouth and she instantly recognized the chloroform smell. Then, she lost consciousness.

Chapter Four

$\mathcal{L}$yon tore through the thick crowd with a boiling rage that made his preternatural skills flare into overdrive. He was halfway to the doors when he realized he was in a half-change. His hands were already claws, and the rest of his body was preparing for his jaguar to emerge. It took everything he had in him to stop and force the change back. He roared, frustration and impotent fury blurring his vision for a long moment. Every instinct in him was screaming at him to change completely and hunt down the bastard who had kidnapped Ariel. But some small amount of common sense told him that suddenly changing into jaguar right in the middle of a crowd filled with humans wasn't the smartest idea.

That and the fact Mason was suddenly by his side shaking him as he yelled in his face. "Damn it, Lyon. Stop the change! Think, man!"

Lyon growled, the sound rough and primal. *Think!* He lowered his arm. Damn, he'd almost hit Mason. He swiped a shaking hand across his eyes, cursing the red rage still blurring his vision. He had to think!

"They can't get far," Mason pointed out. "You have her scent, don't you?"

Lyon forced air into his lungs, cutting off the primal growls still rumbling. Her scent. Thank the Gods. "Yeah. Let me go, Mason. They can't get too far from me."

"I'm right behind you."

They emerged from the club and onto the crowded street. The sounds of the fight still going on inside had people outside pushing to get in to see what was going on. Lyon's fury boiled anew. Damn coyotes had been a distraction! Somehow, Ariel's arrival had been anticipated. It was a too obvious, well thought out plan. How the enemy had known where she was after she'd ditched her watchers was something he planned on finding out. But finding her first was the priority.

He forced a resolute calm into his body and thoughts so that he could control his rage. He stood still, and closed his eyes. Instantly, her familiar scent was in his mind, his nostrils. He carefully sniffed the air. *Come on, sweetheart, which direction did they take you?*

Rage bubbled anew. "Damn it all to hell! The air is full of coyote scents!" Try as hard as he could, he couldn't sense Ariel's sweet scent mixed in with the foul Shifters' scents and that of the countless humans. He wanted to roar again. When he found those damn kidnappers he was going to tear them to shreds. Slowly.

Mason suddenly grabbed his arm and pointed. Lyon looked and saw the back end of a navy blue van as it swerved around the corner street at the end of the block, disappearing from sight in an instant. Despite wanting to chase after it, he knew he'd never catch up. He turned back to the club, fury tightening his muscles painfully.

Inside were five coyotes about to face certain death. But not before he forced them to tell him what he needed to know.

Hang on, Ariel. I'll find you.

•

Kitlene moaned and rubbed her aching temples. She usually didn't have headaches like this unless there had been a storm. And she couldn't remember a storm. She sat up, dizziness swamping her blurred vision for a moment as panic set in. The memory of being at the club with Lyon right before the kidnappers grabbed her came flooding back.

She froze. Where was she? She quickly glanced around the room, looking for her kidnappers. The small area was in semi darkness. There weren't any kidnappers, but she immediately saw the other form lying on the floor in the corner.

"Oh my God, Jade!" She hurried over to her unconscious friend, and came down on her knees beside her. She quickly perused her body but couldn't see any obvious harm. She touched her cheek, and then shook her shoulder. "Jade, wake up. Please." She bit down on her bottom lip for instant pain to keep from breaking down. She had to stay calm. If she panicked now, she wasn't sure she'd hold on to any common sense. And that was something they were going to need.

A moment later, Jade moaned and slowly opened her eyes. Kitlene breathed out a sigh of deep relief. "Are you alright?"

Jade sat up, a foul word slipping from her mouth as she clutched her head. "Ow. I'm going to kill that jerk. He hit me on the head!"

Kitlene's heart stuttered. "Where's Ariel? Who hit you?" The room was small enough to see there wasn't anyone else there with them. She tried to clamp down on the panic rising again. Where was her niece? Was she safe?

Jade grimaced. "I'm sorry, Kit. I stepped out of the room for just a few minutes. I wanted to grab a newspaper. I thought she was still knocked out from the sedative. When I got back, she was gone. She left a note saying that she couldn't allow you to sacrifice yourself. She was running away, and figured Zachary would try to find her, but she was going to disappear until after the Shifter's Moon." She frowned. "The little imp didn't swallow that sedative. She'd planned to run all along."

Kitlene exhaled roughly. She should have known that Ariel was desperate enough to do something like this. She'd hoped that her niece would wait until they had talked to Lyon and Zachary. She looked at the four walls surrounding them in the small room. *At least*, she thought, *Ariel isn't here in whatever danger we are.*

"Where are we?" Jade stood up, pulling Kitlene with her. "Why did those morons grab us? Do you think they were looking for Ariel, or have we just been kidnapped as a random act?"

"I don't think it was random," Kitlene told her. Now that she was thinking clearer, she remembered every detail. "A fight broke out at the club. I was standing near the entrance, but in the middle of a crowd. The men who grabbed me pushed aside a lot of women to get to me, specifically. They had chloroform ready. And they grabbed you from the hotel room, even though no one should have known we were here."

They must have been waiting for her to arrive at the club. *No, not me.* She gasped aloud. Ariel! But why? Did Lyon have enemies that were determined to keep him from marrying Ariel and gaining full Alpha status? But that didn't explain how anyone had known about their arrival. Too many questions. Would Lyon have any of the answers, if she ever managed to see him again?

Lyon. Just the thought of him caused her to calm some. She'd seen the look on his face when he'd heard her scream. Something told her he was even now looking for her. "Lyon knows what happened," she told Jade. "That's one thing in our favor."

"But does he know who kidnapped us and where they've got us?"

Kitlene looked around the room again. Four bare walls. No furniture. No windows. "Where is here?"

Jade walked over to the only door. "Locked. Why am I not surprised?" She banged on the door. "Let us out of here!"

Kitlene shook her head. "Maybe drawing attention to the fact we're conscious again, isn't a smart idea, Jade."

Her fertile imagination could easily come up with a hundred different things kidnappers would do to a victim. And especially to one they thought of as important ...

They waited a few long, drawn-out moments but no one responded to Jade's banging. Kitlene pressed her head against the door, but couldn't hear anything beyond. The implication that their kidnappers had left them alone had her panicking all over again. What if they were out there looking for Ariel?

Anger built past the fear. Why hadn't Zachary warned them that there was the possibility of being in danger from Lyon's enemies? Why would he send Ariel into a situation like this? She frowned. Of course, Zachary had expected the watchers to be protecting them. It wasn't his fault that they had managed to sneak past the guards and disappear before any of the six men realized they were missing. She had thought it such a smart idea. Get to Lyon first, talk some sense into him, and then be back home before anything ... drastic happened. *Yeah, right. So smart. I'm an idiot. And I've put us in danger now.*

"I know I'm stating the obvious, but we've got to get out of here, Kitlene."

Kitlene suddenly smiled. She reached inside her jean's back pocket. She'd stuffed a nail file in there earlier when she'd taken it from Ariel. Her niece had been jokingly threatening to kill herself with it. She pulled it out and waved it at Jade.

"I've always wanted to play the super spy and get myself out of a dangerous situation."

Jade laughed. "Yeah, right. 'Kitlene The Brave'. Aren't you the same woman who runs screaming every time she sees a spider? The same woman who sleeps with a nightlight because she's afraid that 'said spiders' might be lurking in the dark? And don't get me started on the cloud phobia."

"In my defense, clouds herald storms. Not my favorite event." Kitlene studied the door and the keyhole. She inserted the nail file into the narrow hole but it wouldn't turn. Maybe if she jiggled it...

The file broke off into the tiny slot. *Just great. Now what?* But then, the following 'click' announced the unlocking of the door. Kitlene looked at Jade, surprised, and then shook her head. There was no sense in hesitating. They needed to run now while they had the chance. She slowly pulled the door open and peeked out. There was nothing but darkness. Where were they? In a house? Or some other kind of building? Were they even still in Los Angeles? How were they going to find their way out of here, when they didn't even know where they were?

Cautiously she stepped out into what turned out to be a huge, empty room with a two-floor ceiling and four walls. Narrow windows lined the walls, too high to see out but uncovered to allow light in. Yards across the bare cement floor, on the opposite side, stood double wide, garage-style doors. Closed.

"I don't think a broken file is going to work on those doors, " she muttered. There had to be another way out. She went in one direction and Jade the other as they scouted the huge interior. She heard Jade chuckle softly and knew instantly that her best friend had obviously discovered a spider or two. She mentally made a note to get even with her as soon as the opportunity came up. Jade had her phobias too.

The relief-comedy was all too short lived. The loud, grinding sound of metal moving heralded the slow opening of the garage doors. Jade hurried back to Kitlene's side.

Kitlene pulled Jade with her as they backed. "Maybe we should hide as close to the doors as possible. If we're lucky they won't see us when they first come in and we can run out."

It was too far to the doors. They were halfway across the huge expanse of the room when the doors opened wide enough to allow the three men to enter. They were spotted instantly.

"Grab them," the man in the front ordered. They were restrained immediately. Kitlene and Jade struggled but it was useless. The men were burly and large. There was something about their animalistic snarls as they subdued the two women, and their strength was a bit on the super side. She suspected they were Shapeshifters.

"How did you get out of the room?" The one who appeared to be leader, demanded, and then turned to the other two men. "Didn't you idiots check them for anything they could use to escape with?"

The one holding Kitlene tightened his grip, painfully enough to make her utter a cry of pain. She was about to try and get a kick to his knee when a small commotion turned everyone's attention to the doors. She gasped aloud. *Oh God, don't let that be Ariel!*

Two men dragged in an unconscious woman. Blonde. Small. And entirely too pale. When they dropped her to the floor near them, Kitlene released a sigh of relief. It wasn't Ariel. She felt a moment of sadness that another woman was about to share their fate but was so thankful it wasn't her niece.

So, who were these men? Why had they kidnapped Jade and this other woman … if they were in fact looking for Ariel instead? Did they think to use them as bait to bring Ariel running? *Please, no.*

Kitlene cleared a throat gone dry. No time like the present to find out what their fate was to be. She just hoped her voice was hard enough to cover her fear. "Who are you? Why have you kidnapped us?"

Leader laughed. It wasn't a happy sound. Kitlene cringed at the underlying evil in his voice and eyes. "I've been waiting to say this line," he grinned maliciously. "We're your worst nightmare."

"Wanna bet?" Jade muttered. Her captor slugged her arm. She turned eyes of fury on him. Kitlene was glad to see Jade was angry and not afraid. *Not like I am.*

But she couldn't show that fear. There was no telling what these men would do once they discovered they didn't have Ariel. She lifted her head and stared at the leader. "Can you at least tell us why?"

He shrugged as he glanced down at the woman on the floor. Kitlene noticed she was regaining consciousness. She wasn't sure if that was a good thing or not. If the woman panicked, the jerks might react in a purely animalistic way. And she had the feeling the only way they were going to survive this was to remain as outwardly calm as possible.

She noticed the leader was looking intently at her and Jade and then at the woman on the floor. He frowned darkly. "Weren't you both supposed to be blondes?"

Kitlene cringed inwardly. She *had* been mistaken for Ariel. What was going to happen when they discovered their mistake? She could only pray Ariel was safe wherever she was and these idiots couldn't find her. She glanced at Jade and saw her nod her head slightly. They were so close as best friends, it was sometimes very easy to tell what the other was thinking. She looked Leader in the eye and lied with as much conviction as she could.

"I dyed my hair. We both did," she said indicating Jade. "Blondes really don't have all that much fun. And besides that, we figured the charade might give some people a bit of a confusion headache." She purposely smirked at him. "Worked, didn't it?"

"You little witch." Leader stepped forward, his hand raised to strike her.

A rough voice, deadly, deep, and full of danger, spoke up from the direction of the open doors, "You'll be dead before you touch her."

Lyon! Relief flooded Kitlene for all of two seconds. The next seconds, turning into fast-flying minutes, became a nightmare she was sure she would remember for a lifetime.

She'd grown up knowing about shapeshifters. But actually witnessing their instantaneous, supernatural transformation from human to animal was a sight she wasn't prepared for. The men holding her and Jade shoved them to the floor. She looked up to see Lyon and three other men charge in. Instantly they changed to jaguar in mid run. Their challenging roars echoed harshly in the huge room. Her captors changed too, into three wolves and two coyotes.

The nine Shifters came together in a loud, deafening clash that shook the floor beneath them. Kitlene and Jade managed to get the other woman to her feet and they ran across the room to the doors. They stood outside the entrance and watched in horror as the shapeshifters fought. Kitlene knew there would be death, and whatever the outcome was, she would never forget the horrifying sight.

Heart in throat, she couldn't tear her gaze off Lyon. He fought with two of the wolves, his jaguar body moving so fast and so deadly it looked like a flash of color blending in with the flying fur and spurting blood from the wolves. Every few moments she caught sight of his razor sharp claws slicing into one of the Shifters, or saw the gleaming of his large teeth as they tore chunks of flesh. She was too horrified to look away, even knowing that any moment she was going to be sick.

She jumped, startled at Jade's scream of rage and fear. She swung around just in time to see two other men rushing toward them, already turning into wolves as they ran. She barely had a moment to shove Jade from her side and then screamed, "Run!"

She wasn't fast enough to heed her own warning. One wolf lunged straight at her. Excruciating pain sliced through her as his extended claws ripped into her lower stomach. Terror numbed her for one long moment. As she felt herself falling, she looked down to see the river of blood flowing from the long, jagged cut and spilling onto the cement floor. She heard Jade screaming. She heard her own cry of pain and disbelief.

But above it all, she heard Lyon roar. As blackness swirled over her and she hit the ground, her last coherent thought was that she'd never, ever, heard a heart-wrenching sound of such complete and pure anguish and rage. She hoped she never did again.

•

Lyon slashed his claws across the wolf's throat in a deathblow and was dashing across the room to Ariel before the dead Shifter even hit the floor. In all his life, he'd never felt such strength-sapping fear flooding through him as he skidded to a halt beside his unconscious mate.

His Truemate.

If she died, he would too. The sudden, soul-felt realization didn't shock him like it might have before ever meeting her. He knew Truemates were forever, and one didn't survive long without the other; the bond of love was always too strong, too unbreakable. He didn't even know her, and yet he did know that she was meant for him, and he would willingly follow her wherever death took her. The horror of losing her was almost too much to comprehend. Shuddering, he forced the change back to man. Instant clothes covered him without him consciously thinking about it this time; it was the handy bit of magic that every Shifter had.

He carefully lifted her into his arms and held her against his chest. His heart stuttered, and he choked back a roar of fear. The blood from her open wound gushed in a steady stream, immediately coating the front of his shirt. With an iron will of strength, he forced himself to calm down and think. He looked up as Mason came down on his knees beside him.

His Beta was scuffed but not hurt. Behind them, the fight was over and the captors were dead. Lyon moved Ariel slightly in his arms so that Mason was supporting her while he tore off the sleeve of his shirt. Without blinking he instantly changed his other hand into his jaguar claws and ripped a long slice from his elbow to his wrist. He gathered her back into his arms, holding her against his chest. Then, he placed his sliced and bleeding arm across the gape in her stomach, pressing hard.

Shifters carried remarkable, sometimes death-defying healing agents in their blood. It was nature's way of protecting them when the need arose. Since an injured Shifter couldn't go to a human hospital, the healing agents were there in place to help. It wasn't a cure-all, all the time, but it was a crutch they could usually rely on if the injury wasn't too deadly.

He didn't even consider that she wasn't Shifter and his blood might not work. He wouldn't even allow the possibility to surface. He wasn't going to lose her. Not now. Not ever.

He bent his head to hers and whispered softly, "Come on, sweetheart. Hang in there." *I won't let you leave me. You're the one I thought I'd never find. Stay with me, Truemate.* Fear wasn't an emotion he had ever allowed in his life. But it was there now. Howling inside him. And he didn't like it. He couldn't fight it. He'd never faced anything he couldn't fight ... until this moment. The impotent rage threatened to consume him.

Mason muttered something under his breath and Lyon shot him a hard glare. He knew what his friend was thinking. If Ariel had been any other than his intended mate, this blood exchange wouldn't have been allowed. No female, human or Shifter, was thought to be able to safely accept an Alpha's blood. She had to be a close relative. Or his Truemate. Mason was worried that he was being impulsive, the adrenaline keeping him from thinking clearly; his Beta just didn't know yet.

Lyon could feel the warm flow of blood from her wound lessening as his own poured steadily into her and mixed with hers. But he knew the wound was too serious. She would need more blood. A full transfusion. He had to get her stable enough to move.

He'd have to take her back to the club.

"Get the doc to the club," he told Mason. "Now. I want him prepared to treat her as soon as we arrive."

His personal physician, Wren, was always on standby for both clans. Mason nodded his head and jumped to his feet. "My cell is in the Jeep's glove compartment."

Lyon hugged Ariel closer and pressed his bleeding arm deeper into her wound. He had to trust that Wren would be able to save her. There were no other options. Any other time and he would have been shocked at the stark, hot rush of emotions flooding him now. No woman had ever done this to him. He groaned, the acceptance of his feelings burning deeper into him, body and soul. She was his. His Truemate. His blood had to help her.

He kissed the top of her head, burying his face against her soft hair and inhaling her sweet, flowery scent. "I won't let you die, Ariel. You're mine. Stay with me, honey. Listen to my voice and hold on."

He felt rather than saw the dark haired woman who had been with Ariel kneel down by his side. She was crying, her sobs catchy as she tried to speak.

"No," she choked out, "She—"

Lyon growled. "Stop blubbering. She's not going to die. I won't let her." He felt a moment of guilt for his harshness, and calmed his tone, "She's my Truemate," he explained with authority and certainty. "And for that reason alone my blood will save her."

The woman grabbed his arm, and gasped in horror. He tore his gaze from Ariel and looked into the woman's shocked face. His heart did a flip-flop, almost stuttering to a complete stop. He heard her words, but he couldn't force his mind—or his soul—to accept the meaning.

He heard her repeat, "She's not Ariel! She's Kitlene. Ariel's aunt."

Chapter Five

$\mathcal{T}$he low, dangerous growls vibrating from his throat had everyone in the room keeping a cautious distance from him. He didn't care. The rage burning deep inside him was the only thing keeping him sane at the moment. Lyon tore the rest of his shirt off. He glared threateningly at the two men facing him, Mason and Wren.

"She gets my blood. No one else's." It was hard enough allowing anyone else to touch her. But he wasn't going to allow anyone else's blood in her. She was his.

Wren cleared his throat. He was older than any of the other Shifters in the room, had been under Ryan's rule all his life, and now served Lyon and Bryce. His respect was audibly evident in his voice as he tried to reason, "We can safely treat her with a universal blood type. We have plenty in supply. You've given her enough."

Lyon snarled low and took a step toward him. Mason quickly stepped in front of Wren, standing defensively. Lyon met his Beta's hard gaze, and then ground out harsh and commandingly, "I'm only saying this one more time. My blood. Now get that damned transfusion ready and take care of her. If she dies, I'm going to kill." He left the threat hanging in the air and knew they understood. He wouldn't stop at just one killing …

He was so close to turning jaguar and destroying anyone and everything in his sight. He wouldn't even care. Because if she died, he wasn't sure he'd ever feel human again. Only primal. Deadly.

Wren nodded his head, then turned away and started preparing for the surgery. The dark haired woman from earlier—she'd said her name was Jade—was already by the operating table slipping on surgical gloves and mask. She'd told Wren she was a physician and then insisted on helping. She was fierce in her determination to help, and she'd actually backed even tough Mason up a few steps when he'd tried to make her leave. "Try to take me away from her and I'll make you regret it in the worst possible way."

Wren's assistant, a young male, pushed another table next to the other one and motioned Lyon to lie down. Instead of side by side, Lyon positioned his head at the foot, where he would be able to see exactly what was going on. His sliced arm was already healing, the wound closed and a light scar slowly fading, and he didn't even feel the pinch when the IV was put in.

Instead, his eyes never left her face. Jade was leaning over her, whispering, brokenly, in her ear. His sharp hearing picked up the words easily. "Remember, you're 'Kitlene the Brave'. Be strong, please." She took a deep breath, forcing her tears to stop. "I swear I'll never tease you again about spiders or clouds. Survive this and I'll be so lenient. Please, Kitlene."

Kitlene. It was the sweetest sounding, softest name he'd ever heard. It wrapped around his heart and settled deep into his soul, repeating over and over in his head.

And so did the litany: *She's not Ariel. She's not my intended.*

Never one for having nightmares, Lyon felt like he was in one now. What was going on? How could he be so soul-sure about Kitlene being his Truemate if she wasn't the one he was to marry? What did Zachary know about this? Why had he chosen Ariel instead of Kitlene?

And what the hell was he going to do now?

He bit back the possessive growl rumbling up his throat. *She's mine.* He wasn't going to let her go. Damn Zachary for his erroneous decision. He was Alpha and he had the right to choose whom he would marry, not some overzealous, mistakenly superior old man who obviously didn't know as much as he pretended.

Lyon watched as Wren and Jade worked silently, stitching the jagged wound across Kitlene's stomach. Even as they stitched, his sharp sight could see the slow-but-obvious healing taking place across the soft skin of her belly. He sighed out roughly; his blood had accomplished what it was intended to, and saved her. That was all that mattered. For now.

Wren's abrupt words caused his heart to stutter. "There was poison on that damn wolf's claws, Lyon. I can smell it. Your blood stopped it from spreading, but I don't know if it will still cause an infection after we get her stitched up."

"Give her as much of my blood as she can take," he ordered. He'd willingly give her his life if needed to save her. Swallowing back another rough growl, he turned his gaze on Mason standing beside the table bed. "Any reports on who those damn Shifters were working for? I want answers now. If Bryce had anything to do with this, he's a dead man."

He'd kill his brother and not even blink when doing it. There would be no Shifter's Moon marriage, no choosing the true Alpha. He'd kill Bryce and gladly forfeit it all—if Kitlene died from this.

Mason nodded toward Jade and purposely lowered his voice. "No reports in yet. And I put Caleb on the trail to find the missing Ariel. Jade said the girl ran away from the hotel right after Kitlene came here to meet you. And the other kidnapped woman is waiting in your office. I have no idea why she was involved, unless those idiots thought she was actually Ariel."

"This was well thought out," Lyon muttered. "And it has Bryce's dirty scent all over it. He obviously thought that in getting rid of Ariel, he'd be the only one mated the night of the Shifter's Moon. He would win the Alpha title by forfeit." He spit out a round of foul words, then made the effort to calm down when he noticed Wren shooting him an angry glare with the reprimand, "Lyon, you need to stay still."

"Wait on talking to the other woman," Lyon told Mason as he turned back to stare at Kitlene. "I want to talk to her."

An hour later Lyon stood by his bed where he'd insisted they put Kitlene after the surgery. Wren had assured him that she would sleep for hours while healing and that the antibiotics along with his blood would work together effectively. He didn't want to leave her side, but he had to talk to the woman waiting in his office. If there was any chance she knew anything …

He looked down at Kitlene. Her beautiful, but pale, features were in soft repose; she looked like she was sleeping peacefully. Relief lightened his heart, made that gut wrenching feeling in his stomach lessen some. She was already so precious to him, and the acceptance of who she was to him was deeply embedded in him now as though it had always been there. In all his life, he'd never thought he could so easily accept something so shocking. He had a Truemate. The knowledge changed everything. He released a deep sigh and then leaned down and kissed her soft cheek, his lips landing close to her mouth. He lingered there a long moment, unable to pull back. He slowly inhaled, taking her sweet scent deep into him. The scent was a soft perfume of orange blossoms, and uniquely hers. He'd have it in his mind and body forever now.

He kissed her cheek again and then stepped back. "Sleep, baby," he murmured softly. "We'll get this straightened out. Somehow."

He didn't want to leave her until she woke and he knew she was all right. He wanted to lie down beside her. Hold her. Keep her safe. Instead, he forced himself to walk from the room.

Despite the fact she was in his bedroom and safer than any other place, Lyon still placed two of his best Shifter guards at the door of the suite. He wasn't taking any chances. He was going to make sure it was the last time he ever came so close to losing her again.

He walked down the hall, his thoughts forming a strategy. The women's kidnappings had been planned. Someone had known where they were and how to get at them. And he knew whoever was behind it hadn't been working alone. He suspected Bryce, but had to wonder if his brother would be that obvious in any attack. He was going to have to talk to him. Again. And this time, he'd make sure his brother knew he would never win in a fight against him.

He heard the raised voices before he opened his office door. Mason was angry. He recognized Jade's voice and knew his Beta wasn't too happy with whatever she was saying. He shook his head and opened the door.

"Keep your voices down," he ordered, his own low and deep. "If you wake Kitlene up before she needs to awaken, I'll have your hides."

Jade smirked at him, and put her hands on her hips. "You can't have my hide," she stated, "I'm not one of your crazy Shifters."

"*We're* the crazy ones?" Mason shook his head and snarled at her. "The three of you ditch your watchers and then get yourselves kidnapped and nearly killed, and you think that wasn't crazy? Woman, you need a reality check. What the hell were you thinking?"

Lyon seared them with a threatening glare that instantly silenced them both before Jade could reply. They glanced away from him and then sat down. He turned to the silent, pale woman sitting in a chair in the corner. She was pretty, slender, her blue eyes as pale as the shade of her blonde hair, and he guessed about nineteen or twenty. He gentled his tone, so not to scare her. "What is your name?"

She nervously twined her hands together in her lap, glancing at Mason and Jade before finally answering in a low voice, "I'm Niki Teal." She studied him intently. "You're not Bryce. Why am I here? Why was I kidnapped? Is Bryce coming for me?"

Lyon frowned. Damn. A new complication. "You know my brother?" Hell, he already knew the answer to that. Niki Teal was his brother's intended mate. That knowledge threw him. He had to rethink his earlier conclusions. If Niki had been kidnapped too, then chances were that Bryce had nothing to do with it.

Seething rage started boiling in his gut again. Who the hell was responsible for kidnapping the women and trying to kill them? Who else knew how important Ariel and Niki were to the Pride?

"Find Zachary," he told Mason. "Get his lousy hide here. Now."

He turned to Jade. "Tell me what you know about the kidnappers."

She shook her head. "Not much. I was waiting in the hotel room while Kitlene was here. Ariel had managed to sneak out, and left a note saying she was running away until after the Shifter's Moon. They didn't even bother knocking on the door, just broke into the room and grabbed me. They had chloroform. When I woke up I was with Kitlene in the warehouse." She tapped a finger against her chin. "When they returned one of them made a comment that Kitlene and I were supposed to be blondes. I'm guessing it was because they assumed we were Ariel and Niki here."

Lyon ran a hand over his jaw. "How did they know where you were, or even who you were? Your watchers have protected your identity all your lives." He looked at Niki, and watched her closely for any indication of deception. "Where were your watchers when you were kidnapped?"

She frowned at him. He could smell her fear, but she was bravely trying to conquer it. "I don't know. I received a summons a few days ago to come to Los Angeles. The note said Bryce would meet me. And it was signed, by Zachary, so I just assumed it was legit. He had already visited me and told me about the Decree and my part in it, so I didn't even consider that something might be suspect with the summons." She ran a shaky hand through her straight hair. "My watchers didn't show up before I left, so I thought they were just there even though I've never seen them. But when I got here and checked into the hotel room, there were two men waiting for me. At first I thought they were the watchers."

Zachary had told him and Bryce the names of their intended mates, and the only other ones who knew were their Betas, Mason and Holden. *Damn. That leaves the watchers as the only others knowing anything about the women.*

Lyon growled under his breath. He didn't like the answers he was coming up with. If both intended mates had been targeted, then someone else—someone very dangerous—had an ulterior motive to stop the mating on the Shifter's Moon night. He had to find out, and fast. Ariel and Niki's lives were at risk. And Ariel was still in danger while missing. He had no doubt that Caleb would track down Ariel, but would it be in time?

He stood up. "I'll take you to Bryce," he told Niki. He needed to talk to his brother and convince him that they should work together in this. If Bryce balked, then so be it. He wouldn't rest until he found the bastards who had nearly taken the life of his Truemate, and threatened the other women too. He grinned mirthlessly as he realized he was already relishing the kill...

Jade stopped him at the door of the office. "Lyon, I want to sit with Kitlene. You need to tell those guards to let me in."

Mason ended his phone call and spit out a disgruntled snort at Jade. "Why don't you just kick them in the balls like you threatened to do to me?"

Lyon held back his sudden grin. If he didn't know better, he'd swear his 'sworn-to-be-a-bachelor-for-eternity' Beta had just met his perfect match. All the signs were there. Signs he, himself, had instantly recognized when first spotting Kitlene. Mason was just being hard headed and ignoring them. He had a feeling he was going to enjoy watching his Beta suffer. Right along with him. Because, Gods help them both, this new development was about to change everything. They were most likely in for the battle of their lives. Physically ... and mentally.

He shook his head as he escorted Niki out. So much had happened in less than twenty-four hours. Not much of it good, he thought, but at least it wasn't out of control. Yet. Dammit. When he finally confronted Zachary, things were going to get bad fast. He knew the Elder was keeping things from him. He had to have known that Kitlene was Lyon's Truemate. Why the hell did he choose Ariel?

And there was still the mystery behind the women's kidnapping. Right now, he planned to make that a priority. If he had to kill someone to get the answer, then so be it.

At least now, Kitlene was healing. And she was safe with him. He released a long sigh of relief. He'd have to deal with the problem of Ariel being his intended mate, but for now he was content to know his Truemate was safe and under his roof. In his bed.

He grinned again. In his bed. Yeah. He liked the sound of that.

Chapter Six

$\mathscr{T}$he path split into two opposite directions. To her right she could hear the sound of animalistic roars and what sounded like a battle. To her left she heard the soft sound of familiar voices beckoning her. The same contradiction fought for the decision in her soul. She actually took a step to the right, instinctively going toward the roars and battle. Lyon needed her …

Kitlene woke with a fearful gasp on her lips. She let her eyes adjust to the dim light of the room and then slowly turned her head to see the two women sitting side by side in chairs by the bed. Jade and Ariel. "Ariel," she choked out with heartfelt relief.

Ariel and Jade smiled, and Jade quipped happily, "Welcome back to the land of the living, Kitlene the Brave."

Ariel pulled her chair closer to the bed and leaned over her. Tears of happiness flooded her eyes. Kitlene reached up and touched her cheek. "Are you alright, honey?"

"Me?" Ariel clasped Kitlene's hand against her cheek. "Aunty, I've been so worried about you. How do you feel? Are you in pain?"

Instant memories flooded her and Kitlene remembered the last few moments when the wolf had attacked. Her hand flew to her stomach. The first thing she noticed was that her bare skin had a thin line of tiny stitches across her lower belly. The second thing she was acutely aware of was that she was completely naked with the exception of the dark blue, silk shirt she was wearing. And with that knowledge came the realization that not only was it a man's shirt large enough to cover her like a short nightgown, but also that it had a distinctive … scent. Earthly. Male. Unmistakably wild and untamed.

She knew that scent. She didn't understand how she could

be so sure; she'd only been around him for a few minutes. But yet, everything about him had sunk deep into her memory. A permanent record she'd never lose. She knew that with a heart-felt conviction that refused to be ignored.

Jade broke into her troubled thoughts. "It's healing remarkably fast, Kit." She traced a gentle finger across the line of stitches. "Wren said we can take the stitches out by tonight." She shook her head, and Kitlene could see her doctor's mind at work. "It's a freaking miracle. Who knew Shifters had healing agents in their blood?"

Jade was right in that it was healing. She didn't feel any pain, only a slight soreness. And she distinctively remembered the pain when she'd been attacked. How was this possible? What was Jade talking about –Shifters' blood? She sat up and pulled the shirt closed against her naked chest. The sleeves hung down past her hands and she rolled them up. "What happened? The last thing I remembered was that charging wolf." She looked at Ariel, her jumbled thoughts flying in different directions. "And how did you get here? Wait a minute, where exactly is here?"

"Don't panic, Kitlene," Jade calmed, "We're safe. The jaguars rescued us and we're at the Primal Beat now." She briefly explained what had happened, and then ended with, "It was a—uh, the only word to use is 'weird'—sight. He was almost frightening to watch. At first he wouldn't let anyone touch you. Then, he refused to allow the doctor to use anyone else's blood but his. I don't know why that caused friction between him and the other two men, but he made them back down."

"Caleb says he is an incredibly strong Alpha," Ariel said quietly.

Kitlene's pulses jumped just picturing the scene Jade had painted. She whispered his name. Jade nodded and stared intently at her. "You're in his bed."

Her heart stuttered. She took a moment to look around the room. It was definitely male with the décor, the muted blues and browns and sleek furniture emphasizing the clean, uncluttered space. It was a huge room, and the bed she was in was king size. She felt dwarfed sitting in its big center.

And incredibly safe. "Why—" She took a deep breath and willed herself to keep from blushing. This was ridiculous. She shouldn't be reacting this way just because she was in his bed. *And I'm not going to ask why I'm wearing his shirt.* "Why Lyon's bed? Don't they have a guest room, or something?"

Jade stared at her for a few long poignant moments and Kitlene started to feel on edge. She wasn't sure she was going to like what she was about to hear. She glanced at Ariel and saw her lower her gaze. "What is it?"

Jade sighed deeply. "Kitlene, you've been asleep for almost five hours. A lot has happened. I might as well tell you everything and give you the chance to digest it before Lyon decides to throw us out of here for waking you."

Why did that statement make Lyon sound way too ... possessive? She was just imagining it, and so she took a deep breath to calm her racing heart, at the same time she snuggled deeper into the protective feel of his shirt surrounding her.

She forced herself to not think in that direction.

"Ariel, how did you end up here, too?"

Her niece had the grace to look guilty and she quickly apologized. "I'm sorry, Aunty, for running away. I just couldn't allow you to sacrifice yourself for my sake."

"Caleb tracked her down," Jade explained. "He's Lyon's best tracker and it didn't take him more than two hours to find her." She glared at Ariel for a moment. "And good thing he did find her before any other Shifter caught her. When Caleb brought her in Lyon had just returned from talking with his brother and he sat us down for a conference. Do you remember the other woman at the warehouse? It turns out she's Niki Teal, Bryce's fiancée."

"Is she okay?" Kitlene quickly perused Ariel from head to toes then. Her niece looked fine, other than a little tense. "The kidnappers were looking for you, Ariel. I was so afraid of what they would do if they found you first."

Ariel actually grinned. Kitlene wondered at the sudden change in her demeanor. "Caleb would have torn them to pieces first. Lyon is a ferocious force to have to face, but Caleb is just as lethal –only in a different way."

Hmm. Her niece sounded completely enamored of this Caleb. She'd have to talk with her about that later. "You've met Lyon. Does he know now that you're his fiancée and ... not me?" What would happen now? Could she still convince Lyon to accept her as a substitute for Ariel? Would he even listen to reason?

Ariel sobered, losing her smile. "He knows. And after he gave me the longest, nastiest lecture of my life for my foolish escapade, he finally listened to what I had to say. I'm sorry for this mess, Aunty. The guilt is eating me up. All the time we were flying out here, I kept fighting with my conscience. On one hand, I'm young enough to want to be naturally selfish. I want to live before I have to settle down in something as permanent as marriage. But on the other hand, I've always known that my future wasn't really, truly mine to decide. We're special women. The survival of certain people actually depend on us, and that's an incredible gift to have."

Kitlene held her breath. She had the feeling she knew what Ariel was about to say. She just didn't know how she felt about it. And that bothered her more than anything.

"When Caleb found me I panicked. I knew my running was over. I had hoped to stay hidden until after the Shifter's Moon then none of this would be necessary anyway. I figured that even if Lyon accepted your proposal, Jade would step in and stop it before the mating ceremony."

"My plan, exactly," Jade muttered.

Ariel ran a shaky hand through her long hair. "If you think Lyon is tough, you haven't experienced a lecture from Caleb. He threw everything at me. Short of turning me over his knees and giving me the spanking he said I deserved. The short of it is that he made me realize the truth. I was chosen for this. I'm the one destined to unite the Pride by marrying Lyon and giving him the Alpha son. He explained what Grandfather had neglected to tell us. If I give birth to a son bearing the 'moon and jaguar' mark, that child is destined to be a great leader in the future. He will turn out to be their very salvation."

She got up and came to the bed, and then curled up on it beside Kitlene, hugging her close. "I can't let you sacrifice your life for mine, and still go on living too. You wouldn't survive the birth, Aunty; we know that for fact. I've decided to accept the Decree and marry Lyon. You'll be safe, and I will finally fulfill my destiny."

Kitlene felt like she couldn't breathe. She wasn't sure how to feel about Ariel's change of heart, and she wasn't sure what to make of the sudden feeling of … sadness in her own. Was it all so easily solved now? Could she accept Ariel's decision and just go back home?

She finally cleared her throat swallowing the burning, choking feel. *Why do I feel tearful?* "Does Lyon know you've accepted the Decree and that you won't run from him again?"

"Yes." Ariel nodded her head. "Although I'm still not sure how to take his reaction. He's a strange man."

How had he reacted? Kitlene wasn't sure what to think about that. Lyon had thought she was Ariel when they'd first met. Was he angry that she'd tried to deceive him? She hadn't, not really. She just didn't get the chance to tell him the truth before that fight broke out.

Kitlene hugged Ariel close. "Are you sure about this, honey? It's really your decision and no one else's?"

"It's my destiny," Ariel answered with conviction.

Kitlene released a sigh, her heart feeling like it was about to break and she couldn't even explain why. "Then Jade and I will go home. Unless, you want us to stay? We can return the day of the Ceremony, but there's no reason for us to remain here."

Unless…Ariel's life was still in danger. She couldn't leave her niece knowing that there was a chance another kidnapping might happen.

No, she argued mentally, Ariel would be perfectly safe now that she was with Lyon. She knew that, with all her heart.

"We can't leave," Jade said. Kitlene looked enquiringly at her. "This leads me to the rest of the story, and why you're in Lyon's bedroom."

Oh. Was she even sure she wanted to hear this?

"Lyon had a talk with his brother. Apparently they have outside enemies who are, for some unknown reason, determined to stop the Mating Ceremony. Lyon thought Bryce was behind the kidnapping until that woman turned out to be Niki."

"Ariel is still in danger, isn't she?" Kitlene hugged her niece closer.

Jade sighed, the sound long and drawn out. "We all are, Kit. Apparently, it's because of our 'gift'. Those damn jaguar genes. Lyon believes we've been targeted. Not only Ariel, because of the ceremony, but you and me too. He isn't going to take the chance we might be kidnapped again. Or worse."

"We have watchers who have protected us all our lives," Kitlene reasoned. "They will continue to do so. It's our fault they weren't here when all this happened."

"No one knows who they are," Jade answered, "And...no one knows where they are. Zachary hasn't been located either."

Oh God. Could things get any more complicated? "What about the other two Elders?"

"Nowhere to be found."

What was happening? Her fear for Ariel's safety threatened to overwhelm her for a minute. Lyon. She needed to talk to him. She couldn't explain why, only that she needed to. "Where is Lyon? We need to figure this out before Ariel's life is threatened again."

"He's in a conference with several of his men. He doesn't know you're awake yet, and I was supposed to tell him."

Which led her back to the question, "Okay, why am I here in his bedroom?"

Jade grinned. When she had that look on her face, Kitlene always knew Jade's not-funny-at-all sense of humor was surfacing. *Uh oh.*

"Very interesting explanation for that," Jade said, her smile looking more like a grimace. "There are only three main suites here. Two smaller rooms belong to bodyguards. Once Ariel had finally admitted she was ready to accept her role as fiancée, Lyon's attitude changed. Drastically, I might add. He seemed to become ... more 'Alpha' I guess is the right way to explain it. He started issuing orders and everyone scattered to obey him. First he told Caleb to bring up more men for security. He's placed them at each end of the hall where they can keep watch on all three suites. There are also guards at the top of the stair landing, two protecting the front way up and two protecting the back way down."

That sounded reasonable enough. She instinctively had known Lyon would make sure they were safe. "Then why are you smiling as though you're about to reveal a secret?"

"Because I am," Jade told her. "Lyon has placed you in his suite. Me in his Beta's, and Ariel, in Caleb's."

In their suites? "Why?" And where were the men supposed to stay?

"We've become a part of the protection team, Kit. You and I are going to be decoys should anyone somehow manage to get past those guards and get up here. No one would ever expect Ariel to be anywhere else but in Lyon's room. By the time it's discovered, the enemy would be dead."

She suppressed a shudder. When had all this turned into some weird nightmare that felt like it wasn't going to be ending any time soon?

She shook her head at Jade. "You're liking this, I can see it in your eyes. And you accused me of wanting to play the heroine."

"Playing has nothing to do with it." Jade turned serious. "Those kidnapping bastards were planning on killing us, Kitlene. I want to get even. It's bad enough that we've had to live our entire lives with this 'Destiny' crap hanging over our heads, but this is just taking things too far when someone decides we're better off dead simply because we have a 'gift."

Kitlene realized she felt the same way. She was still confused about the part she was to play in all this, but instinct told her it was the only solution for now. If there was a chance that the enemy would eventually be exposed, and in the long run it would take this threat off Ariel, then she was willing to play along.

She just wasn't sure about this new living arrangement …

"Where are the men going to be sleeping while we occupy their suites?" Would Lyon stay somewhere else, instead of being close enough to protect Ariel?

Jade's expression turned angry. That couldn't be good. "That's the part of Lyon's plan I'm not so happy about. In order to protect us, they're staying with us."

"With us?" Kitlene heard the croak of surprise in her voice and shook her head. "As in the same room?" *Okay, I am not going to analyze my reaction to that!*

"Almost," Jade growled out. "These suites are really huge. There is a bedroom, a bath, a kitchenette, a living room, and a den in each one. The men are going to be using the dens as sleeping rooms. We get the bedrooms." She actually growled again and Kitlene couldn't believe the authenticity of the sound coming from her friend's throat. How many more surprises were about to be sprung at her? She gulped when Jade finished her statement, "And these damn bedroom doors do not have locks on them."

Okay. That made her heart speed up again. Not good. She was going to be staying in Lyon's bedroom. He was going to be close by, and …! She shook her head. No way was this going to happen. They could figure out some other way to protect Ariel.

She wasn't about to tell Jade, but she was still stunned by the overwhelming feelings that had hit her the moment she'd met Lyon. Those feelings scared her more than all that had already happened. The sooner this situation was over with, the better.

She couldn't let herself feel anything for the man her niece was destined to marry. How crazy was that?

•

The reports were in and the news wasn't good. Damn it all to hell. What was going on? *Who is behind this?* Lyon snapped the pencil he was holding in two pieces and watched it fly across his desk.

Four watchers found dead, and the other two still missing. He'd let Bryce deal with what ever had happened to Niki's watchers, but for right now he was only concerned with the watchers for Ariel and Kitlene. He wanted answers and he wanted them yesterday.

Three of his men had called from Florida to inform him they had found the elusive watchers, or at least four of them.

Dead. Inside the Skye home.

Granted, they weren't sure the dead men were the actual watchers or the enemy, but it was obvious they were jaguar. Weapons found on the bodies indicated military origins. Since he didn't want to think that a jaguar would be working for the enemy, he had to assume they were the watchers.

And where the hell was Zachary? Or the other two Elders?

His talk with Bryce hadn't been as productive as he'd hoped. His brother was furious that his fiancée had been kidnapped, but didn't seem overly concerned to find out that there was an enemy targeting the women now. Bryce had stated he wasn't surprised. The predicted battle to come was insidiously weeding out the Shifter races, forcing individuals to choose sides. He'd actually expected something like this to happen.

"What better way than to weaken us, Lyon? Are you so willing to take the chance that your woman could be killed any time simply because you've chosen the wrong side to support?"

His woman. Bryce had been referring to Ariel. She was his fiancée.

But, Kitlene was his woman.

He knew that with every fiber of his being. He'd recognized her as his Truemate the first moment he'd set eyes on her and had accepted it instantly. Acknowledged it the very moment her sweet scent had sunk into every pore of his body and settled irrevocably deep into his soul. Grasped at it the truthful moment when he'd watched his blood heal her deadly wound.

He just didn't know what the hell he was going to do about it. He needed to talk to Zachary. He needed to know why Ariel, specifically, had been chosen. Had the Elder been privy to a vision or prophecy that showed Ariel was the only one who would be able to give him that son of destiny? Damn it, would his responsibility to his Pride take away the one thing he knew with a certainty now that he couldn't lose and still go on living?

"Are you going to stay silent, or are you going to talk to me about this?" Mason spoke up, interrupting his thoughts.

Lyon knew what Mason was referring to. It had been more than obvious when he'd turned all primal and possessive over Kitlene after she'd been wounded. He'd given her his Alpha blood. That alone was tell-all. And now, he had her safely tucked in his bedroom.

"Nothing to say," Lyon shrugged his shoulders. He and Mason had grown up close as brothers. They'd shared a lot of things over the years. Lyon just wasn't sure how much of his thoughts and feelings he wanted to share right now. Especially when he hadn't made a decision yet. "She's my Truemate." He didn't have to say her name, Mason already knew. "But I'm destined to marry Ariel. What am I supposed to say to that?"

Mason rubbed his neck. "I'm sorry, brother. This is one crazy, helluva mess."

That was an understatement. He had a looming marriage in less than twenty-six days, a brother who might or might not be plotting to stop the Ceremonial mating any way he could, a possible war on the horizon, and enemies he didn't even know where to begin to look for.

And a Truemate, sleeping in his bed.

"You should have put Jade in your room. I can protect Kitlene just as easy."

"No." She was staying with him, within seeing distance and reach, at all times. He'd kill anyone who tried to hurt her again.

"It isn't your smartest decision," Mason muttered.

Maybe not. But he wasn't going to let her go. Not until there was no other choice ...

"You're just disgruntled because you have to watch over Jade."

"Smart ass. That woman is a walking bomb just waiting for an excuse to explode. Don't blame me if I end up killing her before all this is over with."

Lyon grinned. "I was going to give you Ariel, but I have a feeling your nephew might have challenged that order."

Mason frowned darkly at that. "Yeah, I noticed how he was hovering over her so protectively. He said it was because she was so fragile. And he always feels protective of little women. This isn't good, Lyon. Someone is going to get hurt before this situation is over."

As long as Kitlene stayed safe, one way or another, it didn't matter to him who else got hurt. She mattered.

Hell if he knew what he was going to do to keep her completely safe. Even from him.

Chapter Seven

*W*hen she woke again, Kitlene found the room in complete darkness and no sign of Jade or Ariel. She sat up and glanced over at the clock on the nightstand. Three AM.

That explained why everything was so quiet. Everyone was asleep. "And I've slept long enough to keep me awake for nights now. Great."

She was also a little hungry. She couldn't remember the last time she'd ate, and wasn't even sure what day it was. Jade had mentioned the suite had a kitchenette. Maybe if she was quiet enough, she could sneak in there and find a snack. Suddenly remembering that Lyon was most likely sleeping in the den, her heart started racing.

How was she going to face him? He thought she'd tried to deceive him into believing she was Ariel. Then, in order to save her life he had to give her his blood. What did you say to someone after that? *Thanks for the blood. Sorry about all the mix up.* She grimaced. *Yeah, right.*

Her stomach reminded her she was hungry and she got off the bed, went to the door and slowly opened it. The living room area was dark as well. Her tummy grumbled again and she hoped it remained quiet long enough for her to reach the relative safety of the kitchen. She'd heard that Shifters had excellent, supernatural hearing. The last thing she wanted to do was wake Lyon. Clutching closed the silk shirt she tiptoed across the living room to where a dim light glowed from an open doorway indicating the kitchen. She was halfway there before she squealed and stopped immediately.

His voice was low. Deep. Almost a sensual hum. "Where are you going, sweetheart?"

Lyon turned on a small lamp next to the sofa he was reclining on, illuminating the room. Her breath caught. His long, jean clad legs were stretched out in front of him, and he was reclining back, arms behind his head. Shirtless. *Oh.* Heaven help her. He was one perfect specimen of the male species. A broad, tanned chest, lightly dusted with dark tawny hair. Muscled arms, flat washboard stomach. She hastily pulled her gaze upward again. His sensually handsome face was so compelling the bad-boy looks alone could make a woman willingly melt into a puddle at his feet. *Sigh.* She was in so much trouble. She'd never reacted to any man this way; so acutely aware of every lethal inch of his hard, toned body. Her breathing escalated.

"I didn't know you were out here," she said quickly to hide her embarrassment. "I wanted something to snack on. Sorry for waking you." *Oh sigh, Kitlene. That sounded so juvenile.*

He stared at her, his dark turquoise gaze intense and thorough as it roamed over her scantily clad body. *Puddle forthcoming.* She self-consciously clutched the shirt tighter closed.

"You didn't wake me," he murmured gently. "How do you feel? Wren said he took the stitches out and the wound was already fading." His eyes darkened and he slowly sat up straighter. Kitlene felt the sudden need to run. No man had ever looked at her like he was doing right now. "Come here."

"What?" She gulped and her heartbeat sped up.

His grin was slow, but that made it all the more sensuous. "Come here, I want to take a look. I trust Wren, but I'd rather be sure."

Heart racing way too fast, breath suddenly catchy, she shook her head. "No need to check. Your doctor was telling the truth." God help her, but she wanted to obey his oddly sexy command. Not good. But … she didn't have any panties on. Or anything else! She wasn't about to lift that shirt just to appease his curiosity!

His eyes narrowed, the turquoise turning brighter in vivid intensity. "Come here," he said deceptively soft, "Or I come get you."

He wouldn't! She took a step back when he slowly rose to his feet. Suddenly panicking, she held out both hands to stop him from getting any closer and balled them into fists. "Don't you dare touch me," she warned. He looked very much like a dangerous cat on the prowl right then. Determined in his intent. Sensual in his moves and narrowed gaze. She didn't know whether the shiver that danced over her now overly sensitized nerves was from fear ... or excitement. She only knew she didn't like it.

He raised tawny brows. "Now, sweetheart," he drawled softly, "Is that any way to treat the man who saved your life? You're acting like I would hurt you if I touched you."

Kitlene studied his face closely, trying to decipher his thoughts. Was that just a tinge of regret in his tone? "I didn't say that. It's just," She said a silent prayer he wasn't noticing her blush and rushed on, "That I'm completely naked under this shirt."

Oh great. She couldn't believe she'd just blurted that out. What was it about men and the word 'naked'? Did they all have to automatically react so primal-male whenever they heard it? If she hadn't been standing so close to him she might have missed hearing his low rumbling growl. And she certainly didn't miss the look on his face, or the darkening of his cat-eyes. She took two more steps back. Running back to the safety of the bedroom was looking like the best of all ideas right now.

"Stop, Kitlene," he commanded softly, a dark frown marring his handsome features. "I'm not going to touch you, so stop backing away." He ran a hand over his face, and then sighed out roughly. "Come on, I'll get you something to eat."

Surprised at the abrupt change in his demeanor, Kitlene cautiously followed him to the kitchenette. He pulled out a bar chair from the breakfast counter and waved at her to sit. It took a bit of maneuvering to get up on the high-seated chair and still keep the shirt from coasting up her hips. She noticed him watching her endeavors from under lowered lashes as he sat a glass of milk down in front of her.

"My shirt looks good on you," he murmured in a sexy rasp.

Her entire body responded instantly. Shivery. Alive. She'd felt those same feelings when she'd first met him. Panic tried to set in again. This couldn't be happening. And it certainly wasn't going to work. She couldn't stay here, under his watch. There had to be a better solution.

"What happened to my own clothes?" *Okay. Calm voice. That's good.*

He turned back to the refrigerator and pulled out a carton of eggs. He shrugged those wide, bare shoulders and she immediately chewed on her bottom lip to keep from sighing in appreciation. It didn't help that he had the sexiest body she'd ever seen on a man. *Stop, Kitlene. Stop thinking in that direction.*

"They were ruined from the wound and blood. I had them thrown out. Sorry. I'll have someone get your suitcases from the hotel tomorrow."

"Why didn't you, earlier?" Wouldn't that have made more sense than clothing her in one of his shirts?

He sighed, the sound so soft she wasn't sure she heard it. Or the incredibly low murmured words, "Because I wanted you wearing my shirt." She had to have imagined he'd said those words. He turned back to her. "Because my men have been going over your hotel room, inch by inch, to make sure we don't miss any clues. I want to know who those bastards were that kidnapped you. I don't want any evidence lost, so that meant leaving everything as is."

Would they find anything? Something else had been bothering her ever since she'd talked to Jade and Ariel earlier. "Lyon, how did they know or suspect Ariel might show up at your club right when I did? No one knew we were here. We made sure even the watchers were left clueless."

"Yeah," Sudden anger darkened his features now and his voice roughened. "About that." He placed his hands, palms down, on the counter in front of her and leaned close. A muscle clenched in his strong jaw. His entire body language shouted anger. She stared, a bit stunned. One minute he was a concerned host and the next he was an aggressive Shifter showing his Alpha nature at its best. *Whoa.*

"I've had this urge ever since meeting you to turn you over my knees and spank the hell out of you for being so foolish." Once again those mesmerizing cat-eyes made a thorough sweep over her before coming back to snare her gaze with his. His voice hardened. "Those damn watchers protected you for a reason, Kitlene. You knew that. Ditching their security was beyond stupid." He snarled low, his upper lip baring his teeth. Very strong, sharp teeth. "What the hell were you thinking?"

"Stop cussing at me," she told him, straightening her shoulders. Two could play at this angry word game. After all she'd been through the last few days, he had no right treating her like a child that needed scolding. "We had legitimate reasons for doing what we did. How were we to know someone would guess and be waiting to kidnap us? We're not psychic."

He growled. Low and rough. "Damn it, I'll do more than just cuss at you if you ever even think of doing something that crazy again."

"We're back to that part where I'm telling you that you better not touch me," she gritted out, hands clenching. How had this conversation gotten so out of control?

"Put yourself in danger like that again," he drawled dangerously, "and you'll quickly find out that telling me not to touch you will be a waste of breath."

Okay, reacting to that primal male threat shouldn't feel so exciting. What was wrong with her? She wasn't exactly sure what was happening between them but it was more than a little overwhelming. She knew then that she needed to diffuse the oddly sensual tension before things got out of control. She prided herself on being able to remain calm in most situations, but she wasn't so sure she'd succeed around someone like Lyon –he was too intense in everything he said and did. "We didn't deliberately set out to get into danger, Lyon," she said quietly. "Ariel was upset about this Decree and the only solution to the situation was to talk to you first before this went farther."

He straightened, and then leaned back against the counter behind him. He crossed his arms over his chest. "Why ditch the watchers?"

She relaxed; at least he was willing to listen now. "We didn't know who they were or where, and we couldn't contact Zachary. Ariel was making herself sick. She wasn't eating or sleeping, she cried all the time. The only solution was to talk to you about a compromise."

His brows arched. "Compromise?" He shook his head. "I wasn't happy about this damn Decree, either, but it's a done deal. The only way to protect and unify my Pride is to follow through with it."

Kitlene took a deep breath and then released it on a shaky sigh. She'd been so sure that sacrificing herself in Ariel's place was the only solution. Now, she wasn't so sure. If Ariel had already decided to accept the Decree and marry Lyon, then was it necessary to even bring up the crazy plan she'd thought was the right decision?

"Ariel is only eighteen," she explained instead, purposely ignoring his question about the compromise. "She has her whole life ahead of her. Zachary should have chosen someone else. I thought we could convince you to wait until we could talk to Zachary and have him pick another woman. There are others, almost twenty of us left."

She felt, as well as saw, the way his entire body tensed at her words. His cat eyes suddenly gleamed with an inner fire that felt physically scorching as it roamed over her body again. And darn it, her body reacted instantly. She felt sensually tingly all over.

"Why didn't he choose you, instead?"

A hard shiver streaked over and through her at the deep, sexy huskiness of his voice. Her hands shook as she clutched the opening of the shirt tighter closed. She couldn't answer that. Couldn't tell him the truth. She broke free from his captive stare and looked down at the glass of milk on the counter. She shook her head. "Zachary is a wise Elder. He must have believed that Ariel was the one for you. Just as he picked Niki for Bryce. I've never pretended to understand his motives, or his powerful knowledge." She shrugged. "And the fact that Ariel is so young wasn't a problem he acknowledged."

"You've always known that your destiny was bound with the Jaguar." Lyon's voice roughened. "And you accepted that. Why would you think to change the Decree if you already knew that Zachary's choice was the final word?" He stared at her for a long moment, and then his voice deepened as he asked, "What was the compromise, Kitlene?"

"It doesn't matter now," she said. *Please don't keep asking.*

"The hell it doesn't," Lyon muttered. "My intended mate made herself sick and then ran away to avoid marrying me. I take that personal. Now, she suddenly changes her mind and is ready to follow through with the Decree. Her only answer was that she wouldn't allow you to sacrifice everything. What did she mean by that?"

He wasn't going to allow her to not tell him. She could hear it in his voice, could see it in the aggressive way he held himself. He was so Alpha right then, it scared her a little.

No, if she admitted the truth, what really scared her was just how primal male he was. She couldn't get past that, and how much it kept her so intensely aware of his every move, his every look.

She cleared her suddenly dry throat. "Ariel is a bit dramatic in some things. You usually have to take what she says or does and try to make sense out of it first. In her defense, she's still very young. I'm sure she'll settle down once she's ... married."

"You didn't answer my question."

She raised her head and met his hot stare. "Sorry. That's all I can say. And it doesn't matter now. She's accepted the situation."

Lyon slowly shook his head. His voice lowered, sexy and rough at the same time. "Sweetheart, you can tell me the truth, or I'll get it out of her. Your choice."

He would, too. Instinct told her he wasn't a man easily pushed around. If he wanted something, he got it. "That's not the sexiest trait to have, you know."

Oh, heaven help her, she'd said that aloud! She could feel her cheeks heating immediately.

"Your eyes are the most expressive I've ever seen, and I can almost see the countless thoughts running around in your mind." He roughly swiped his hand across his face and then into his hair. "But, I'll be damned if I know what you meant by that remark." He frowned at her. "So stop stalling and tell me what Ariel was talking about, before I forget what's important at the moment."

It was time to retreat. Ariel was right. She was a coward in many things. "I'm not saying anything else. And you can forget about bullying Ariel into telling you. She's impulsive and hyper at times, but she's also a very stubborn woman."

"Why is it a secret?" He straightened, dropping his arms to his side. Cat sighting prey was her automatic thought. A thrill of excitement shot through her before she could suppress it.

"You're not my Alpha, Lyon Savage," she stated with as much bravado she could force out while staring at his muscles as they tensed and bunched. "You're not my fiancé. I don't have to obey you or cower to your arrogant demands. If I want to keep my personal reasons to myself, then you just have to accept that."

He growled low. Actually growled at her! She started to get off the bar chair.

"Don't even think about running, little kitten," he murmured in a dangerously sexy command. "You're not going anywhere until we finish this conversation."

She couldn't stop herself and muttered Jade's favorite words, "Wanna bet?"

Uh oh. Big mistake. He was around the counter and had her grasped in his arms before she could blink twice. He grabbed her by the waist and lifted her off the chair and swung her up straight into his arms. Shocked, she squealed and then pounded at his chest.

"Put me down!" She couldn't believe he had just caveman-grabbed her simply because she'd challenged him. "What do you think you're doing, you egotistical cat!"

He ignored her struggles and carried her into the living room, back to the sofa. He suddenly dropped his arms so that her feet hit the floor. Just as quick, he was sitting and grabbing her again. Before she could even squeal again, Kitlene found herself face down across his knees. He wouldn't!

"Don't you dare touch me! I'll scream this place down. I mean it, Lyon! Ow!"

His hard hand came down landing a stinging smack across her butt cheek. Right on her bare butt! She screamed in outrage. She couldn't believe this was happening.

She kicked and squirmed, trying to twist out of his hold. Another hard smack landed and she screamed again.

Before she could open her mouth for another screaming protest he grabbed her waist and flipped her over. One moment she was laying across his lap and the next he'd pulled her straight up into his arms against his chest. One hand behind her head, the other arm wrapped around her back, Lyon jerked her closer. So close she could clearly see the fire burning in the turquoise depths of his eyes.

Snarling, he muttered, "Hell."

She had only a second to see the dangerous intent in his blazing eyes and then he was kissing her.

He silenced her whimpered protest, his lips capturing hers in a hot, open mouth kiss that stole her breath and every coherent thought she had. For one long minute she was shocked. And then she was drowning in incredible, breath-stealing sensations she never knew existed. His mouth feasted on hers, deepening the kiss by pushing his rough, cat-textured tongue in to entwine with hers. She couldn't think, didn't want to.

Before she even realized she was doing it, she whimpered an acceptance into his ravaging mouth and melted against him. He growled low in his throat and the primal, sexy sound rumbled up into her mouth. His hand beneath her hair on her neck tightened.

His other arm against her back tightened for only a moment. Then, he was slowly smoothing it down her back, over her hip, and straight to the bottom edge of his shirt. The moment his caressing palm lifted the shirt and touched her bare bottom she uttered a small scream of pure pleasure into his devouring mouth.

Suddenly, a loud pounding on the suite's door broke them apart. Kitlene gasped in a deep breath and stared into Lyon's glittering eyes as he made the effort to control his own breathing.

"Lyon, what's going on? Everything okay?"

Lyon cussed under his breath. "Fine, Mason. Nothing to worry about."

Kitlene wanted to moan. Nothing? That kiss was nothing?

"We heard a scream."

"Yeah," Lyon coughed out a chuckle, sounding suspiciously like he thought it all a big joke. But she saw the deception in his burning eyes, the strained look of passion still keeping his features hard. He never took his gaze from hers. "Kitlene had a fright when she woke and found herself in a strange bed. She's fine now."

She heard Mason mumble something as he left. Breathing erratically she tore her gaze from Lyon's hot, penetrating stare. Reality hit her, hard and fast. She was sitting in Ariel's fiancé's lap, nearly naked and cuddled against his bare chest. *No. No. No!* Kitlene pushed against his restraining hold. Somehow, she managed to slip from his grasp and still maintain her dignity and keep the shirt closed as she stood. Once again on her feet, albeit unsteady feet, she backed away from him.

"I can't believe you did that." She groaned under her breath. Her voice sounded way too breathless and soft. That wasn't good. Ha. There wasn't anything good about her reactions to this man and what had just happened.

"It's been inevitable since the moment we met." His voice was low and sexily hoarse. She shivered in reaction, and wanted to ask him what he meant by that but was afraid to. He ate her up with his hungry stare and it was all she could do to stand there and pretend to be as calm as she could manage.

"Don't ever touch me again." There, that sounded brave enough.

His grin was more than sexy; it was downright dangerous. "Sweetheart, you'll learn fast that I'm not one to take orders." His hot stare raked her from head to toes. "And no one tells me not to take what I want."

He wanted her. How had this situation got so out of control? She couldn't think straight with him eating her up like that with his hungry gaze. She shook her head. It was time to retreat. She saw it in his expression. Knew she was in danger if she stayed a moment longer.

"This is crazy. You're Ariel's fiancé." If she kept saying that aloud enough, she just might convince herself that having these out-of-place feelings for this Shifter was more than just crazy. She had to get control now. "I can't believe I was planning on sacrificing myself as a substitute for Ariel. I've had too many crazy plans in the last few days, but that was definitely the craziest." *Oh no.* She hadn't meant to blurt that out. She quickly followed with, "I'm not staying here, either. I'm going back to the hotel."

Lyon growled warningly, coming to his feet in a surge of sleek power. "Think again, sweetheart. You're not getting out of my sight. Try running from me and I'll hunt you down. You don't want to have to deal with me, then." He frowned, his sensuous lips thinning in anger. "And what the hell are you talking about, substituting yourself for Ariel?"

"Nothing now." She backed her way to the bedroom door. If she could just get away from his captive stare, she could think clearer. "Everything has been solved and Ariel is willing to marry you." *Please don't ask anything more.* She'd die of embarrassment if he knew the full truth: *I thought it a great idea to give myself to you as a sacrifice. Smart, huh?*

"Kitlene," he growled her name so rough she shivered again. "Don't walk away from me without explaining that. My bedroom door doesn't have a lock. And I don't think you want me following you in there—or want me anywhere close to my bed right now." He gave her a look so thorough and so hot she felt scorched all over. "Believe me."

Gulp. That was a threat she knew she'd better take seriously. Time to diffuse this situation, if she could. And hopefully talk to a calmer Lyon tomorrow. When she was fully dressed. She couldn't stop herself, and she glanced down at the obvious erection straining against the flap of his jeans. Yep. Later was definitely better. When he wasn't so fully ... aroused.

She let her shoulders slump dramatically and sighed as tired-sounding as she could. She even made her voice soft and weak. "I really need to lie down, Lyon. Can we call a truce and talk tomorrow?"

He stared intensely at her for long, strained moments. She was afraid he was about to say no. She wasn't sure what she was going to do then. The man had her scared and excited all at once. *Heaven help me. I've got to get out of here.*

Lyon lifted his hand–and what she was beginning to suspect was a habit whenever he was vexed –ran his fingers over his face and then through his hair. He exhaled roughly.

"Go to bed." He spit out a few foul words she clearly heard. "And do us both a favor. Don't come out again until I can get you some decent clothes. If I see you wearing nothing but my shirt again and looking so damn sexy in it, I won't promise to not repeat what happened a few minutes ago." He growled low, a clear warning. "And Kitlene, nothing will make me stop next time."

She fled. He didn't have to tell her twice. As soon as she could, she was going to do an "Ariel trick' and run. She wouldn't stop until she was as far away as she could get from too-sexy-for-his-own-good Lyon Savage. She had the feeling her sanity would depend on the long distance.

She just wished she didn't feel so sad about that thought.

Chapter Eight

*H*e'd told her she wasn't getting out of his sight. He'd lied. If he'd stayed in that room with her so temptingly close another minute, he would have done something he knew was life-changing wrong. His conscience told him it was wrong. His heart and aching body told him different.

So, he'd run. After entrusting Mason to guard Kitlene, Lyon left the club and got in his Jaguar. Minutes later he was speeding through downtown L.A. and heading to the ranch. The pre-dawn morning made traffic lighter than it would be later and he made it out of town in less than a half hour.

He could still taste her mouth. She had the softest lips, and the taste was like the sweetest of creams. Addictively sweet. He could have kissed her senseless and still wanted to taste her more. Hell. He hadn't meant to kiss her. Shouldn't have even touched her. But she'd pushed him too far, telling him she wasn't his in any way.

Hearing her say it had only made him want to turn primal and prove her wrong. And then, dammit, she'd melted into his kiss and immediately turned his insides into molten lava. Another minute and he would have had that damn shirt off her and...

He didn't even brake as he turned off the freeway onto the road leading to the ranch. For a tire-spinning moment the Jaguar tilted before he regained control and righted it back onto the graveled road.

Lyon prided himself on the steely control he had over everything in his life. This wasn't control. From the first moment he'd looked into her beautiful dove-grey eyes and inhaled the undeniable scent of his Truemate, he'd lost control of everything.

And he had no idea how to get it back again.

The road came to a branch. The right led to the ranch house, another two miles in. The left faded off into the countryside, leading to horse trails and mountainous areas. He stopped the car on the left side and got out. Once a week he and his men came out to the ranch to train. Other times, anyone of them used the area for running in jaguar form. It was the only time they could escape the city and be able to run free without fear of exposure. The vast ranchland belonged to the Pride, but his brother ran it and Lyon respected his space by keeping his men as far from the main house as possible. Either side very seldom managed to cross paths, though once in awhile a lone jaguar might come across another pride member running.

He hoped this wasn't one of those times. The way he was feeling, he'd probably attack with very little provocation. He changed to jaguar, and relished the wildness that swamped his senses as he fell to all fours. He lifted his head and sniffed the cool morning air. Various scents came back to him of other animals, though all of them were natural beings. Good. No sense in pissing off Bryce by attacking one of his men if the chance came up. He prowled off the road and headed east toward the training grounds. In a few moments, he was running full-out, his jaguar speed eating up the miles as he ran effortlessly, tirelessly.

He ran for two hours. And for the first time in his life he discovered he couldn't turn off his human thoughts while he ran free as jaguar.

•

The Lion Shifter lowered the binoculars he was holding and sat back. He was in human form, as were his two companions, but the three other men behind them paced in their lion forms, restless to start the hunt.

"Does he come out here often, alone?"

"Yeah," the man standing beside him answered. "He trains his men here, and comes out almost every other night to run." He chuckled as though it was really amusing. "Damn city life keeps them feeling caged, yet they prefer living there. Go figure."

Cats were nocturnal animals. Bred hunters. They needed space to roam. The Lion understood that need too, and nodded his head. "Good. This opens up a possibility I hadn't anticipated."

The other man in human form shook his head. "I'm surprised he's out here this morning. He usually comes at night. And after all that's happened, I didn't think he'd leave his woman under someone else's protection while he ran."

"How many men does he have following him?"

"Trained as warriors, less than fifty. Employed at the Club, about twenty."

"She'll be too protected now at the Club. We'll have to figure another way to get to her. Who were the other two women with her?"

"Kitlene Skye, her aunt. And Jade Tempest, best friend and physician."

"Hmm. Physician. That might be a idea to stew over." The Lion raised the binoculars again and located the running jaguar in his sights. "Incredible speed," he murmured in admiring respect. He turned to the three young male lions pacing behind him. "Think you can catch him? We'll see. But! Don't attack. Aggravate him all you want to, but don't lay a paw on him. Not yet. Now, go."

With roars of overzealous youth and the scent of prey in their nostrils the three lions sprang off the small hilltop and hit the trail following the jaguar.

The Lion nodded his head in satisfaction. "Step one."

•

Lyon smelled the lion Shifters before he saw them. He skidded to a halt, sides heaving from his run, and waited for them to show themselves. Stinking ambushers were waiting just beyond a clump of trees. He growled low. Where had they come from? Caleb said he'd seen Lions arrive at the ranch a few days before, but he'd only sighted four full-grown males. The ones hiding in the trees were young; he could tell by their scent and the amateurish growls of aggression they weren't bothering to keep low. He counted three. Damn cubs didn't even know how to stay concealed.

Good. He needed a fight. He calmed his breathing. He was winded from the long hard run and that wasn't the best condition to fight three, but he knew he was seasoned enough to whip them if he took them on one at a time. And they were probably stupid and inexperienced enough to let him do just that. His feline lips peeled back in a feral grin. *Come on, kits. Let's get this over with.*

He roared a challenge.

The three young male cats hit the ground simultaneously and stalked toward him. Lyon braced his body, ready to spring into attack. Yards from him they stopped and hissed threats. Lyon mentally chuckled. They knew he was in prime condition and wouldn't go down without taking one or two with him. So they waited. And they taunted.

Then, as one, they slowly moved forward. Lyon watched each one closely for any sign of sudden attack. Instead of attacking, they split up and circled him. He growled and stood his ground. They slowly closed the circle around him. As they moved closer, he finally got tired of the game and struck out with his long claws extended. He slapped one male across his face. The lion reared back with a cry of rage.

But he didn't attack. And neither did the other two. *What the hell?* Lyon swung his body around to face one of the others and then struck at him too, landing a deep slash across his shoulder. Although enraged and growling like they were going to tear him apart, they still didn't attack.

He was just a game to them. And that really pissed him off. He struck the third lion, this time across the throat. All three were bleeding from his strikes but they still hadn't hit back. Okay, if they weren't going to oblige him with a fair fight, it was time to send them running with their tails tucked behind them. With a roar of warning, Lyon launched into the air and landed full body on the closest lion. He took him down, slashing as he rolled clear.

In the blink of an eye he was on the next lion, dealing him the same damage. Before that one gained his feet, Lyon had the third lion down and bleeding. Sides heaving, blood dripping from his claws and mouth, he stared them down.

They got to their feet, whining with pain and frustration. Hell. They were ... frustrated? Why weren't they fighting back?

If he hadn't witnessed it, he'd have never believed the story if someone else had told him that three lions would walk away from a fight with one jaguar. But they did. They turned and ran. They were still running as he finally lost sight of them.

Exhausted but satisfied, Lyon trotted back where he'd left his car. He didn't know what exactly had just happened, but he wasn't about to let it go. Bryce was about to get a visitor. And when he left here today, he was confident that his brother would know that he wasn't going to tolerate any more. Whatever Bryce was planning, it was ending here and now.

•

As it turned out, Bryce wasn't there. Like most cats, the jaguar was a nocturnal animal that slept late in the morning after staying up all night. His brother should have been in bed since it was only seven in the morning, but Lyon found the ranch house oddly empty. And there were no signs of the visiting Lions, either. Lyon didn't like the gut feeling that something was seriously wrong. He changed back to jaguar and spent the next half hour searching for any of Bryce's men.

He was coming back from circling the five-acre perimeter around the house when he saw Bryce, Niki, and five other jaguar Shifters going inside. He changed to human and clothed himself. A minute later he strode in, unannounced, and went straight for his brother.

Grabbing him by the throat he shoved him against the nearest wall.

"What the hell!" Bryce struggle. Behind them, Niki screamed and the bodyguards surged forward.

"Call them off, brother, or I'll rip your throat out before they reach me."

Bryce choked and squirmed a minute before he ordered his men, "Back off."

Lyon slowly released him. "In your office. Now." He didn't wait for Bryce to follow. He stomped into the large room and swung around to face him as Bryce sauntered in, Niki at his side. Lyon nodded his head toward her. "Send her out."

Bryce whispered low to her and after a moment's hesitation she turned and left, closing the door behind her.

"What the hell do you think you're doing?" Bryce demanded as he rubbed his bruised throat.

"I've decided to give you a warning, brother, instead of beating the hell out of you. If I find any other Shifter species on this ranch again and they attack any of my men, I'll come back here and rip your throat out. I don't give a damn what the consequences will be. This land belongs to the Jaguar Pride and I won't tolerate you bringing in other Shifters to roam free on it."

"What are you talking about?" Bryce spit out a few foul words. There were times when he could out-swear even Lyon, and he was obviously trying that now in an effort to show bravado in the face of Lyon's fury.

"I found three young male lions on the property earlier. Why were they here?"

"How the hell should I know?" Bryce muttered in defiance. "Did you ask them?"

"They ran off after I bloodied them up," Lyon told him. It still bothered him that they hadn't fought back. Something was definitely ... off. And he was sure his brother knew exactly what it was. Maybe he should just beat it out of him and get it over with. "Did they come in with those other four? Don't look so innocent, Bryce, it isn't working. You know I'm aware of everything that goes on here. Four male African Lions arrived a few days ago. The same day the women were kidnapped. I find that interestingly curious. Now, start talking or get ready to fight."

Bryce scowled at him and spit out a cat-huff of aggression. "I don't have to explain my actions to you, you egotistical bastard. Until one of us is declared reigning Alpha, neither has control. If I want to invite anyone to my home, you have no say about it. But if you have to know, those Shifters were visiting Dignitaries from a large Lion Pride in Kenya. They're planning to purchase property in the area. Like most of us, they prefer to live in the country. They wanted my opinion on the area around L.A."

"Yeah, right. Bryce 'The Real Estate Shifter'. Why don't I believe you?"

"Because you're looking for a reason to fight me," Bryce scoffed at him.

"I don't need a reason." Lyon clamped down on the fury and aggression building in crescendo deep inside. Tearing his brother to pieces wouldn't exactly solve anything. His brother's death would only force the Elders to take over as reigning rule of the Pride. He wasn't going to allow that. So, that meant he had to back down. For now.

He unclenched his fisted hands and forced a calm he was still far from feeling. "We're brothers and that means you know me better than anyone," he stated, holding Bryce's gaze in the Alpha way. "So, you know I won't give you another warning. I'll strike. Don't be stupid enough to doubt that, Bryce. Ever."

He stomped out of the room and out of the house. He was still in the dark about what his brother was planning, but at least now

Bryce knew he would be watching him.

As he jogged to where he'd left his car, he thought back over the morning's events. It was possible the three lions were simply trespassing and that's the reason they hadn't attacked him.

There were other possibilities, but he didn't like them. His brother was a rash, impulsive man but he wasn't as stupid as Lyon sometimes called him. Bryce wouldn't be foolish enough to jeopardize his Alpha status before the Shifter's Moon Ceremony.

Damn. He just had to think about the Shifter's Moon, didn't he? It took a lot of willpower then to keep from letting his thoughts stray to the woman he'd left this morning. Nearly naked in his shirt, and sleeping in his bed. He groaned loudly as the relentless ache he'd been fighting all morning abruptly renewed with a hot rush and started torturing him all over again.

It didn't help his restraint any when he arrived at the car and heard his cell phone ringing. He grabbed it off the car seat and answered, "What?"

In the background he could hear raised voices and loud crashes. His heartbeat increased. Mason's voice came on the line, shouting obscenities over the noise.

"Give me permission to kill," Mason yelled angrily. "I swear, I'll try and spare Ariel. But Jade and Kitlene are as good as dead if you don't get back here now, Lyon. Grab her, Beau! Kitlene, put that vase down, now! Lyon, I mean it. They're dead."

Lyon shook his head as he stared at the cell phone, the call now disconnected. He didn't know whether to be very worried … or to laugh.

He started the car, stepped on the gas, spinning the tires as he peeled back onto the road. For some reason, his mood was suddenly a little lighter. All the way back to the freeway and home, he was picturing small, delicate Kitlene using a vase to threaten his mean, tough Beta. Her lovely features would be set in that touch-me-and-you-die look and her beautiful dove-grey eyes would be sparkling with the fiery anger he'd already seen.

He couldn't help it; he grinned. And then he started laughing. Man, he loved fire in a woman.

Chapter Nine

$\mathcal{S}$he tried. She failed miserably. She'd spent the next few hours until morning curled up in that king-sized bed, *his* bed, and tried to think of all the logical reasons why she had to stay here.

Ariel needed her. That was the first and main priority. Although her niece had finally come to terms with her destiny, she was still young enough to be in an absolute panic the closer it came to the wedding day. It was only natural, especially considering she would be marrying a man she didn't know and starting a life that was too surreal at times. Chances were, Ariel would finally panic at the last minute and run again. Kitlene had to be here for her. She had to find a way to help her through this and prepare her for what was to come.

Ha. How do you prepare for marriage with a man like Lyon Savage? She shivered, just thinking about him. And then she had to admit it wasn't fear—or anything near revulsion even—that made her react that way with just the thought of the enigmatic man.

He'd touched her. And it wasn't just his physical touch, although that had nearly melted her completely, but something he had touched deep inside her the moment their eyes had met. He'd touched her with the intense, breath-taking, heart stopping, deep-in-the-pit-of-your-soul invisible touch that had, some strange way, irrevocably branded her. Forever.

Heaven help me. How could she feel this way about him? It was more than crazy. It was suicidal to her very sanity.

And when he'd pulled her against his chest and claimed her lips in that devouring kiss, she'd known then she was as good as lost. If Mason hadn't interrupted them, she would have willingly given him anything he demanded. That should shock her. But she was being honest enough to admit the truth to herself. Shock had been the last thing on her mind while she willingly melted in his strong, possessive embrace.

And therein lay the best argument for leaving. The jerk had kissed her! And he was engaged to Ariel! What kind of man was he who would kiss another woman like that and then threatened to do it again?

No, she couldn't stay here. She didn't understand this strange pull, this odd connection, lying between them, but she wasn't going to stay long enough to let it reveal itself. She'd go home, back to Florida, and then return the week before the wedding to help Ariel. Her niece was well protected and guarded to keep from running again, and she was a sensible, strong enough woman to adjust to all this.

She'd already noticed that Ariel hadn't argued about being under Caleb's protection, staying with him in his suite. Kitlene wasn't sure what to think about that. Maybe it was simply because Ariel had instinctively learned to trust Caleb after he'd found her. Maybe Ariel needed this time separate from Lyon to get used to their upcoming marriage. If she'd been forced into close proximity with him, she might have balked even more. This way, she had her own space and time to get to know him.

But I don't have to get used to him. No, the sooner she was away from him, the better for her. Heart. And soul.

So, even though he'd threatened her about coming back out of the room until she was properly dressed, she'd decided to confront him about leaving. She braced for his anger and marched out of the bedroom, head high, shoulders back.

Only to find a stranger lying on the sofa, sleeping. Surprised, she quickly looked around the suite but Lyon was nowhere around. The door to the den was open and the kitchenette was empty too.

He'd left her? After he swore he wasn't going to let her out of his sight? She shook her head; she didn't want to dwell on why that bothered her. Instead, she started tiptoeing to the suite door. She'd find Jade and they'd leave.

"Cats aren't heavy sleepers, Kitlene," the man drawled behind her. "We hear every sound around us. Where are you planning to go, especially dressed like that? Lyon would skin my hide if I let you walk out into that hall and parade around in front of his guards wearing nothing but, hell. Is that *his* shirt? Well, damn."

Kitlene swung back to face him. "Who are you?" She made her voice as firm as she could, "I want to talk to Jade and Ariel. Now." She clutched the shirt closed tighter. "And speaking of clothes, I need my suitcase from the hotel." Darn if she was going to let these arrogant Shifters make her feel so—so vulnerable and so woman-weak. They acted like all women were not only to be overly protected, but also had to be told what they could do and when. Ha. She'd been independent all her life and she wasn't about to let things change now.

"My name is Mason," he answered. "I'm Lyon's Beta." He nodded his head, indicating the bedroom door. She turned and saw her suitcase sitting by the open door. She'd been so intent on confronting Lyon and getting out of here, she hadn't even noticed the suitcase sitting there. She walked, with as much dignity as she could, considering he was staring at her in calculating intensity, to the suitcase and grabbed it. She even refrained from slamming the bedroom door behind her. She dressed quickly, pulling on a pair of hip hugging jeans and a peach, silk T-shirt. She and Jade had only packed for a few days stay, and had decided on the most casual clothes. Now she wished she'd had the foresight to bring something more mature and a little less form fitting. All her clothes were ultra-feminine, clingy, soft and sexy. She preferred her jeans and silk blouses, but her skirts, dresses, and all her underwear were all just as sensual. Soft and sensual was an addiction when it came to her clothes and her wardrobe at home was full proof. Pushing aside the thought of home for the moment, she slipped on heel-less sandals, and then brushed her hair. She closed the suitcase, leaving it on the bed. She had no intention of unpacking those few articles of clothing. She was not staying here.

She looked down where Lyon's shirt lay on the floor at her feet. She couldn't stop herself. She picked it up and held it against her breasts for a long minute. She brought it up to her nose. Even after she'd slept in it for hours, it stilled smelled like him. Earthly. Sensual. Primal. All male. She inhaled deeply, taking that scent deep into her. Holding it there. Knowing with a soul-felt conviction she would always remember it.

She heard Jade's angry voice in the other room and with a sigh carefully folded the shirt and placed it on the bed near the pillows. It was time to leave. While she still had the will to.

"I'm leaving, you shrill little cat," Mason growled out at Jade as she stood at the door of the suite and pushed him into the hall. "But, I'm staying right here at the door."

"Why, because you want to eavesdrop on our conversation? That is so rude. Why don't you go find something—cat to do instead of playing at guard kitty? What do you think we're going to do, jump from the balcony and escape?"

"It occurred to me," he muttered. "I'm not giving you much credit for being too smart."

Jade screeched at the insult and balled her fist. Ariel, standing next to her, grabbed her swinging arm just in time. Kitlene stared at Mason. He'd seen that punch aiming for him and he hadn't moved a muscle, much less blinked. Whoa. She was learning fast that these men weren't the type easily controlled. Lyon hadn't liked her warning him to not touch her, and Mason wasn't even the least bit afraid of Jade's fury. She had the bad feeling that leaving here wasn't going to be as easy as saying it.

Ariel closed the door in Mason's face and turned Jade back into the room. "Good morning, Aunty. We brought breakfast." She waved her hand at the meal spread across the small table near the kitchenette. "We raided the downstairs kitchen," she explained and then laughed. "Caleb nearly had a stroke when Jade and I ganged up on him and threatened to faint if we didn't get a decent meal fast."

Kitlene studied her niece closely. She was wide-awake. Ariel hated mornings, and she was downright perky. What had changed? "Who are you and what did you do with my niece?"

Ariel giggled. "She grew up, Aunty. Overnight."

"Why don't I like the sound of that word—*overnight*?"

Ariel blushed. "Aunty! I can't believe you of all people would even think such a thought! I was perfectly safe with Caleb. He did sleep outside the bedroom door—on the floor of all things—but he didn't even come near me the entire night. He's the perfect gentleman. And he takes his duty as protector very seriously."

That's not what she'd been thinking. Kitlene frowned. Or had she? After this morning's run-in with Lyon, she wasn't sure what to think anymore at this point. Ariel had always been a natural flirt, and had gone through countless boyfriends. She hoped her niece wasn't already setting her sights on an unsuspecting Caleb, thinking she could flirt a little before settling down as a married woman in less than a month's time. Kitlene sighed. When had this entire situation become so complicated?

They sat down to eat. Jade remained oddly quiet since the incident with Mason. Kitlene finally asked her what was wrong. "You're only this quiet when you're worried. After we get Ariel completely settled in, we're leaving, if that's what you're worried about."

"That's not it, exactly." Jade frowned. "When they brought our suitcases in this morning, I discovered my medical bag was missing. I really do need to get you home where I have more serum supplies. You'll need an injection in two more days."

She'd almost forgot about the injections. In all that had happened, even considering offering herself as replacement for Ariel, she hadn't once thought about missing an injection. Granted, nothing Jade had tried was working yet but she held a little spark of relentless hope deep inside her that one day it just might. She couldn't miss that injection or they'd have to start all over.

"No problem," she told Jade and then looked at Ariel. "I know you are still adjusting to this situation, sweetie. But, you've always been the stronger of the two of us, and I have a feeling you're going to get through this fine. Accepting the Decree was the major hurdle. I think it would be better if Jade and I went home and then returned before the wedding."

Ariel vehemently shook her head. "No! Aunty, the truth is I'm only being brave for you. I'm still scared to death. I don't even know the man I'm destined to marry. I need you here with me to get through all that's to come."

"You'll be completely safe, you know that," Kitlene said, already knowing she was about to make a decision that would change things, possibly in all the wrong ways. "You'll get to know Lyon, and by the time the wedding day arrives, you'll be comfortable with him." She took a deep breath and released it on a shaky exhale. Her next words struck at her heart, and she didn't want to figure out why. "There's time for you to even learn to love him. And how could he not fall in love with you?"

Silence lingered between them. Kitlene determinedly forced back the little hurt that suddenly surfaced from her soul. What was wrong with her? She couldn't have feelings for Lyon. *No. Never.*

"What about the fact that Lyon said we're all in danger until the Shifter's Moon Ceremony?" Ariel asked, "They've got us under their protection twenty-four-seven. You can't go back home, Aunty. We don't even know where our watchers are."

She'd thought about that. "I'm sure the watchers are probably scrambling around trying to find us, so all we have to do is return home back to everything normal, and they'll be there. They've always been there, and there's no reason why they still won't be."

"She's right," Jade said and stood up. "Let's go now, Kitlene. The sooner we're out of here, the better."

Kitlene retrieved her suitcase from the bedroom and Jade opened the suite door. They came face to face with Mason and Caleb blocking their way. Both men stood stiff, arms folded across their chests, determined looks on their handsome faces. Kitlene had the brief thought that all shapeshifters must be genetically handsome; and there was definitely an overabundance of that gene here. Mason and Caleb were about the same height of six-one, both wide shouldered, muscled. Mason's dark honey-brown hair was shorter than Caleb's darker brown. Mason's eyes were typical cat-green, and Caleb's were a darker hazel.

And right now, those handsome faces wore expressions that said they were ready for a fight.

"Be a sweetheart, and call us a cab," Jade said too-sweetly. Kitlene bit her lip to keep from laughing. "Kitlene and I are leaving. It's not that we haven't enjoyed our stay it's just that we have better things to do than be lazy in this lap of luxury you've forced on us."

"You're a cab."

Kitlene laughed anyway. Who would have thought that this big, tough Mason would have a sense of humor?

"Now, get back in that room," he ordered. "I don't have time to deal with your escapades this morning."

Uh oh, Mason. You were doing so good until that remark. "Seriously, Mason," Kitlene lowered her voice to the soft and soothing tone she'd always been able to calm other people with. "We can't stay here. Jade and I have nothing to do with this, not personally anyway. And we have our lives to get back to. I've promised Ariel I'll be back the week before the wedding."

"Ariel needs you here," Caleb stated, his voice hard. "And you'll both be safer here, too."

"Our watchers will be there, as soon as we get home," Jade argued. "And I need to get Kitlene home now."

"Why?"

Kitlene shook her head. They didn't have to know the reason. It was too personal. But she knew they wouldn't accept a lame excuse so she told them a half-lie. "Jade gives me special injections for a personal, woman's problem. I can't miss one or it will be like having to start over. And unfortunately, her medical bag wasn't with the suitcases you retrieved from the hotel."

"Give me the name of the injection medicine and I'll get it," Mason said. "But you can forget about leaving. As long as you're in danger, you're staying under our protection."

"Wanna bet?" Jade muttered her usual challenge and then backed up a step. Kitlene knew that look on her face. All hell was about to break loose. She briefly thought about stopping her. But, her need to escape here … away from Lyon was enough to help her decide it was the only way out. She pulled Ariel back a step.

Jade swung first, her fisted hand aiming at the side of Mason's head. Kitlene struck at Caleb. Both men were caught off guard with surprise. They both jumped back and ended up colliding with each other, almost losing their footing. Their cussing was so rough and filthy, all three women gasped.

Ariel launched herself on top of Caleb and screamed, "Run!"

Kitlene and Jade raced out into the hall. Only to be met by two guards. They were backed into the room again. Mason and Caleb had managed to get to their feet. Caleb had one arm wrapped around a struggling Ariel and Mason was slowly advancing on Jade. Kitlene faced the two guards.

She looked at Jade, and just like they had all their lives, they read the other's thoughts. Moving suddenly and fast, they grabbed the nearest objects within reach and started throwing vases, books, personal items, all the food and dinnerware off the table, and even small chairs. The men cussed up blue streaks as they dodged the various missiles, every now and then howling out roars of anger above the chaotic noise of the battle.

The guards managed to back Kitlene into the den. She looked down and saw a huge vase sitting on an end table next to the door. She grabbed it up, with the brief thought it looked incredibly expensive, and held it high. Just about that time, Mason yelled at one of the guards named Beau who had entered the fight, to stop Jade as she made a run for the unprotected suite door. He was holding his cell phone and he turned to see Kitlene aim the vase straight at him. He actually paled.

"Grab her, Beau!" he yelled as he waved at a fleeing Jade, then "Kitlene, put that vase down, now!" She didn't hear the rest of his words. She threw the vase as hard as she could. She had a moment to admire her aim. She didn't realize she was that good.

•

Lyon was glad he had the chance to enjoy that laugh on the way home. He was far from laughing now. He stood in the doorway of his suite and surveyed the mess inside. The fact that there was dead silence, despite having eight people sitting around the wrecked room, was amazing in itself. But the fact that his Beta, Caleb, Beau, and two of his men looked like they had just been bested in a fight was beyond comprehension.

He looked over at the three women sitting together in one large overstuffed chair. A thorough glance assured him they were okay. His glance lingered on Kitlene. But she refused to meet his gaze. Her lovely face was flushed with a pink glow that made her look incredibly guilty about something. She looked adorable and angry at the same time. The burning ache in his lower body renewed. *Dammit.*

"Okay, start talking," he ordered. "What the hell happened here?"

"We had a disagreement," Mason spoke up, his tone hard. Lyon noted the big angry welt on his forehead. He saw similar wounds on the other men. Caleb was sporting a black eye.

"Whatever happened to talking like adults?"

Mason actually growled at him. Lyon hid his grin. But he lost all thoughts of fun when Caleb spoke up.

"Kitlene and Jade decided they were leaving. We told them they couldn't. Someone threw something." He looked embarrassed as he rubbed at his black eye. "Kind of lost track of what happened next."

A red haze of fury misted Lyon's sight for a moment. She'd tried to leave? After he'd warned her he wouldn't let her? He settled his hard gaze on the object of his anger. "I thought we discussed this. You're safer here with me."

Kitlene's head jerked up and she met his gaze with fire in her own. "Safer with you? Ha. Your men are barbaric. They actually tried to physically restrain us. And besides, Ariel is the important one here, Lyon. We have watchers to protect us, and there's no excuse for you to keep me and Jade here."

He'd deal with his men making the mistake of touching her later. Right now, he had to get control of the possessive fury that was trying to make him forget all logic. "Your watchers are dead, Kitlene," he stated abruptly. He watched her turn pale and forced himself to stay where he was. "We found four dead in your home, and the other two are still missing."

"How?" She clasped her hands together in her lap. He hated seeing that look of fear on her face and in her eyes. His heart clenched. On one hand, he wanted to protect her from the cruelty of the situation. But on the other hand, he knew he had to be tough enough with her to make her understand just how dangerous this was.

"Shot in the back of the head." There was no sense in trying to sugar coat anything; she needed to know the extent of danger she was in. He had to make her see that staying here was the only protection she had right now.

"Who is doing this?" She placed her arm around Ariel. "Do you know yet?"

No. But he was sure as hell going to find out and fast. He knew, despite wanting to, he couldn't keep her in his sight at all times. She was relatively safe here at the club, under constant guard, but he wouldn't be there every minute. Hell, there'd be times he'd have to run. For the freedom his jaguar soul needed. For the freedom he knew he would need from her.

Because he had to remember she wasn't his. He was going to marry Ariel. His Pride was depending on him.

"We haven't been able to contact Zachary or the other two Elders, either. Until we can, you might as well figure you're staying."

She frowned at him, her fear seeming to disappear at his arrogant tone. Again she was showing that fiery spunk he was discovering he liked—a lot.

"There are still a few unbroken things in this room," she said, her tone too sweet and innocent. His body tightened in sexual reaction.

She'd just threatened him, and he liked it. Damn.

He studied her closely. She wasn't that brave, was she? Someone should have warned her about baiting him. He was still aching with the sexual adrenaline from this morning's hot, devouring kiss. He already knew his restraint around her wasn't as strong as he wanted it to be, and if she challenged him it would only make his primal side more dominant around her. Not good.

He shook his head. "You aren't serious, are you? You would try that, again?" Placing his hands on his hips he widened his stance. He purposely roughened his tone. "You might have bested my men. Once." He speared a reprimanding glare in their direction, and then turned his hard stare back on her. "But, kitten, you don't stand a chance of getting past me."

He wasn't surprised at her reaction to his words. He'd instinctively known she'd rise to his challenge. His blood heated instantly, lust and primal emotions swamping him as he watched her stand.

But the look she was spearing him with almost made him wish he hadn't pushed her. She looked oddly confident. He bit back a groan, suddenly realizing why. If she tried to get past him, he'd have to touch her. And touching her again was the last thing he should ever do. They both knew that, already.

"Would you really physically restrain me, Lyon?"

Damn but her voice was pure silk. He cringed. He was in trouble. He thought fast. "I'll make you a deal, sweetheart. If you can break out of my hold, without me hurting you, then I'll let you walk out of here." He grinned, his thoughts suddenly way too hot, considering what he was about to do. "Come here."

He'd have to touch her, but there wasn't any other way. He realized he was holding his breath as he watched her, and he released it on a long sigh. Her eyes darkened and she chewed on her full bottom lip. His gut clenched in reaction, heat searing his groin as he watched her mangle that same, soft, sweet lip he'd chewed on for too short a heated moment just hours earlier.

He swore his heart stuttered when he saw the moment she'd made up her mind. Her lovely eyes narrowed in challenge and his body reacted instantly hardening even more. She slowly walked toward him. She stopped less than a foot away from him. Their gazes locked. For one long, tense minute, it felt like they were the only two there. Lyon shook his head to clear the wayward thought.

Then he grabbed her.

Kitlene squealed in surprise. In a split second he had her swung around, her back to his chest, and his arms locked around her waist with her arms trapped under his. For one long moment she remained frozen, and then she started struggling.

"That wasn't fair," she bit out. "Let me go."

Never. "Make me."

She kicked back with one of her feet but he easily dodged the blow. She tried to pull her arms out from beneath his, but he tightened his hold painfully enough to make her gasp.

God help him, but she felt so good in his arms, every feminine inch of her warm body pressed against his. Her struggles were making him hard and achy all over again. She was so delicate, so soft. He bit back a groan and forced himself to concentrate on why he was holding her like this in the first place. He bent his head to hers, his mouth close to her ear.

"Make me release you, kitten." *Before I can't.*

She tensed for a moment, and he could hear her breathing increase. He could feel her heartbeat under his arm, racing alarmingly. Then she suddenly went limp. Completely relaxed against him. Soft. Calm. Breathing slow and easy. It surprised the hell out of him.

But not as much as her next action.

She moved her hand from beneath his captive arm when he loosened his hold ever so slightly. With the softest caress he'd ever known, she smoothed her palm across his hand, then up his bare elbow, and farther to the sleeve of his T-shirt. That searing touch shot through him like lightning, leaving a trail of fire in its wake. He almost stopped breathing as he watched, and excruciatingly felt her caress sweep over his arm all the way up and then down again. And then caress back up, straight to his neck.

He was that close to turning her into his arms and kissing the hell out of her. Audience and consequences be damned.

She sighed, the sound so incredibly sexy he groaned raggedly. Hell. He moved his arms to turn her around.

When he did, she spun around, slapped both hands against his chest and pushed. Impossibly hard.

Shocked speechless at being caught off guard, Lyon landed on his butt at her feet.

"I've been told you are a man of honor, Lyon." Her words were quiet. Firm. They tore straight into him. "That means you have to keep your end of the deal. I'm out of here."

Chapter Ten

*K*itlene was aware of everyone surging to stand, but all she could do was stare down at Lyon and try to force her body to take in a much-needed breath. If she didn't breathe soon she was going to end up on that floor next to him.

She hadn't meant to touch him like that. God only knew what possessed her to. She didn't want to accept what she thought had happened; it scared her more than anything ever had.

She'd heard his voice. In her head. Heard his agonized words as clear as though he'd whispered them in her ear. "Before I can't."

No. It wasn't possible. He'd told her to make him release her, and nothing more. He wouldn't have said those words.

And never mind her instant reaction to the breath-stealing words. Just like before, when he kissed her, she found herself melting into his arms, against his hard body without conscious thought of consequences. Found her hand moving before she even realized what she was doing. Touching him. Caressing him. Willingly relaxing into the strength of his captive embrace.

When she'd felt the way his body instantly reacted to her touch, hardening even more against her, she'd been stunned back to reality. Shoving out of his suddenly lax embrace was her only choice. The instinctive thought to escape had her striking before she realized it.

Never in a million years would she have thought she'd see someone like Lyon Savage on the floor at her feet.

And by the look on his face she was hoping—no, praying—that it would be the last time.

Lyon gracefully surged to his feet, his gaze locked on hers. His handsome features were flushed with anger, his cat eyes narrow and glinting turquoise fire. Not for anything would she back away, but it did take a lot of willpower. She met his gaze with what she hoped was an angry one too. *Heaven help me, but he's sexy even when he's obviously furious!*

Before he could move or say a word, a choked out screech followed by loud wailing broke the tense moment. Behind them, Ariel covered her face with her hands and was suddenly bawling so hard it shocked them all speechless.

"No!" She cried in harsh, choking sobs. "You can't leave me, Aunty. I need you. I can't believe you would desert me like this. I'll be alone. I can't bear it, I just can't."

Her niece had always been one for dramatic statements, but this time Kitlene knew it wasn't theatrics. She clearly heard the fear and anguish in Ariel's voice and it hit her hard. Guilt, and her own fear for Ariel's wellbeing, rolled over her like a ferocious tidal wave. All the adrenaline from the fight earlier, all the stark emotions swamping her from the incident with Lyon, and all her conflicting thoughts on whether to stay or run, suddenly combined to rush like an arrow slicing through her entire body. She nearly doubled over, and just barely managed to swallow it all down. Instead, she hurried over to Ariel and gathered the sobbing woman into her arms.

"Hush, honey. Everything will be all right. I promise." Ariel sobbed harder and Kitlene felt like crying with her. If she stayed...

She took a deep breath, released it on a shaky sigh and then swallowed back the fear, the dire warning persisting in the back of her mind. She made the choice. She could only pray it wouldn't be a decision that would destroy her in the end. "Stop, Ariel. I won't let you go through this alone. I'll stay here. I promise."

She felt Lyon move up next to her. She had the brief moment to realize he had been as silent as the cat he was, but she'd still known he was there. She didn't like the way she reacted to him, every time he was near her. Heaven help her if she didn't manage to get control soon.

Before she could dwell on it longer, Lyon reached out and untangled Ariel from her arms. And pulled her straight into his. The air rushed out of her lungs as she stared at him holding her niece so gently, his features completely clear of his earlier anger. She told herself it was only shock at his sudden, obviously gentle action but a voice deep inside her consciousness scoffed. She wasn't prepared for her reaction to seeing Lyon and Ariel together, even in this situation. She bit back a groan of dismay.

"Your aunt is right, honey," Lyon said, his voice gruff but gentle. "You have to stop crying now. You're not alone in this, and there's no reason to be afraid." Placing his hand under her chin he raised her face. "There's not a man here who would hurt you in any way. We cherish and protect our women. This Decree has us all a bit off, but we're in it together. You have to trust me and believe that I'm going to make everything right. Can you be brave enough to face what's to come?"

Ariel gulped several deep breaths and started hiccupping. She finally managed to squeak out an answer, sounding very much like the too young eighteen-year-old she was. "If Aunty stays, then I'll be fine. I need her here. Will you please make sure she stays? Then, yes. I fully accept the Decree and what's to come. And I trust you, Lyon."

"Good." Lyon released her and stepped back. His tone changed as he abruptly barked out an order to Beau, "Get housecleaning up here to clean this mess." He looked at the men, his stare hard. "And pass this on to the other men," His voice turned deadly, "No one touches Kitlene again. And if she decides to walk out of here, then she does on her own free will."

Kitlene barely held back her gasp of shock at his words. She suddenly felt lightheaded. Ariel moved away from Lyon and put her arms around her. For a moment she was sure it was the only thing keeping her standing. *Why am I reacting like this to his statement?*

Lyon turned slowly to face her. She couldn't read his expression, but something in his eyes made her shiver. There was danger glinting in the dark depths, and something more. *It can't be what I think it is.* But she couldn't ignore it; every feminine instinct in her recognized that look of lust.

"That was an interesting move of defense, Kitlene," he stated, his voice controlled yet husky. "Still, it won't work every time. If you hadn't taken me by surprise, you wouldn't have broke free. Because of that, I'm assuming none of you have had any training to protect yourselves, have you? Zachary was lax in thinking those incompetent watchers would always keep you safe."

Jade spoke up. "Don't think we're completely helpless, Lyon." She smiled, her tone sarcastic. "Sorry—oops, I mean not about wrecking your room."

Surprising Kitlene again, Lyon actually laughed. This man was going to drive her crazy if she couldn't manage to keep up with his mood swings.

"I wouldn't laugh, Lyon," Mason muttered. "Notice anything missing from that end table by your den?"

She cringed, biting her lip at his reaction. *Uh oh*, she thought in surprise, *Cats really do roar when they get angry.*

Lyon choked the angry words out through thinned lips. "What the hell happened to my vase?"

Mason, Caleb, and the other men as one pointed straight at Kitlene. Tattle-tales! So much for that statement about protecting their women. They'd ratted her out instantly. She raised her chin and glared at them.

"That damn vase cost me thirty thousand dollars," he snarled low. "It was going to be a gift for my great-aunt on her one hundredth birthday this month. Dammit, Kitlene," he growled out her name and she almost cringed again. "Tell me they're pointing at you because you can give me a logical explanation, and not that you destroyed it."

"I did it," Ariel spoke up quickly. "Sorry."

The way he was staring at her, Kitlene knew Lyon wasn't buying Ariel's confession. She straightened her shoulders. "They tried to restrain me. I didn't have a choice." *Just like I haven't had any choices these past few days.*

At her words, his tense body language suddenly changed. He shot a hard glare at the two guards. And then murmured low and dangerous, "Never touch her again." He nodded toward the door. "Get back to your posts."

When he turned back to her, Kitlene almost took a step back in surprise again. His look was so hot she felt the heat waft over her in a hard wave. Hot? Why was he looking at her like that? She wasn't sure she really wanted to know. She'd had enough surprises to last a lifetime already and they all revolved around this enigmatic man standing so close and looking like he was ready to eat her or something. And she was so not going to think about that 'something.'

"Since I don't want you using that defense move you used on me, on my men, then there's only one solution to your protection.

I take my men out to the ranch every weekend for training. You three are going with us. I'm going to make sure you're trained in self defense, and as soon as possible." He kept his hot, hard stare on her although he was talking to Ariel and Jade as well. "Make no mistake, my men will guard you twenty-four-seven and do whatever they must to protect you. But, in the next few days you're going to learn how to defend yourselves too. Without breaking anything."

"Where's the fun in that?" Jade's voice was low but the words clear.

Lyon's upper lip curled in a slight snarl. "Oh, it's going to be fun all right," he promised silkily, his glance searing over Kitlene from her head to her toes. "For us. But definitely not for you, ladies."

Kitlene managed to break free from Lyon's captive stare and lowered her eyes. She was feeling way too hot, and hoped he wasn't noticing. If it took only his heated stare to make her feel like she was burning from the inside out, just that easily, then she was in so much trouble.

Unfortunately, Jade noticed her discomfort too. "Kitlene, you're flushed." *Great. Thanks, Jade, for making that more obvious.* Lyon's eyes narrowed as he studied her closer.

"I'm fine," she lied quickly. "It's been a long morning, already."

"Maybe you should take a nap," Jade suggested.

Lyon nodded his head, his eyes still drinking her in. "A catnap sounds good." He ran his hand over his face and then through his hair. "Mason, Caleb. They're still in your care." He shot them a warning look. "But don't start another damn battle if one of them decides to leave. Come and get me first." He turned to Ariel, his voice gentling, "We're settled on this, right?"

She nodded. "You keep Aunty here, and I promise I'll do everything it takes to fulfill my end of this bargain."

Lyon smiled at her niece, though Kitlene noticed it never reached his eyes. His sensuous lips barely moved when he stated low and deep, "I'll keep her, Ariel. Trust me."

Kitlene decided she'd better find someplace to sit. Before she fell. Lyon Savage was wreaking havoc on her emotions and she wasn't sure she could take twenty-six more days of this. She had this feeling his words to Ariel was saying more than just a simple promise. Every womanly instinct in her knew it was a vow.

•

Everyone cleared out when housekeeping showed up to clean the wrecked room. Lyon crooked his finger at Kitlene, indicating he wanted her to follow him to the bedroom. He watched her eyes darken, and then she bit at her bottom lip again. *Sweetheart, you'll never have a poker face.* He knew he was being contradictory, keeping her off balance with his attitude changes every few minutes, but it was the only way he could maintain his distance. And stay sane.

He was still reeling from that move she'd made to break free from him. Part of him wanted to be furious that she'd dared use a feminine trick like that. Part of him admired her bravery. But part of him, the part that still had his blood heated, was shaking in fear. He'd reacted to her caress instantly. He'd lost all thoughts of anything but holding her, touching her, kissing her. He hadn't cared that there were other people in the room, hadn't cared that everything—*everything* was at stake if he lost control and took what he most wanted at that moment.

And then Ariel had fallen apart in heart-wrenching sobs. She'd unknowingly saved them all by that action. Because nothing else would have stopped him from picking Kitlene up in his arms and carrying her to his bed, claiming her in every possible way. Mason would have tried, but he would have fought his Beta and been forced to hurt him. And in claiming Kitlene, he would have destroyed the hope of his people.

Too many would have been hurt. In more ways than one. So he'd desperately grasped at the chance to regain control, and had used Ariel's distress to his advantage. He couldn't help but wonder if the young woman had deliberately staged that sobbing scene in order to force Kitlene to stay. Obviously the niece was just as spunky as her aunt. *Some man is going to have his hands full with that one, one day.*

He readily admitted the truth to himself, something his soul had already accepted. Ariel had been chosen as his intended mate, but he would release her from that debt when the time came. Kitlene was his Truemate and he wasn't going to let her go. He would keep up the pretense of accepting Zachary's choice, but when the time came he would claim Kitlene and marry her on the night of the Shifter's Moon.

He turned to look at her as she followed him into the bedroom and he closed the door to enclose them in privacy from the housekeeping staff in the next room. He had less than twenty-six days to make her permanently his. Just by her stiff stance now, he knew he had his hands full. She was going to fight him. His body hardened at that thought. He was already relishing the sensual battle to come. She wasn't immune to him; he'd felt her responses every time they'd touched. Even now her soft skin was still flushed and the more he looked at her the more he wanted, ached, to touch her. To hell with holding back. He was going to use her responses to his advantage in every way possible.

The only problem was that he would have to take things slow enough so she didn't balk and decide to run, this time for good. If he pushed too fast, she'd break her promise to Ariel.

Ha. I'll never let you run from me, kitten. You're mine.

He watched her move to the foot of the bed where her suitcase lay. Everything about her was soft, sensual, and it called to everything primal male in him. He forced his gaze away and walked over to the closet, and then pulled open the double doors. "There's room in here for the clothes you brought. We'll get you more in the next few days. You can use a few of my drawers too; just empty the stuff out and I'll find a place later."

"I don't need you to buy me more clothes." Her voice was low but firm.

He hid his grin. "It's the least I can do," he answered smoothly. "In thanks for agreeing to stay for Ariel's sake."

"That's all I agreed to."

He clearly heard the warning in her tone. He turned away to grab a clean shirt and jeans so she wouldn't see his expression when he lied to her. "No one will touch you again, Kitlene." That much was true. He'd kill the next man who laid a hand on her. "If you decide to leave, you won't be restrained." *Unless I have to.*

"Does that 'no one' include you?"

Damn but she was easily keeping one step ahead of him. Okay, time to change tactics. "No. It doesn't." Let her think on that for a minute.

"Why?"

Lyon faced her. She looked so beautiful, so fragile, standing there with confusion stamped on her flushed face. His heart did a double beat. He wanted nothing more than to take her in his arms and kiss her. He stifled a lustful groan. Okay, honest time. He wanted more than just kisses. *Slow, man. Don't rush this.*

"I don't think you want that answer right now, kitten." He walked to the bathroom, purposely keeping his distance. "I'm going to take a shower. Housekeeping should be done in the living room in awhile, so you won't be shut up in here much longer." When he reached the bathroom door, he turned to look back at her confused expression. His heart softened but he kept his voice firm. "And the next time you decide to start a fight with some of my men, do me a favor and keep your soft paws off anything expensive."

It took every ounce of willpower he had not to laugh out loud at her muttered comment as he shut the bathroom door.

"I don't have ... paws."

•

Half an hour later, Lyon came out of the bathroom refreshed and a little more relaxed. Cold showers were good for accomplishing at least that. His gaze fell on the bed. Damn but he was tired. He hadn't slept in over two days, since Kitlene's arrival and kidnapping. The strain of all that had happened in so short a time was finally taking its toll. Cats could stay up all night and not tire. But come early morning they needed their catnaps. Despite his tough attitude, he was definitely one cat needing a long nap right now. He grimaced at the thought he'd be sleeping on the sofa in the living room instead of his bed. Kitlene or housekeeping had already made up the bed from when she'd been in it. Pity. He'd have loved to stretch out on the same sheets she'd no doubt left her sweet scent on.

His erection strained against his jeans. Again. So much for going slow if all he had to do was think about her and he was instantly hard and aching. It was going to be harder than facing hell to take it slow.

The bedroom door was open and he heard low murmurs coming from the living room. He immediately zeroed in on Kitlene's soft voice, and then realized she was talking to Wren. His heart stuttered. Instantly his mind cleared of tantalizing, tempting thoughts of touching her, and instinctive protectiveness swamped his senses. Maybe that flush on her skin hadn't been just a reaction to him. Maybe something was wrong. He hurried into the living room, and came to a sudden stop when he saw Wren bending over her and inserting a needle into her bare arm.

His instinctive growl was out before he could stop it. "What's going on, Wren?"

The doctor straightened and looked at him. "She's fevered, Lyon. I suspect it has something to do with that damn poison from the wolf. I've taken a blood sample, and now I've given her an antibiotic boost."

Fear hit him like a punch to the gut. He wanted to kill again. "How soon will you know the results to the blood test?"

"An hour or two. Jade knows her medical history, so I'm going to have her help me in the lab. She's told me—"

Kitlene gasped and grabbed at his arm to stop him from finishing his sentence. "I'm really fine. It's just a little fever."

Lyon instinctively knew she was lying. He tore his gaze from her and turned it on Jade standing next to Wren. "What doesn't she want me to know?" he demanded in a not-so-calm tone. "Spill it, Jade, or I swear I'll find out another way." He looked at Kitlene's flushed face and saw something deep in her eyes he didn't like. His gut clenched and he added roughly, "And she doesn't want me to do that."

Jade hesitated for a moment and Lyon forced himself to control his temper. Something wasn't right here, and whatever it was threatening Kitlene wasn't about to be allowed. He'd protect her from Hell itself if he had to.

"Kitlene has a—woman's condition," Jade finally answered. "It's really personal, Lyon, so don't glower at me thinking you'll make me regale you with every tiny detail. Needless to say, it's something that needs to be monitored. I've been her personal physician for years now and I know what needs to be done. I told Mason I need my medical supplies and he's already working on getting them brought from my lab in Florida. He said your three men were still down there searching for the missing two watchers, and keeping watch over our houses, so they can get what I need and send it immediately."

Medical condition? Fear rose in him again, and he swallowed it down with a hard mental shove. Jade sounded calm enough, but he didn't like the sound of "immediately." He was more than ready to do battle against anything that threatened his Truemate. Whether she wanted him to or not.

"Do you have what she needs now, Wren, while the supplies are on the way?"

Wren shook his head, a hard frown creasing his brows. "Jade says I don't. And she won't tell me exact details. I realize this is personal, like she stated, but I don't like being in the dark."

"Jade—" Lyon snarled low. He wanted answers. *Now, dammit.*

"Stop it," Kitlene muttered, her voice strained with tension and something else he couldn't decipher. "Lyon, don't you dare threaten her for keeping my personal stuff personal. This is none of your business. Jade has taken care of me for years, and she will do so now. So back off. I mean it. I won't stand your bullying much more."

Ah, sweetheart, you haven't seen me bully. Yet. When it comes to you, I'll do whatever it takes to keep you safe. From anything. Including yourself. "Don't expect me to just ignore the fact that something is wrong, Kitlene," he said sternly. "And don't spout that you're-not-my-Alpha crap again. As long as you're under my care, you're my responsibility."

Damn. He hadn't meant it exactly like that. And the last thing he wanted was to see her lovely dove-grey eyes tear up. He'd discovered earlier that he could easily contend with Ariel's tears. But he knew, with everything in him, he'd never be able to handle Kitlene crying.

"She needs to rest a few more hours, Lyon," Wren interrupted.

He didn't hesitate. He moved forward and then scooped her up into his arms. She made a little gasping sound but automatically put her arms around his neck. He cuddled her close, his heart melting at how delicate and vulnerable she was.

"Wren, get those damn tests done. Let me know as soon as you get a result. And Jade, let me know when your supplies arrive."

He carried his precious burden back to the bedroom and kicked the door closed behind him. He moved to the bed and lowered her onto it. Before she could make a protest, he climbed in beside her. He turned her to her side and then spooned in behind her, closing his arms tight and secure around her.

She froze, then choked out a soft, "Lyon,"

He aligned his body so that every inch of him touched every sweet inch of her. One arm rested under her head, the other was tight across her slender waist. He dropped his head to hers.

"Shhh. Just rest, kitten," he soothed. "I'm only going to hold you while we both get some much-needed rest. We'll talk about this later." Later, when he could talk calmly enough to get answers out of her without making her cry. Whatever this medical condition was, she was determined to keep it secret. She could try, but he was as determined, if not more, to find out what was wrong and fix it. He wouldn't allow anything to harm her. The sooner she learned that, the better for them both. He just hoped she never learned what her tears could so easily do to him; that she never knew what a blow those tears could render.

Her soft sigh moved over him like a fleeting caress. Against his will, his body tightened. "There won't be anything to talk about later, either," she said, her voice tearful but nonetheless firm.

"You will tell me," he told her, trying hard to keep his voice gentle while his body steadily burned. He instinctively knew she needed gentle right now. But holding her like this had his body warring with his conscience and trying hard to win that battle. He wanted her so bad the ache was eating away deep inside him. And he needed her with a passionate, soul-felt strength that scared the hell out of him. Claiming her, taking her body and soul, would reaffirm the Truemate connection. It took a hell of a lot of willpower to force down the burning, aching need to just throw caution to the wind and make love to her. Here. Now.

He'd never wanted anything or any woman with the ferocity, the soul-deep craving that he wanted her now. *Mine. No matter what.*

"No. I won't tell you, so let it go." She was still challenging him. Even when her voice was slurred and she was already half asleep from the shot Wren had given her.

He smiled and kissed her soft hair beneath his cheek. "Sorry, sweetheart. 'No' isn't a word I'm going to allow you to use often, so you'd better accept that now and give us both a break."

"Egotistical cat."

He couldn't stop his chuckle. She made him smile even when he was choking with fear for her safety, or when he was quietly burning up with desperate, hot need. "Yeah. I am."

She made a move to turn out of his arms, so he tightened his hold with the hoarse warning, "Don't move."

"This isn't something you should be doing," she protested but she stilled instantly. He knew she'd felt the ridge of his erection pressing intimately against her bottom. It took a strong dose of willpower to stop from rubbing against her again.

"I'm only holding you," he murmured.

"Why?"

Man, he hated that vulnerable sound in her voice. It nearly killed him. He wanted her fiery, not compliant. "Because I'm an egotistical Alpha cat and I can do whatever I want." He growled low to get his point across. "Now go to sleep."

She remained stiff for long minutes. He refused to loosen his hold, and even managed to pull her closer against him. Finally, exhaustion and the fever allowed her to relax. He knew the exact moment she fell asleep.

And he knew the exact moment when he realized that no matter what he had to do, he was going to spend the rest of their lives holding her.

This felt too damn right. And he knew he'd fight Hell itself to keep her, here with him. Forever.

No matter the cost.

Chapter Eleven

She slept most of the day, and woke late afternoon alone in that big bed. She could still feel his strong, protective hold as though he was still there beside her.

Kitlene slowly sat up and looked around the bedroom but found it empty. She sighed and leaned back against the headboard. Remembering earlier, she shook her head. Had she really fallen asleep in Lyon's arms?

She was so sure when he settled in behind her and pulled her close that the odd, sensual heat between them would keep her tense and fully awake. She could only blame it on the fever and that shot Wren had given her. She wasn't ready to accept the fact that she'd immediately felt safe and even *right* enclosed in his strong arms and held tight against his body.

His aroused body. She groaned. That alone should have kept her awake. And she should have been stronger and pulled away. Should have. But hadn't. *Why did I let him hold me? And why did he do it?* Why would he hold her, kiss her, go all protective and possessive over her like that? He was engaged to Ariel. Granted, he'd thought she was Ariel when they'd first met and that would explain why he'd shown interest then. But later?

The picture of him holding Ariel while she cried came back into her mind and she clenched her hands together. Her heart had nearly stopped when he'd taken Ariel into his arms. She hadn't expected her reaction to be so strong. What was wrong with her? She couldn't be attracted to her niece's fiancé.

Attracted? Ha. It went deeper than that, and she knew it. Knew it and feared it. She could have fought him when he'd kissed her. Instead she'd melted into his embrace and whimpered for more. Then, when she'd touched him as he held her in that defense hold, she'd lost all sense of reason. And this morning sleeping in his arms she'd subconsciously allowed herself to accept that she was right where she wanted to be. In his arms.

No. No. Stop this right now. How crazy was this? Restless, Kitlene got off the bed. She couldn't let her thoughts go in that direction. If she allowed her feelings for Lyon to go on, she knew it would only result in heartache later.

As she stood, dizziness swamped her. A sudden, sharp pain in her stomach hit so hard she doubled over in a loud gasp.

The bedroom door flew open as soon as she cried out. Lyon rushed in. "What's wrong? Jade, get in here." He hurried over to her and pulled her upright. His features were creased with worry and his grip protective. "Kitlene, what is it?"

The odd pain rolled through her lower stomach again and she bit down on her bottom lip to keep from crying out. Lyon cursed low and swung her up into his arms. He sat down in a chair, holding her close. Kitlene wanted to curl up against him but fought the urge. But she didn't fight his hold. Right then it felt too good, too right.

"Kit," Jade hurriedly knelt by the chair. "Where does it hurt?"

"Stomach," Kitlene gasped out as another pain hit. If she didn't know better, she'd have sworn she was having monthly cramps in the ultra-extreme mode. But it couldn't be. She hadn't had her monthly cycle for over a year since Jade had been giving her the injections. They'd assumed it was because the serum was working to repair her female organs and eventually, hopefully, eradicate the defective gene.

"Do something," Lyon demanded to Jade in a low snarl. He ran his hands soothingly up and down Kitlene's arms. When she gasped in pain again, he moved his warm hand to her stomach and pressed gently there. "What the hell is wrong with her?"

Jade jerked open her medical bag and pulled out a syringe and the serum. The moment Kitlene saw it she groaned and pushed farther into Lyon's protective hold. The last thing she wanted or needed right now was one of those extra long needles poking into her stomach. "No. Can't it wait?"

Jade shook her head. "You're overdue. I'll give you something for the pain first, and then the serum."

Kitlene wasn't sure she could take two needles right then. She knew she was being childish, but couldn't stop herself. She blamed it on the pain making her common sense fly right out the window. She saw Jade tap an air bubble out of the first needle and she cringed. Without thinking, she wiggled around in Lyon's hold and hid her face against his chest. She felt his arms tighten instantly. Right then, gasping with pain again, she wasn't ashamed of using his protectiveness to her advantage. "I hate needles," she told him, "And they hurt. Make her go away. I'll take the serum later."

She heard Jade's loud gasp. "Kitlene Skye! I can't believe you'd use feminine tears to get out of a little shot. This is a new one, for you."

Lyon growled. Kitlene shivered at the dangerous tone. "Is this really necessary right now?" he asked gruffly. He moved his hand underneath Kitlene's hair and gently massaged her neck. His other one, around her waist, kept up a steady warm pressure against her stomach. Kitlene wanted to melt into him, let him take away the pain, and then just hold her. Keeping her face against his chest, she swallowed back a groan. It had to be the pain making her so crazy, thinking thoughts like that.

"Yes, it's necessary," Jade answered brusquely. "She needs something for the pain, you know that."

"It's easing already," Kitlene quickly told her.

"Liar."

Kitlene knew Jade wasn't going to give in. But she'd told the truth; the pain really was already lessening. Whatever had caused it wasn't letting it stay long. Just as she was thinking everything was back under control, Lyon moved slightly, his body tensing, yet his arms loosening a little. He pulled her back, just enough for his mouth to touch her cheek.

"Kitlene," he whispered her name softly, huskily. "Sweetheart, look at me." He put his hand under her chin and forced her face up to his. She wanted to close her eyes against the strange look she saw in his turquoise gaze. She saw protectiveness. Authority. And something she hadn't expected: fear.

What was he afraid of?

"Look in my eyes," he said, his tone low and deep. So husky it caressed over her in a rough wave of sensual heat. "Concentrate on what you see there. Look deep enough, and you'll see the truth. I would never allow anything to hurt you, if it was in my power to stop it." His voice deepened, roughened. "Do you believe me?"

She couldn't pull her gaze from his. She lost every bit of common sense she had then. Something invisible and irrevocable moved from him and into her in that suspended moment their gazes locked. She lost her breath, and all thoughts of time or place. All that she could see, hear, smell, feel, was Lyon. She'd never experienced anything like it. And she realized she wanted it to last forever. Searching deep into his dark eyes she thought for one brief, heart stopping moment that he wanted it, too.

Moments or minutes later, she heard Jade's light laugh. It instantly broke the odd sensual spell cocooning her and Lyon. "You can breathe again, you coward," Jade said with another chuckle. "All done."

Shocked, Kitlene looked down and saw Jade lowering her blouse. Her mind and senses cleared as realization hit. While Lyon had kept her mesmerized with his captive gaze, Jade had given her both shots. He'd deliberately tricked her.

And it had worked. She'd willingly lost herself in his eyes, losing all thoughts of anyone or anything else around her. She didn't know whether to be angry or embarrassed. She sat up straighter, pushing away from Lyon's arms. She decided anger would be the better choice.

"That wasn't the least bit funny," she muttered as she glared at Jade. She couldn't bring herself to look at Lyon. Not yet.

"Ha. It worked, didn't it?" Jade closed her medical bag. She glanced at Lyon. "You're hired. She gets these shots twice a week. Just let me know when your schedule allows you to be here for her."

"Any time," Lyon murmured.

Did he have to sound so sexy when he said that? Okay, time to get off his lap. Before she hit him. Or … before she burrowed back against him. She pushed his arms away and stood.

Lyon stood too, close behind her, and placed his hands lightly on her waist. He leaned down, his mouth close to her ear. "Were you telling the truth when you said the pain was gone?" His voice was still low, still deeply husky. Just the sound of it was enough to make her want to turn back into the shelter of his arms.

Instead, she nodded, unable to answer. This was embarrassing enough, without him asking more questions about what was going on in her body.

He released a rough sigh. "Then, I'll leave. I have work to do." His tone was suddenly firm. "But if you need me or something just have one of the bodyguards come get me."

Kitlene stared at his back as he quickly left the room. She abruptly realized her mouth was open in shock from his statement and his suddenly fast retreat. She swallowed tightly and then shook her head. "I don't think I can stand this confusion much longer. What just happened to make him practically run from the room?" One moment he'd been so overly protective. The next moment he was acting as though he couldn't get away from her fast enough.

Jade's expression turned serious. "You're going to be mad when I tell you this. So sit down. Over there."

Kitlene didn't like the tone in her voice. *What now?* She remained standing. "What are you talking about?"

"It's not really my fault," Jade said, a frown creasing her brow. "Mason should have told his men not to be snoops."

Kitlene's heart raced. "I've had enough confusion to last a lifetime. Spit it all out, Jade, and spare me any more."

"Mason's men went to my house, the lab, to get the serum supplies. He ordered them to get everything on the list I gave him. The good news is that as soon as they obtained everything one of the men rushed back here. He arrived less than a hour ago."

"Okay. That's good, isn't it? You were able to give me the injection in plenty of time. Why are you still frowning?"

"I had the serum supplies in a refrigerator and safe combo. The only other things in there with the serum were … your medical records."

Kitlene felt the room spin for a moment. "Oh, God. Tell me he didn't grab the records too and bring them." This wasn't happening.

Jade spit out a foul word and Kitlene cringed. If her friend was talking that bad, then it was worse than she was holding out hope for.

"He brought back the entire set of records."

Okay, now she felt like sitting down. Before she fell. "Did anyone else see them when he arrived?"

"Wren was here waiting, and so was Lyon. You were still sleeping and Lyon was trying to browbeat me into telling him what he wanted to know. We were right in the middle of a standoff when the man arrived. Wren was telling Lyon that even though your fever was completely gone, he didn't like the looks of your blood tests. He said he had found an anomaly he couldn't pinpoint or explain. Lyon was furious, especially when I refused to explain anything. Then, in walked the man with not only the serum supplies but also your medical records file. I'm sorry, Kit. My expression at seeing your records must have been a giveaway. Lyon grabbed them before I could."

She was going to be sick. Of all the things that could and had went wrong these past few days this was the last thing she'd ever expected to have to worry about. Her knees gave out and she slumped down on the edge of the bed. "He knows?"

Jade shook her head. "Not exactly." Jade's tone was a mixture of anger and smugness. "I showed him what an angry woman is capable of when she's pushed too far. I marched up to him and smacked him across the face so hard he actually reeled backward."

Kitlene covered her face with shaky hands. "You hit him? And you're still alive?" It would be truly funny if she weren't so sick to her stomach right then.

Jade grinned. "Yeah, my thought too. So, then I grabbed the file away from him and started cussing up a blue streak at the top of my lungs. By the time he realized it was all a ploy to distract him from the importance of the files, he had managed to gain control of his rage."

Kitlene lowered her hands. "And you're going to tell me the not-so-funny part next, right?" She was really sure she didn't want to hear it.

"He's frightening when he's angry," Jade commented, shaking her head. "These nasty, deep growls come from his throat. His eyes gleam with fire. You can actually see the glow. And then his voice gets really low and dangerous sounding. Any sane person would run when confronted with that."

"So you ran with the records?"

"Ha ha. No, but I did back away as far as I could. Then I told him that he had no right interfering in your personal stuff. I told him that if he forced me to show him your records then it would be the final straw for you and you would leave. I told him that nothing would keep you here."

She wanted to leave now, anyway. Her feelings for Lyon weren't something she was willing to accept but she knew she couldn't deny them. And now her embarrassing secret was too close to being exposed.

"What did he do?" She knew there was more bad news coming; she could see it in Jade's expression.

"He was silent for long minutes. Then, he told Wren to find out what that 'anomaly' in your blood was. He told me that I could either help or just stand back and wait for Wren to find out what he wanted to know." Jade sighed. "Either way, Kitlene, it's not good. Wren is a very intelligent physician. And he has blood samples from you. Sooner or later, the truth is going to come out. I'm sorry."

Did it really matter? It wasn't something she wanted to share with anyone. Especially Lyon. But, it wasn't a secret that would cause any harm to anyone but her. She had lived with the curse all her life, had gradually accepted that it made her less of a woman. If Lyon found out, it wouldn't change anything. Not really. He was engaged to Ariel, and it shouldn't matter if he knew. It would embarrass her, but it's not like she was going to be staying here long.

"It's up to you, now," Jade told her. She came over and sat down next to her on the bed. "I can work with Wren after I tell him the full truth, or we just sit back and wait to see if he figures it out. I have to tell you, Kitlene, that working with Wren on this just might be the opportunity we've needed all along. You know, the old saying 'two heads are better than one'. He's jaguar and knows practically everything there is to know about their DNA and health."

Kitlene was suddenly tired. Not so much physically, because she'd slept enough to last a week. But, mentally she was worn out. "I don't know that I have much of a choice, Jade. Lyon is determined that Wren will find out what we were trying to keep secret. And then we'll have to assure him that Ariel doesn't suffer the same defective gene, that she's from my dad's side of the family."

She rubbed at her stomach when a sudden, little twinge reminded her of the pain earlier. "And what about this sudden pain? I thought I was having major 'kill-me-now' monthly cramps. Why now? Did my blood tests show anything else wrong?"

Jade shook her head. "I haven't had time to study the results. Wren had just printed them out when the guy arrived with the supplies." She pondered for a minute. "Maybe it was a reaction to the fever. Or even a reaction to having Lyon's blood transfused into your system. He's full jaguar. Maybe it was your body's way of adjusting to the strong potency of undiluted jaguar blood." She reached for her bag. "I know you're going to whimper about this, but I need to get another blood sample. I need to check things and see if there was any particular reason for the strange cramps."

Kitlene groaned. Loud. "Fine. But trust me when I say that I'm going to find a way to get revenge for all these needles."

Jade grinned, the look on her face way too devious for Kitlene's peace of mind. "Want me to call Lyon back in here to hold you and distract you while I draw the blood samples?"

"Funny. You're just adding to the list."

"I wasn't being funny." Jade readied the syringe. "That man has a serious 'protect-Kitlene-from-all-harm' attitude. Makes you wonder. Doesn't it?"

"Ow! And no, it doesn't. You're just imagining it."

She was lying to herself. And if Jade was noticing it too ... how many others were? Aloud, she asked, "How many more days until the Shifter's Moon?"

•

Primal Beat was packed tonight. Lyon had given orders to the extra bouncer/guards at the doors to stay alert and not allow any Shifter in that smelled the least aggressive. Either they were all on their best behavior tonight, or there wasn't a Shifter present that had anything on his mind other than having a good time.

Of course, it could be that the news of what had happened to the five coyotes had made its rounds among the other Shifter races in L.A. and everyone knew better than to enter the club with any trace of intent to harm on their scent.

He'd had the mangled bodies returned to the coyote pack. Their Alpha would get the message without Lyon having to say a thing. No one came into his territory and dared harm one of his own.

Targeting his Truemate was enough to start a war. And every Shifter race in the area knew it. Since the Alpha Coyote hadn't responded aggressively after the death of five of his men, Lyon knew his suspicions were right. They'd been rogues. Working for someone else.

After thoroughly glancing around the crowd one more time,

Lyon relaxed back against the booth's cushions. The large, round table was located in a secluded, strategic area of the club where he could see the entire room. He held a lot of his non-private meetings there, and it offered him a chance to keep a covert visual on everything. The lighting was discreetly low, keeping the area private, and effectively discouraging patrons of the club from venturing near.

"We tried asking questions of the other coyotes there when we took the bodies back," Beau said, "but they weren't talking. Damn dogs are the most stubborn of the breeds. The Alpha wasn't being helpful either. He denied having anything to do with the rogues' actions, but he also refused to allow us to question any of the family members."

"I haven't seen any coyote breed on the ranch," Caleb stated. "So, if they were working under Bryce's orders, he kept it secret and away from the ranch."

"What other breeds, besides the African Lions, have you seen there?" Lyon wasn't ready to accept Bryce's innocence in all that was happening. He had the feeling it wasn't going to be long before he had to beat the truth out of his brother.

Caleb frowned. "Interestingly enough, just the Lions. But I heard through my sources that other cat breeds were slowly filtering in to the city. A cougar pride from Arizona moved into the east district of L.A. last week and then announced they were looking for mountainous property to buy. They're a small pride, less than twenty. Bryce said that the Lions were looking to do the same."

His brother had sworn his innocence, but he'd lied about other things before. Bryce stood to profit in more ways than one if he became Alpha of the Jaguar and then joined the opposition preparing for a future war against the humans.

"That leaves the wolves who helped kidnap the women." Lyon swallowed back the sudden rage that tried to surface the moment he thought of Kitlene nearly being killed by that rogue wolf Shifter. "Since we don't have a full, Alpha-ran wolf pack in the area, Caleb send your searchers out to the smaller mountain cities and have them locate the nearest Alpha. Have them take the message that he can either come talk to me here, or I go to him. But, either way, he will talk to me. My gut is telling me that those damn wolves at the warehouse weren't rogues."

He looked over the crowded club once again. Almost every Shifter race around the area was represented here tonight. He could smell the various breeds, knew most of them by familiarity, and could guess at the others. What the hell was going on? "Beau, you and a few other men circle the crowd tonight. Find out what the general mood is among the Shifters."

Mason nodded his head as Beau left the table. "You're thinking that some of them might be planning to join our side, aren't you?"

"Damn the fact that we have to have a side to begin with," Lyon muttered. He'd known a future war was inevitable, but he didn't have to like it. His Pride's security was his responsibility, and he'd fight to protect them, but he still harbored the small hope that he wouldn't have to fight against his brother or his men. They were Jaguar too.

"I've made arrangements to take the women out to the ranch tomorrow for training," Mason said, breaking into his thoughts. "We'll have an extra guard for each woman. Since the rest of the men aren't training until the weekend, I've pulled in three from Bryce's ranks."

Lyon had ten of his own men, undercover, who worked for an unsuspecting Bryce. He'd placed them there the year before when Bryce had tried to recruit some of Lyon's males to join him. "Are they still loyal to me?" He wasn't about to take a chance with Kitlene's or the other women's security.

"Yes," Caleb assured him. "They report to me every week and I'd sense it if they weren't."

Mason lifted his drink and took a sip. And then choked on it, spitting the liquid out with a curse. Lyon followed his shocked gaze and nearly ended up choking, too, without benefit of liquid. He spit out a rough cat-huff of displeasure as his gaze zeroed in on the object of his now intense, undivided attention.

Damn, his little kitten was really pushing her luck right now. She had to have known he wouldn't have allowed her downstairs. It wasn't safe. She was most likely challenging him to see how far he could be pushed. He knew his abrupt leaving her earlier must have left her confused; especially after that brief heart stopping moment they'd been lost in each other's eyes, as he'd held her. He hadn't wanted to leave. But his feelings then had been too close, too primal and he wasn't sure what he would have done if he'd stayed.

Hell, he knew. He'd have carried her to bed. His protective instincts might have been strong enough to stop him from claiming her then, but he hadn't wanted to take that chance. His feelings for her were growing more possessive and too close to being out of control every time he touched her.

Pushing away the blood stirring thoughts, he suddenly grinned as he stared at her. His body came instantly alive, muscles tensing, groin tightening. Damn, he had it bad for this woman.

Kitlene, along with Jade and Ariel, glided across the club's main floor, heading straight to their table. His hungry gaze caressed over her and he swallowed back a groan of pure, hot lust. She looked too damn sexy. He wanted her with a need so hot and potent it nearly took his breath. He choked out a cough, and straightened in his seat as he drank her in.

Her incredibly tight, black jeans molded to every enticing curve of her hips, tiny waist, and long legs. The blouse she was wearing was clingy silk, pale lavender, and cut daringly low. Her arms were bare, and the straps on her shoulders were so thin they were barely noticeable. Her cleavage was mouthwateringly tempting, and shouting *look at me.* He had to forcibly drag his gaze upward to keep from drooling right then and there. She looked good enough to eat. Her soft, thick hair was piled high on her head, a few stray curls hanging down next to each cheek. It made her look a little more mature, but her innocence shown like a light across her ethereal features, and he suddenly groaned in disgust at his erotic thoughts. He had to keep reminding himself to go slow. He frowned at the thought. Dammit, she wasn't helping him any. If he didn't know better, he'd swear she was deliberately tempting him. If she kept pushing his buttons, he wasn't going to be able to hold onto his iron control much longer. Then, the gods help them both. He let his hungry gaze eat her up as she walked toward him. She glided with an enthralling, sensual grace that left him breathless, and he could only stare as she finally came to stand in front of the table.

Then, he found his voice. He cleared a throat gone dry and managed to drawl out, "If you're thinking of making a run for freedom, kitten, you'll never make it." He seared her with a long hot look from head to toes. His groin tightened painfully, need burning deep. "Not dressed like that. Every damn man in the place has his eyes on you right now." He swallowed down the possessive growl that rose in his throat. He was ready to fight every man there for doing nothing more than being male and staring at a beautiful woman.

He abruptly stood, possessive and protective instincts roaring to full force. Mason and Caleb stood too, subtly moving to flank Ariel and Jade. Kitlene smiled at him—so incredibly sweet and sensual at the same time—he nearly lost all control right then. He'd promised himself earlier, after Jade's threat that Kitlene would run if he kept pushing, that he'd try and be less Alpha around her. But right now, feeling the threat of other men around her, he couldn't control his primal instincts. He wanted to turn all cave man and throw her over his shoulder and take her out of there. He could just imagine her reaction. His delicate little Truemate had already shown she had a temper to match her red hair and she wasn't afraid to use it. He frowned. Hell, there was enough attention on her right now. Carrying her out of here and back upstairs was feeling more and more like the best idea but not the smartest he'd had.

He had no choice for the moment but to play this out and see where it led. "What are you doing down here?" He moved aside and indicated she was to sit down where he'd been sitting. She gracefully slid into the booth and he followed. He made sure he was close enough that their bodies were almost touching. He felt her tense immediately.

"We were feeling claustrophobic upstairs," she answered. But she wasn't looking directly at him and he wasn't going to let her avoid eye contact for long.

"I know I said no one would restrain you, Kitlene," he murmured, leaning close to her, "but that won't prevent my men from following orders and protecting you. They'd be forced to stop you if you placed yourself in danger." He leaned closer, his mouth next to her ear and said low, "And if they touched you, I'd have to punish them. Do you want to be responsible for that?"

She gasped lightly, her cheeks turning a pretty shade of pink. He held back his satisfied grin. She was so responsive to him, whether she wanted to be or not. His body tightened again, hard lust boiling anew deep inside him.

"Aunty worked in a club in Stuart," Ariel spoke up, effectively breaking the sexually charged moment. "But it wasn't as big as this one."

Lyon leaned back from Kitlene but placed his arm on the booth's headrest right behind her shoulders. "Oh? What did you do?" He resisted the urge to tangle his fingers in her soft hair. He wanted to pull the clasp out and let the long strands flow over his arm. Damn, but he had it bad; he couldn't even keep a normal thought in his head around her. He wasn't even sure of what he'd just said, his mind was so centered on her every breath.

Kitlene shrugged, and he almost groaned. Even that movement was sexy. "The owner was an old family friend, so I helped out in his office whenever he needed it."

"Zachary didn't tell us much about your family, Ariel." Lyon deliberately turned his attention to the other woman. Sitting this close to Kitlene, his body was on fire, and he wasn't sure how much more he could take. He kept breathing in deep inhales of her enticing, orange blossom scent. It kept his blood heated, stroking his overly sensitized nerve endings with torturous licks. At this rate, he wasn't going to last much longer. That cave man idea was looking better by the moment. "Where is the rest of your family? Your parents?"

"Mine died when I was eleven," Ariel answered. "Aunty's father died when she was younger and her mother died when Aunty was born. We've been together since then, and Jade's been our only other family."

Lyon felt the instant Kitlene's body tensed at Ariel's comments. He slanted a glance at her and saw her face pale. Protective instincts flooded him. Why had Ariel's statement made her react that way? Damn it, he was getting tired of this mystery. If something was bothering her, something she was keeping secret that might eventually harm her, then he was going to find out what it was. She might as well give in now.

"We were told there are only twenty of you left, who carry the jaguar genes," he said to Ariel while carefully watching Kitlene. "Did you inherit it from your mother, or your father?"

"Mother. All of us. Every female has at least one daughter and the gene is passed that way."

"Why are there so few of you left?" Shouldn't the fact that each woman had a daughter, keep the lines carrying on? But then, his own mother had given birth to twin males and not a daughter.

Maybe there were exceptions, circumstances they didn't know about. He'd have to get Wren to check into it later.

Jade made a loud coughing sound and Lyon looked away from Kitlene to stare at her. The woman was a ferocious mama bear when it came to protecting her friends. He had a feeling she was about to deliberately change the subject, and the reason had everything to do with the way Kitlene was subtly squirming beside him.

"We don't know," Jade answered for Ariel. "And let's talk about something more interesting. Like, for example, when can we go shopping?"

Lyon shook his head. Fine. He'd drop the subject, but not for long. He'd have Kitlene all to himself later and he'd get answers then. One way or another. "You'll have to wait a few days," he stated. "I want you trained to protect yourself should the need arise. So until you can, I don't want you out in public."

"Fine. Whatever." Jade frowned at him. "But don't plan on keeping us prisoners here for long. We need to go shopping. Ariel will need a wedding gown, and other things."

A long minute of strained silence lingered around the table after her statement. Ariel blushed a deep red and subtly scooted closer to Kitlene. Lyon studied the two women, his thoughts and mood abruptly dark now. His intended mate was a lovely young woman that any man would be proud to marry. He'd already discovered Ariel's sweet temperament and her loyalty. But she wasn't his Truemate.

Damn, this was too messed up. He looked at Mason, and tried to keep the growl out of his voice as he asked, "Have we heard anything about Zachary's whereabouts yet?"

Mason shook his head. "I've sent a group down to South America, to the area we know the Elders live. We should be hearing something in the next twenty-four hours."

And if they didn't? Where the hell had the Elders disappeared? And why? Lyon didn't like the bad feeling that kept persisting in the back of his mind. Every instinct in him was screaming at him to prepare for the fight of his life. He looked again at Kitlene. No matter what he had to do, even if it meant marrying Ariel, then he'd make sure she was safe from this invisible threat.

Even if it meant he had to give her up to protect her.

Chapter Twelve

The sexual tension arcing between them slowly built as the night wore on. The sensual heat radiating off his hard body enclosed her in an intimate cocoon, threatening to overload her senses. Kitlene was finding it hard to even concentrate on anything but Lyon.

And he knew it. She felt his acute awareness of her, almost as though he was constantly touching her and gauging her every reaction. Even though he talked to the others at the table, his gaze was always straying to her. Without her realizing it he had somehow managed to move close enough to her so that their bodies were touching, subtly, and she could feel his every breath. Her every breath made her brush against him. It was nerve wracking ... and erotic all in one.

Her overwhelming sensual awareness of him scared her. She knew it was wrong, but she couldn't stop the wanting. *Oh God.* She almost gasped aloud with the mental admission. When had her feelings changed from being attracted to him ... to wanting him?

He felt her tense and without stopping his conversation with Mason he turned his turquoise gaze on her and his brow rose in silent question. And God help her, but she saw more than just a question there in the depths of his dark gaze.

She saw primal male desire. Simmering hunger. It took her breath away.

Her entire body reacted, every feminine instinct in her reaching out. It left her reeling with the knowledge that this man wanted her and he wasn't hiding it. He hadn't, since the first moment they'd met.

This can't happen. Lyon was engaged to Ariel. It was in the Decree, the very Law that had been put into place to save the Jaguar people. No matter how she felt or what he wanted, their personal feelings had no place in the Destiny that was already playing out.

Even if she wanted to be his more than she'd ever wanted anything in her life.

Panic hit. She couldn't stay here. Ariel would just have to understand. She wasn't even sure she could return at the end of the month and watch her niece marry Lyon ...

"What's wrong, kitten?" Lyon murmured the words next to her ear as the others talked around them. "Are you feeling sick again?"

Sick. Yes, but it wasn't what he thought. It was a heart felt sickness that was already reaching down to her soul. She knew then, right there at that very moment that she was falling in love with him. And knew in the next moment that it was so wrong in every way.

"No," she managed to whisper back, avoiding his searching gaze so that he wouldn't see the tears she felt burning there. *I can't cry. This is crazy. I've got to leave. Now.* A little stronger she stated, "I'm tired. I'm going back upstairs."

She pushed against him. "Move, Lyon."

"No."

The word was stated with male stubbornness. She glared at him. "Why not?"

She was afraid to try and decipher the look in his eyes right then. Her entire body was reacting to the savage gleam of warning shining in the dark depths.

"If you go back upstairs now, Kitlene, I'll follow." He let that murmured statement sink in. Around them the others kept up a conversation that effectively shut them in a private cocoon, and she had a brief moment to be very thankful no one else was noticing the strong tension between her and Lyon. He smiled, but it didn't seem to reach his eyes. "Cats get tired by early morning, sweetheart, and need their naps. It'll be easier then."

Okay, she was not going to ask what he meant by that remark. "What's that suppose to mean?" Darn. Not so smart.

He was silent for a long poignant moment, their gazes locked. It took a lot of willpower to keep from squirming under his intense stare. Especially when those mesmerizing eyes slowly caressed over her face, down her throat, and straight to the low vee of her blouse. Her entire body tingled as though he'd physically touched her.

He suddenly frowned. "When you go shopping, I want you to get some decent clothes."

She blinked rapidly to clear the sensual fog that moments ago had kept her a willing prisoner. "Who do you think you are, telling me what I can wear? When did you get it in your head that you own me?"

His eyes narrowed and his voice lowered, became dangerously sexy and rough. "You're just asking for trouble, aren't you, sweetheart? Do you really want me to answer that right here and now?" He leaned in and his mouth touched her ear, sending sensual shivers straight to her womb. "As long as you're here, Kitlene, you're under my protection. I'll fight or kill if I have to, to protect you from anything or anyone. But I'll be damned if I'll be happy about having to fight my own men for doing something so male as staring at you because you like to wear provocative clothes."

"You are one egotistical cat," she muttered, anger and desire vying for dominance deep in her. "And I'm getting tired of your Alpha attitude. Now move, or I swear I'm going to hit you."

His grin was too sexy, too confident. It unnerved her. Heaven help her, it actually excited her. "Try it, kitten. I can take the punch. But are you willing to take the consequences?"

"Are you threatening me?" She balled her hand into a fist when he grinned again.

"Promising."

Okay, that was it. She couldn't stand much more of this sexually tinged conversation. Someone else was going to start noticing the tension and what was going on between them. "Fine." She purposely turned away from him and said aloud to Jade, "It's getting late. Are you and Ariel ready to go upstairs?" She stared hard at Jade to get her silent point across and saw her friend nod her head in understanding.

Lyon had no choice but to move and the men stood politely as the three women left the booth. Two guards fell into place behind them as they crossed the main floor and climbed the stairs. Kitlene was very aware of the stares of some of the club patrons as the three women were flanked by the two burly guards and escorted across the room. But she was even more aware of Lyon's hard stare. She knew his gaze never left her. She felt it like a hot, caressing physical touch. It left her with an ache she wasn't too happy with.

Upstairs she said goodnight to Jade and Ariel, shaking her head when Jade asked her if she wanted to talk. She couldn't talk about it, not even to her best friend. Everything she was feeling was so wrong. But she couldn't stop it.

She was falling in love with Lyon. And she wanted him with a need that swamped her senses, flooded her body, and threatened her in more ways than she was ready to accept. It was though she was finally awakening after a too long sleep that had kept her a prisoner in her own mind and body. Every feminine instinct and need inside her was coming painfully alive.

She leaned back against the door, her breathing choppy. She didn't even have to close her eyes to see his face in front of her. His hungry eyes devouring her. His hard body sexually tense and aggressive. His rough voice sensually melting her with every word he said. She wrapped her arms around her waist and moaned.

The door behind her pushed open, and she stepped back a few feet. Her gasp echoed in the room as Lyon walked in and closed the door behind him. They faced each other, gazes locked in a silent admission neither could deny.

He didn't give her time to say anything. He strode to her and grasped her upper arms in a hard grip. Then, just as fast he swung her around and pressed her back against the door. He released her and slammed his hands against the door's wood, on each side of her face. He stopped short at leaning into her.

Breathing harsh, his eyes gleaming with a hungry fire, his features hard and flushed, he muttered roughly, "Touch me, Kitlene." He growled. "If *you* touch *me*, then I don't have to hold back any more."

She tried. She really did try to be the strong one. She made one last, desperate effort to stop what was sure to happen, knowing it was so terribly wrong and the results would be far more disastrous than either of them could comprehend. "We can't do this, Lyon." She stared into his stormy glare. The hunger reflected there struck an answering spark in her, making her words seem too weak even to her own ears. "I can't."

He growled, the sound low and dangerous. "You're one stubborn little kitten," he muttered. "I know you feel what I'm feeling, Kitlene. I'm attuned to your every reaction to me." He groaned. "Baby, I can even see it in your beautiful eyes. I feel it when I'm near you. When

I touch you. When I kissed you."

He leaned in as though he was going to kiss her and she panicked. If he did that, she was lost and she knew it. She said the only thing she thought would diffuse this volatile moment. "I won't have sex with my niece's fiancé."

His face flushed darker, obvious fury narrowing his eyes. "Damn it all to hell." He swung away from her and stomped across the room. His words had been uttered in a dead, darkly dangerous pitch and she shivered in reaction; she'd never heard that tone from him.

She wanted to go to him. She wanted to touch him. Beg him to claim her, body, heart and soul.

But the consequences would be unbearable. He was going to marry Ariel. And ... if she gave herself to him, risking everything, she wouldn't be able to live with herself. He risked all that he held dear. His Alpha status. The salvation of his people.

He risked all that and more. Because she knew deep inside her soul that he wouldn't give her up if she gave herself to him. She knew it.

Kitlene wanted to cry. Her heart felt like it was breaking. She finally pushed away from the door and slowly walked over to him. Taking a deep breath then exhaling slowly, she forced out the words she'd never wanted to tell him.

"Lyon, there's something you need to know about me."

He slowly turned to face her. The look in his eyes was frightening. He looked like a man on the edge, not caring if he fell or not. "Do you know what the term Truemate means, Kitlene?"

The question threw her. She shook her head. Why was he asking this? "Is it a Jaguar term?"

"Shifter." He ran a hand over his face and through his hair. "It means soul mate. Shifters usually mate for life, but can have more than one spouse in a lifetime if something happens and they lose one. Divorce. Death. Or just falling out of love. It happens in every race, or species. You know that. But finding your Truemate is a rare occurrence. A Truemate is a soul mate. The two are bound together for eternity. The love between them is indestructible, a force nothing can fight against."

"How rare?" She took another calming breath, suddenly realizing where this conversation was leading. And scared to death with that realization. "How rare is finding your Truemate?"

He looked at her for the longest, poignant moment. Her heart stuttered, almost stopping. *Please don't say it.*

"So rare that it's almost become a fairy tale idea that Shifters tell their children, never believing it to be true any more."

She actually bit her tongue to keep from asking, but the question burst out of her mouth before she could stop it. "Why are you telling me this?"

He closed the small distance between them, and for a moment it looked like he was about to take her in his arms. She clearly saw the intent in his eyes. But he suddenly tensed and muttered so low she wasn't sure she heard right, "I won't touch you, first."

Instead, he said louder, "Ariel was chosen for me. I didn't have a choice in the matter. I agreed to marry her because our union will mean the salvation of our people. But I won't love her. I can't. I had every intention of giving her all the respect, protection, and care she would deserve. But the moment I met you, everything changed." He sighed roughly. "You can deny it all you want to, kitten. But you felt it too. That first moment of recognition. You've felt it since, with every touch, every breath we've taken. You are my Truemate, Kitlene. You are the only one I will ever claim." He growled, deep and long. "And no one will stand in my way."

She felt the truth in his words, all the way to the very depths of her soul. It made her heart ache so much she thought she could stop breathing right then and not even care.

"There is someone who will stop this from happening, Lyon." She closed her eyes tight for a moment, trying hard to keep the tears from falling. She failed. The hot tears leaked down her cheeks. "I will."

He roared. The sound shocked her. She took a step back.

"Why the bloody-damn-hell are you being so stubborn about this? Didn't you just hear what I said? Damn it, Kitlene!"

A loud pounding on the door startled her. Mason yelled out, "What's wrong, Lyon?"

"Go the hell away, Mason," he muttered dangerously. She was reminded that cat Shifters had excellent hearing when Mason muttered back, "Fine. Your battle." and she heard his steps retreat. She almost called out for him to stay.

"I heard every word, Lyon." She squared her shoulders, biting back the anger that made her want to punch him for pushing this when they both knew it was so wrong, so dangerous. "Now it's your turn to hear me." It was time. She had to tell him everything. Never mind how much it hurt her. Or him. "Do you remember when you asked me why Zachary didn't choose me instead of Ariel?"

He nodded his head, lips thin in anger, eyes glinting. "Yeah. And you conveniently skirted around answering." His breathing became harsher. "What are you trying to tell me, Kitlene? You're not available? Are you already destined to be some other Alpha's mate?" His rough growls rumbled, one after the other, for long frightening moments, preventing her from answering. "Too damn bad. I don't care who the hell Zachary chose for you. You're mine. My Truemate. I'll kill Zachary or any other damn Shifter who tries to claim you now. I mean it, Kitlene. I'll kill."

"You can't fight fate." There. The words were said.

"Watch me."

No more time. No more hiding. "If you claim me, Lyon, if you make me your mate, I'll die. It won't be Zachary or any other Shifter you kill. It will be me." She didn't try to stop the tears. It wasn't worth the effort any more. She rushed on with the fateful words, knowing they had to be said before her broken heart stopped beating right then and there. "I have a defective gene from the Jaguar DNA. All the women in my family line have had it. The gene is responsible for causing every woman, every generation, no exceptions, to … die … the minute they give birth to their first child.

"You can claim me. I can give you that destined Alpha son. But I'll die doing it. And there's nothing you or anyone can do to stop that. I'll die because of you, Lyon."

Chapter Thirteen

$\mathcal{L}$yon felt his whole world crumble and disappear right before his eyes. His legs wouldn't even hold him up. He fell to his knees, shock reverberating through him with waves so cruel and painful he couldn't catch his breath. Her horrifying words screamed through his numb mind, and his vision darkened.

Anguish, and a rage so deep, frighteningly feral and uncontrollable, built from the very depths of his soul and rose up. He lifted his head and roared.

And roared.

The suite door flew open and Mason, Caleb, Beau, and two other guards came rushing in. Shocked, they stared at Lyon, then at Kitlene. He managed to choke off the roars and then lowered his head. He felt like slumping in defeat. Surprised he could even talk, Lyon finally muttered hoarsely to his Beta. "Take Kitlene to Jade. Keep her there." He lifted his head to stare at the white-faced woman standing in front of him. "Mason," he choked out, "keep her safe."

He wanted to take her in his arms. He wanted to erase the fear, the anguish he saw reflected there in her tear-streaked face and beautiful haunted eyes. But if he touched her now …

He'd never let go. And he would willingly kill himself before ever hurting her.

He watched Mason escort a silent, crying Kitlene from the room and had to choke back more roars. Feral, primal rage was blurring his vision again. He had to get out of here. Now.

He struggled to his feet. He heard Caleb's calm voice as if from a distance. "You're in half change, Lyon." Caleb purred soothingly. "You need to change back before you leave."

He couldn't. His jaguar soul was pushing forward. The rage

was controlling the change, demanding dominance. He needed the change. Needed the change to take away the all-too human emotions bombarding him and trying to destroy his very sanity.

His voice gruff from the half change, he told Caleb, "Get me to the car. Take me to the ranch." *Get me out of here before the pain kills me.*

In jaguar form he paced back and forth on the back seat of the car Caleb was driving. Every now and then he'd release a roar of rage. Caleb would soothingly purr back at him, coax him to calm. But he knew he would never feel calm again.

His world was destroyed. He'd found and lost his Truemate before he'd even had the chance to claim what was rightfully his and should have been his forever.

He wanted to kill. And unfortunately for the Elder, Zachary was foremost on his mind. Gods help the man if Lyon ever faced him again. Lyon wouldn't care that his own life would be forfeit. Without Kitlene, it wouldn't matter any way.

At the ranch, Caleb released him from the car and he ran. Hard. Fast. Mindlessly.

He ran for pain-filled hours. Pushed the limits of his strength, his endurance. Ran until his legs collapsed and his heaving sides couldn't pull enough air into his lungs. Until his human sanity finally submitted willingly to let the jaguar's soul take complete control.

The jaguar roared into the night. He was enraged. Hungry. Exhausted.

But at least the human part of him had already forgotten why.

•

Mason let him stay out there for four days before he finally went in search and found Lyon, still in jaguar form.

It took a physical fight between them, both in jaguar forms, and then a mental argument that nearly scorched the hides off each other before Lyon finally conceded and changed back to man. Naked, he slumped to the ground.

Mason willed clothes on and plunked down next to him. "Lucky for you, I was too tired to beat you bloody."

Lyon growled, the sound too close to full jaguar still. "Not in this life time." He made the mental effort to will on clothes. He turned a nasty stare on his Beta. "What the hell are you doing here, any way? I gave you an order to stay with Kitlene and keep her safe." He ran a hand through his tangled hair and sighed roughly. "You're the only one I trust with her, Mason."

"She's safe," Mason assured. "In fact, I took her some place where she is completely safe." He looked long at Lyon before adding quietly, "Even from you."

Lyon stiffened. His tone dangerous, he demanded, "You took her from the Club? Damn you, Mason. Where is she?" A touch of panic shivered through him and he swallowed it down. The thought of Kitlene not being near him wasn't something he wanted to accept.

"At your great aunt's estate," Mason answered. "That place is like a fortress. And Gwendolyn guards her loved ones with a ferocious danger no sane man or Shifter would ever willingly go against. Ariel and Jade are there too. I didn't want to take any chances."

Lyon's shoulders slumped as some small amount of relief shot through him. She was safe. And Mason was right. If there was any place on earth Kitlene was safer than with him, it had to be with Gwendolyn Savage. That woman was the most vicious Shifter alive today. She had the strength and attitude that could put any tough Alpha to shame no matter how strong he thought he was.

"I even refrained, though it was hard, from telling Gwen that Kitlene was the one who broke her birthday gift. Wasn't that nice of me?"

Lyon spit out a few nasty, foul expletives. He wasn't in the mood for this. "The humor isn't working, Mason. Explain why you're so tired and why you thought to take Kitlene to Gwen."

Mason's features hardened. "We've had more fights at the Club. Various Shifters, and some of them definitely out-of-towners. They're working in groups, Lyon. And not with their own species. Wolves with cats. Hell, even some bears came in looking for a fight and they had deer Shifters with them. I don't know what the hell is going on, but it's escalating."

Lyon's anger simmered, belying his oddly calm tone, "There's only a few weeks left before the Shifter's Moon. It's tied in with that, I'm sure of it." Someone was working toward stopping the Mating Ceremony that night. He just wished he knew who it was exactly. If his brother was innocent, then who else stood to gain any profit? He growled. He needed to fight. He wanted that enemy under his paws right now. Maybe then, he'd be able to fight all of this soul destroying rage out of his system. "Let's get back to the Club. I'm calling in all our warriors." He stood, his shoulders back, head high. "If it's a war our mysterious enemy wants, then he'll get one." He started walking. "But he might as well concede that he'll lose. Nothing is going to take what rightfully belongs to me. I'll kill anyone I have to, to protect what's mine."

"You mean that you'll protect our people and your mate. Ariel. Right?"

Lyon shot a hard glare at Mason walking by his side. Mason knew the whole story. He could see it in his eyes. "Kitlene can never belong to me." Saying it aloud nearly choked the breath out of him. He cleared his throat. "I know that, Mason. But I can't let her go. I have to have her near. Don't think I haven't thought about the consequences. These last four days have been torture. She's my Truemate and I can never claim her. So, I'll keep her near, and I'll protect her for the rest of her life. No one will ever touch her. Ever hurt her in any way. Most of all ... I will never hurt her."

The two men walked the rest of the way in silence to where Mason had parked his jeep. He'd told his Beta the truth, and in his mind he knew it was the only way things could be. But damn if his treacherous heart and his hurting soul didn't disagree.

•

Returning to the Club, Lyon and Mason went into war preparation mode. All the warriors under Lyon's rule were called in from their various places around the city. Caleb called in the ten men working undercover at the ranch. Lyon questioned them thoroughly about the events going on at the ranch and what his brother might be doing.

He wasn't surprised to discover that Bryce seemed to be getting ready for some kind of battle too. "Are they all cat Shifters with him?"

All ten shook their heads but only one answered. "No. We've scented wolves, coyotes, bears, and those African lions are still there too."

"Any Alphas among them?"

"That's what's so strange," Caleb interrupted. "They're all rogue. We're sure of it. I've had the chance to check most of them out, one time or another, as they've come and gone on the ranch. I've tracked them back to their dens. Not once have any of them been in contact with an Alpha. The only ones who haven't left the ranch in the past week are the lions."

If there were no Alphas present, it had to mean that Bryce was playing leader. Lyon's jaguar soul stirred in readiness. He was going to have to confront his brother one final time. And this time maybe even kill him.

Through long hours and quickly passing days of preparation, plans, and meetings, Lyon concentrated on the battle that loomed so close. But try as hard as he could, he still couldn't stop his thoughts from straying to Kitlene. Even when he fell into exhausted sleep for a few short hours of regenerative rest, he dreamed of her. He'd wake, sweating, swearing, and his soul crying out.

He didn't think he could live without her. He wanted her, needed her with a soul-searing ache that ate at him day and night. He wanted to hold her. Protect her. Cherish her. Love her.

Claim her.

But he'd kill himself first before he ever made her his. He would willingly sacrifice his own life for hers.

When she'd told him her secret, he had almost gone crazy. How cruel was Fate to finally deliver his Truemate into his arms and then force them to deny their bond? He'd never felt such a killing rage as he had then in that moment he fully realized that Kitlene would never be his.

He knew then that he would never allow her to risk her life, not for him or for anyone else. She'd stay near him and let him protect her from anyone who dared to even touch her. The thought of another man touching her, wanting her, nearly caused him to lose his mind with the stark possessiveness painfully clenching his gut.

Because, gods help him, he needed her. And he knew that need would never die. It would only grow, eating away at his soul, and his control. And then the only fear would be in the question: How in this world was he ever going to keep her safe—from him?

Chapter Fourteen

*K*itlene couldn't believe she'd find anything ever again to laugh at. But watching Jade get thrown into the mud, only to come up sputtering swear words she shouldn't have known, and then fly back into her opponent, became more comical each time it happened.

The three women were in the training area, in the back yard of the huge mansion Lyon's great aunt humbly called her 'home sweet home'. Ha. It was more like a four story castle sitting on a fortified mountain, with more security than even a king or queen could boast.

Mason had delivered them into Gwendolyn's care two days after Lyon had left the Club. He had his hands full with the fights and odd events happening and was worried about keeping the women safe.

Before leaving he had muttered a side note to Kitlene, "You owe me one, honey. I could tell Gwendolyn you broke that expensive vase by throwing it at me. She really wanted that vase for her birthday." He'd winked at her. "But your secret is safe with me. Just remember that, in case you get any crazy ideas in the near future." She knew he was teasing, in his own odd way, but she thanked him anyway. She'd taken one long look at the woman whose care she'd be under for a few weeks and she had to admit she was just a little bit intimated.

Gwendolyn Savage was six and half feet tall. Slender yet muscled. She looked like a walking tree that could easily squash anyone or anything in her path and not even blink doing it. Her features were harsh and beautiful at the same time. She had narrow cat eyes that were the darkest shade of green, almost black. Ice and an iron-will glittered in those depths. Her features were patrician; long nose, wide thin lips, high cheekbones. She wore her starkly white hair braided and curled on top of her head like a crown. She was elegance and menace all in one.

And the first thing she'd done the morning after their arrival was to put her trainers to teaching the three women self protection techniques.

"I don't know what my nephew was thinking," she'd commented in a voice so contradictory to her harsh appearance that it had shocked the three women when they'd first heard her. It was soft, elegant, and slightly musical. "He should have been training you immediately. We can't have the Alpha's mate unable to protect herself if the need ever arose."

That was the first thing that had happened to make Kitlene want to cry all over again. After the introductions, and after settling in, Gwen had gathered them together for a get-to-know-you tea in a quaint drawing room that was oddly frilly and ultra feminine. Gwen had looked from one woman to the other, studying them so intently they begin to squirm.

And then she'd abruptly announced, "You're all full human. So odd. In all my years of studying our heritage I never knew about the special women who carried the jaguar genes yet were not Shifters. My nephews' mother was one of those women and I didn't even know it." She'd frowned ferociously for a moment. "Ah, that old man Zachary has a lot of explaining to do."

She handed a cup to Kitlene. "And since you're human, that explains why Mason brought you here for protection. It's two weeks before the Shifter's Moon and you're too vulnerable there at that overly populated Club. I'm assuming you don't have any training in fighting skills, dear?"

Kitlene looked at the other two, confused at where the conversation seemed to be going. Then she answered, "No. We don't. Lyon—he planned on training us. But we never saw the need. Especially considering that Jade and I will be going home after the marriage."

Gwen's aristocratic features darkened for a moment with a flush of anger, her eyes gleamed with an odd calculating look. Kitlene's heart raced for no known reason she could understand. Then again, it may have been because of the hard tone of the woman's voice when she demanded, "What do you mean...you will be leaving after the marriage?"

Jade, always ready to come to Kitlene's aid, spoke up, her own voice hard. "Ariel won't need us here." She turned to Ariel. "Right, sweetie? You're a grown woman now and you won't need us hovering."

Ariel slowly nodded, staring wide-eyed and a little afraid, at Gwen. Kitlene felt the same way. The sudden, obvious anger coming off the woman was palpable.

"Ariel?" Gwen sat her teacup down with a hard snap of her hand. The fragile china on the tray clattered, sounding overly loud in the room. "Some one should start explaining. Now. Why is Ariel staying behind and not you, Kitlene?"

Kitlene exhaled, wanting to suddenly cry and hating herself for the weakness. She'd been so tearful since those last moments with Lyon. It took a lot of willpower to keep from just giving in to a long crying spree. But now certainly wasn't the time. She cleared her throat and answered, "My niece will be a married woman. And my life, my home, is still in Florida." She bravely looked Gwen directly in the eyes and asked, "Why are you upset about that?"

"Because, damn it, Ariel is not Lyon's Truemate!" Gwen surged to her feet and shouted out, "Celeste, get Lyon on the phone. Tell him I want to talk to him immediately." She turned back to them and stared hard, shaking her head. "Who made this mess? I'm betting Zachary. Damn the man to hell. I'll kill him myself before Lyon even gets the chance."

Kitlene felt faint. Gwendolyn's shocking words echoed all around her. She looked at Jade and then at Ariel. They looked as stunned as she felt. She was afraid to ask Gwen to explain her statement. Jade caught her gaze and mouthed silently, "We'll talk later."

The maid, Celeste, came hurrying in a minute later. "Madam, I could only reach Beau at the Club. He says Lyon hasn't returned from the ranch. He's been there for two days now. I left the message that he was to call you."

Kitlene was shocked at the unique swear words that came out of Gwendolyn's mouth then.

The next morning, listening to Jade repeat most of those same words Gwen had used the night before actually had her laughing again. Gwen had let them retire for the night, setting them up in bedroom suites that looked like palatial rooms fit only for royalty.

But as she bade them goodnight she'd made the comment that she would "fix the damn problem as soon as possible" and adding, "Be prepared to start training tomorrow. All three of you."

Kitlene had managed to avoid Jade's questions, claiming she was too tired. She couldn't talk to her just yet. The hurt was still too painful. And besides, it wouldn't change anything. Lyon knew the truth now, and he would finally realize that he would have to marry Ariel. Remembering those last moments with him, she knew he had accepted that. He'd sent her away from him. And even though it had nearly killed her, she had willingly left. Destroying them both served no purpose, and nothing could change the truth...or change Destiny itself. Even if it killed them both with the inevitable soul-felt pain, they couldn't change what was. They both had to go forward.

She was determined to try.

Now it was early morning, and already they'd been put through countless self-defense moves that had all three women bruised and muddy. Nearby, Gwen watched with eagle eyes and nodded her approval. Kitlene watched the elderly woman under lowered lashes. That morning at breakfast, Gwen had acted as though the night's previous conversation had never occurred. She treated them as though she was their elderly aunt and she had nothing more to do than spoil them while they visited. Other than the insistence that they train, she was more than sweet to them for the rest of the time.

Kitlene was still feeling the shock from Gwen's statement the night before. And even though she found herself determinedly concentrating on the training, her thoughts kept straying back to the words. How had Gwendolyn known about her and Lyon? How was it even possible, when she hadn't even known herself until Lyon had told her?

It didn't matter. Nothing could come of it. She would spend the rest of her life with a broken heart, loving a man she could never be with. Her soul was sick. And she didn't know how she was ever going to live through the pain. She only knew that somehow, she had to.

"Ariel, honey," Gwen called out from where she sat in a lounge chair under a huge umbrella yards away. "You've done enough today. Come sit with me, while Kitlene and Jade finish their lessons."

Kitlene was immediately suspicious of Gwen's motives. And she hated feeling that way. Her emotions since she'd been taken from Lyon that fateful night had ranged from one extreme to the other and she couldn't control any of them. Telling him the truth had been the hardest thing she'd ever done. But facing his reaction was the most gut wrenching, heart breaking, soul-destroying thing she'd ever witnessed.

In the depths of his eyes, in the rage of his roar, she'd heard his defeat. And his acceptance. It had nearly killed her.

She watched Ariel settle in the chair next to Gwen and suddenly wished she had the distance-hearing talent Shifters had. The two of them looked way too serious to be having just a simple get-to-know-you talk.

Kitlene's trainer called for her to step forward and she reluctantly pulled her gaze away from the disturbing scene of her niece nodding vigorously at something Gwendolyn Savage had just said. She pushed the worry away and resolutely listened to the trainer explain the next defense move. *I'll learn this*, she mentally declared with determined heartfelt conviction. *And then, heaven help anyone who tries to stop me from leaving...*

It sounded like a good plan. She just wished her heart and soul agreed with her mind.

Chapter Fifteen

$\mathcal{A}$ week passed, with the women training hard, and Kitlene's heart refusing to mend while she made secret plans to disappear after the Ceremony on the night of the Shifter's Moon. She didn't know exactly where she would go because she'd already decided that returning home wasn't the best idea. Her watchers were dead, and she didn't know where Zachary was. That caused her more than one twinge of worry and guilt. What would the Elder do if he knew what she was planning?

On the sixth night, a storm blew in from the Pacific coast. Its ferocity was surprising. Hurricane force winds shoved against the castle-like mansion, rain beat down unmercifully hard. Lightning and thunder vied for attention, each strike and boom louder than the last. The fortress estate was older than Gwendolyn Savage and had withstood countless storm attacks over the centuries, but still, Kitlene was beginning to feel like this would turn out to be a battle against all odds.

Her head pounded, and nausea rolled through her. She'd always had this physical reaction to storms. Ever since that fated day she'd lost her brother, his wife, and her aunt and uncle in that car accident during a dangerous storm. Doctors had told her it was all 'mental' and that one day she would get over it. Years later, and she still suffered. And she knew from experience the headache would only get worse as this storm raged on. It wouldn't be long before she'd be suffering excruciating pain and begging for relief.

Jade came into her bedroom without knocking. Kitlene was relieved to see she was carrying her medical bag. Uncurling from her fetal position on the bed, she sat up.

"Please tell me you have something, sans a needle, for this headache."

"I had a few pain pills earlier," Jade answered with a frown, "but they're not in my bag any more. Sorry, honey. That means a shot."

Kitlene shook her head. "I'd rather suffer." *Lyon isn't here to hold me through it.* The unspoken words rolled around in her mind and she felt tears burn in her throat, then eyes. She'd been so angry with him when he'd distracted her while Jade had given her the shots that morning. But she couldn't forget the incredible tenderness, the strong protectiveness he'd surrounded her with while he held her safe in his arms.

She wanted his arms around her now. She needed him. So desperately. And it wasn't entirely because she'd had to endure Jade's sadistic needles twice already this week. No, her heart readily admitted she just simply needed Lyon to hold her. Aching with that relentless need, she wrapped her arms around her waist. "Will you ask Gwen if she has something for a headache?"

Jade grumbled but left to find Gwen. Kitlene sighed, the sound ragged. Thunder boomed so loud it felt as though the rafters of the mansion shook in shock. She couldn't stop it, she brokenly murmured his name aloud, "Lyon."

And suddenly in the utter stillness that followed the last thunder boom, she heard his whispered answer.

"Kitlene."

She bit her lip to keep from crying out. She hadn't really heard him. It wasn't possible. It was only wishful thinking. She rubbed at her aching temples. It was just the headache making her whimsical. Crazy.

But you didn't have a headache that time when he was holding you and taunting you to break free ...

She'd heard his desperate plea, "Make me release you kitten. Before I can't."

The memory shook her, stuttering her heart. She tried to force logical reasoning into her befuddled, pain filled mind, fighting against the harsh pounding in her head as it steadily increased. "Truemate means soul mate." Lyon had uttered the words as though they held a magical meaning deep beyond simple explanation. Was it possible that Truemates could sometimes hear the other's thoughts?

Even knowing she shouldn't, she wanted that to be true. She knew it would only cause heartache and pain if it were, because it would be one more connection between them that couldn't be broken despite the necessity.

Still, she couldn't stop herself. She mentally called his name again, suddenly feeling very frightened and achingly alone at the same time. *Lyon.*

As though from a long distance, as though it were a litany that had already been repeated many times over, she heard him whisper in her mind, *I'll keep you safe, kitten. I swear it. Always.*

Thunder boomed over and over, shaking the big mansion with the reverberations. Kitlene gasped with the excruciating pain that hit her between the eyes, and she doubled over as her stomach heaved in warning. She was blinded as her vision went black, and the room spun around her. She fell to her knees, crying out.

A hand touched her shoulder. A voice soothingly coaxed, "Take this. It will stop the pain."

She didn't argue. She opened her mouth and let the woman place something on her tongue. She swallowed automatically, hoping it would stay down despite her heaving stomach. She staggered to her feet as the woman put her arms around her and helped her to the bed. There, she fell back on the bed and barely managed to say a heartfelt thank you to her unseen helper. In the back of her mind she had the thought it was probably one of the maids sent with medicine from Gwen.

Just when she thought she couldn't hold back the scream of pain from the pounding in her head, she suddenly felt a strange weakness flow over her. The pain receded, slowly, but surely. She would have been very thankful for that fact. If it hadn't been that as soon as the pain disappeared, she suddenly realized she was quickly sinking into a terrifying black pit of nothingness.

Kitlene struggled, trying to push back the blackness. Panic hit her like a physical blow. She was falling. Fast. Hard. Deep into something she knew, deep in her soul that she would never rise from again.

•

Lyon jerked to a sitting position and rubbed the sleep from his eyes. He glanced at the clock on the wall. He'd only meant to rest a few minutes; exhaustion had pushed at him so relentlessly, he hadn't had a choice. He needed to be alert. Ready. But as soon as he'd fallen asleep, he'd dreamed of Kitlene. Just like he did each time he closed his eyes.

Now, a strange fear echoed through his mind and he abruptly recalled what he'd been dreaming this time. Kitlene had been lying on a bed crying out for him. And he'd tried desperately to reach her, but something kept him rooted to the spot he was standing in. He'd called out to her, trying to soothe her, trying to let her know that he heard her. I'll keep you safe, kitten. I swear it. Always.

He growled and then spit out foul words as his own vow mocked him. He leapt from the bed, grabbed his jeans and pulled them on. He knew she was safe at Gwendolyn's fortress. Hell, he'd already decided that it was the only place to keep her from now on, whether she agreed or not. There, she'd be protected and loved. She'd be within distance, but yet far enough away from him that he wouldn't be tempted in doing something he would never have the right to do.

He thought back to the phone conversation with his aunt late last night. After berating him for not answering her call sooner, she'd proceeded to lecture him about his duties. His duties, damn it!

"A Shifter takes care of his Truemate," she'd scolded. "You didn't even make sure she was trained in self defense."

"Aunty, calm down." He'd taken a deep calming breath too, then exhaled roughly. "I had already planned to train Ariel as soon as possible. Something came up first."

The long silence on the other end had actually made his nape hair stand on end. His aunt was a formidable woman and could scare the hide off you if she ever got angry. Her ice-cold tone proved it when she said too quietly. "I wasn't talking about Ariel."

He'd cursed a blue streak then, albeit only in his head. No sense in angering the woman any more than necessary. But damn it, he was Alpha and his word was law. If he told her to get her busybody nose out of the situation, she would have no choice but to obey. He groaned. He loved Gwendolyn and respected her. So he bit back the angry words, and mocking her quiet tone he said, "Ariel is my intended mate, Gwendolyn. There are circumstances that you aren't aware about, and don't concern you."

"Don't give me that crap, young kit," she stated, tone hard. "I had a long talk with your intended. She finally told me about her aunt's...health problem. Where the hell is Wren? Why haven't you got him working on the situation? He's one of the best physicians the Jaguar Pride has ever had and if he set his mind to it, I have no doubt he would solve the problem. Have this Jade woman help him." She hadn't given him the chance to say anything as she rushed on, her anger growing, "I can't believe you would give up this easily, Lyon Savage. Your parents were the staunchest fighters in our history. You should be ashamed. She's your Truemate, damn it." She paused long enough to let her anger settle, then asked, "Don't you love her?"

Rage exploded, deep inside him. Love Kitlene? Hell, he loved her so much it was destroying his soul. He had kissed her only once, had all too briefly held her while she slept, had touched her too few times. Yet, he loved her with a love so deep, so real that he couldn't even think about it or he'd go insane.

He hadn't answered Gwen, but he knew she heard the truth in his silence. "I am going to marry Ariel on the destined night, Gwendolyn," he finally said. "There is too much at stake now. Zachary chose her because she is the one who will give birth to the destined Alpha son. You, out of us all, know what it means to protect our people's future. "

"What if Bryce's mate has the destined child, instead?"

He'd ruled his half of the Jaguar Pride since the death of his father, had killed to protect them, and had sacrificed more than he thought he'd ever be asked to do. And now he had to rely on Fate to help him. He wasn't going to accept any other outcome. Ariel would give him that son. And he'd live with the fact that he'd never really live again … without Kitlene by his side instead. "I thought I was your favorite nephew, Aunty. How can you even think of him winning the title of reigning Alpha? You are always the one touting positive thoughts are the best defense." He tried to make his voice sound teasing, but failed. He wanted to rage at her, and at Fate.

"Don't use that tone with me, son." Gwen coughed out a soft chuff. "You know exactly how much I love you. I love Bryce too, but he isn't the right choice for reigning Alpha. He's too volatile, too unstable in his beast's nature."

If she only knew that those words were describing him all too much right then …

"You accepted me as Alpha the day my father died," Lyon said then, his voice commanding her to accept his authority now. "And as your Alpha, I'm asking that you respect my decision in this. I want you to do me a favor, Aunty. Kitlene is a fragile woman. She's so innocent of the world around her despite everything. She needs you now. And I need you to take care of her for me. Keep her there, safe in that damn fortress you call a simple home, and protect her. For me."

"I can sense her innocence and her fragility," Gwen answered, "But she's stronger than you give her credit for." She laughed lightly. "She's been a very quick learner in the self defense training. Her trainer says she's a little spitfire, a feminine stick of dynamite. But even more important, Lyon, is the fact that she is a grown woman and she has a mind of her own. I can't keep her here a prisoner, you know that."

"I can't keep her safe, Gwen, if she's anywhere else. I'd go crazy not having her within distance of my protection." Lyon bit back the expletives he wanted to spit out. "And I can't keep her here with me. I'm not that strong."

"Then," Gwen's voice was soft but full of an anger that spoke volumes. "You'd better decide right now whether you want to fight for her—or against her. She's going to leave after the Ceremony, and she has every right to. If you don't claim her as your Truemate, then you have no right in any of her decisions. She doesn't belong to you, Lyon. She never will. The choice, my dear nephew, is yours. Only."

"I won't claim her," he growled out, his beast raging to break free, his soul mocking his words. "I won't kill her. I'll die first. That's my final decision."

And he would never break that soul-vow. Never. No matter how much it destroyed him.

•

Mason met him in his office and announced abruptly, "Zachary is on his way to Gwendolyn's estate. My man called in a few minutes ago and said he was to give you a message from the Elder." He looked angry as he continued, "He said you are forbidden to fight with Bryce. No matter the provocation or the reason."

"Zachary can go to hell," Lyon told him. He sat down in his desk chair and punched on the speakerphone. He couldn't get the thought out of his head that Kitlene was upset about something, and he needed to know she was all right. He dialed Gwen's number.

His heart stopped the moment he heard his aunt answer on the first ring and say, "She's not here, Lyon. Something is not right. Jade swears Kitlene was stricken with a debilitating headache and wouldn't have left the house for any reason during this storm. She's not in her room. And she's not in the house."

He surged to his feet, heart racing, his breath nearly choking in his throat. "Search for her, Gwen. I'm on my way now."

He'd never before felt this unbearable punch of cold fear that struck his mind and body now and he couldn't breathe through the force of it. For a long moment he couldn't even think straight. Kitlene was missing. The fear almost brought him to his knees. Luckily, Mason was thinking clearer. He leaned over the desk and barked at Gwen, "Call in the men I have guarding the estate, Gwendolyn. I left four there, without your knowledge, to stand guard outside the gates. All four of them are trackers."

Lyon was already out the door, shouting to Beau, "Call Caleb. Have him meet me at Gwendolyn's estate. Now!"

He'd never driven so fast. Lucky for him there wasn't much traffic or people out in the nasty storm that seemed to hover over the city, and he didn't run into a cop either. Lucky for the cop, too. He'd rip through anyone who tried to stop him.

Hang on, kitten. I'm coming. He wished to the gods she could hear his mental vow. He'd promised to keep her safe. Twice now she'd been taken from him. And damn it that was two times too many. Never again. He didn't care what he had to do, who he had to fight, he wasn't going to ever let her out of his sights again. He'd find a way for them to live under the same roof. Even if it killed them both.

It normally took an hour to reach the outskirts of L.A. where Gwendolyn's mansion was situated. It took Lyon less than thirty minutes. And it was the longest thirty minutes of his life. He died a thousand deaths every time he was forced to slow the car down when the storm pushed dangerously enough to knock if off the road. The delays were killing him. *I'm coming, Kitlene. Stay safe, for me, sweetheart. I'll have you back in my arms before you know it. I promise.*

He knew the promise meant unbearable heartache to them both, but he didn't care. He meant every word. When he got to her, he was going to take her in his arms and keep her there. Then, gods help them both, because he would willingly die with her when the time came.

The mansion came into view. He slammed his foot down hard on the car brakes just as he reached the entrance to the estate, and the car skidded straight into the large metal gates blocking his way. *Damn it, Gwen should have had the gates open.*

Mason shook himself like a cat shaking off water as they climbed out of the crashed car. "Damn, Lyon. You do realize you need to be alive to save her, don't you?"

"Shut up," Lyon growled. He was already sniffing the air, already searching for clues. Rushing adrenaline pumped through him, shaking his body from head to toes. "You have her scent. Start at the back of the house. I'm taking the surrounding woods. Do your men have radios on them? Good. Go, Mason."

Both men shifted instantly into jaguar. They jumped over the mangled gates with little effort. With a roar, full of promise to Kitlene, and full of deadly retribution to her kidnapper, Lyon took off in a fast run across the front grounds of the estate and straight into the dark woods. The storm had abated some, but it wasn't long before his fur was soaked and the muddy ground slowed him.

He finally stopped and carefully took in his surroundings. He growled under his breath. The damn rain was keeping his sense of smell from being as strong as he needed. And if there had been any tracks to follow, the rain had cleared them too. He remained perfectly still, expanding his senses, reaching deep inside him to find the help he desperately needed then. *Where are you, Kitlene?*

His mind went over all the possible scenarios. Someone had known she was at the mansion. Someone had access to her that Gwen wouldn't suspect. Who? Who else knew she was here?

The truth hit him hard. Zachary.

The missing Elder had suddenly, without any hint of intention, showed up after missing for weeks. What the hell was the old man up to? When he found him, Lyon was going to have a long … *talk* with him. After, he was sure the Elder would think twice about ever interfering in his life again.

He started forward once more, thoroughly searching the muddied ground and carefully sniffing the air for any signs of Kitlene. Instinct led him on, the jaguar determinedly tracking his mate. He was at home in the wilds, and there was no place the enemy could hide where he wouldn't be able to track him down. Minutes later he found himself standing in front of a small cave cut into the side of a hill. There was no indication anyone had been in the area for a long time. But he knew. She was in there.

And so was Zachary.

His elation at finding her matched the killing rage he felt toward the old man. If Zachary had harmed her in any way …

On silent tread Lyon moved into the dark interior of the cave. He remained in jaguar form, better to fight if he had to. His jaguar sight adjusted instantly to the blackness but it wasn't necessary. Farther into the cave a pale light shone from around a corner. He moved toward it, acutely alert to any danger. Kitlene's scent beckoned him, stronger now, yet Zachary's faded. The old man had left her alone.

Lyon rushed forward, rounded the curve of the cave wall and then skidded to a halt. Kitlene was on the floor, lying on a blanket, her eyes closed. His heart stopped and he had to choke down the instant icy fear that she might not even be alive.

He changed to man and rushed to her. He fell to his knees, reached out a shaky hand and touched her pale face. "Kitlene."

She opened those beautiful eyes and lifted her head the moment he touched her. Lyon had never felt such immense relief as he did then. He took a deep breath to calm his racing heart. He exhaled roughly and voice hoarse, asked, "Are you okay, sweetheart? Tell me he didn't hurt you."

"Lyon," she uttered his name in a worshipful whisper that caressed over his senses in a rushing wave, instantly leaving stark desire and hot need in its wake. His body hardened painfully. Just the sound of her sweet voice and he wanted her. *Damn. Now isn't the time for this.*

He was shaking again as helped her sit up. "What happened, Kitlene?"

She shook her head as she relaxed against him, curling her arms around his neck. "Zachary—"

"Is a dead man," he interrupted, dangerous promise in his tone. "Why did he kidnap you?"

"He didn't, Lyon." She looked a little confused but then shook her head again, wincing. "Ow. My head still hurts."

He pulled her closer and gently pushed her head against his bare chest. Sliding his hand beneath the heavy weight of her tangled hair, he rubbed her nape with soothing strokes. His other hand stroked firmly up and down her back. "I'm sorry about that, baby. But you've got to help me understand here, what happened. Where is Zachary and what part did he play in this?"

Kitlene's voice was muffled against his chest. Her words slowly registered and he suddenly choked out a gasp at what he thought he heard her say. "What?"

She lifted her head, her smile so sweet and sexy at the same time that he nearly forgot where he was and what he'd been asking. "I said: do you realize you're naked?"

Hell! In his need to reach her he hadn't even thought about clothes. He stared down into her eyes. Clearing a throat gone dry he murmured huskily, "Sorry." A little voice taunted him as soon as he said the word: Are you really sorry? She was looking into his eyes, her own darkening with something he was afraid to decipher right then or they'd both be in trouble. His voice was gravelly as he said, "Let go of my neck, and I'll get clothes on."

"I can't."

Gods help him but those soft, sensual, wicked words nearly killed him. He managed to choke out, "Why?"

Kitlene tightened her arms around his neck. Her dove grey eyes darkened even more, her cheeks flushed, and her mouth opened on a ragged sigh. He wanted to groan and growl at the same time. "I'm afraid to let go," she admitted. "If you're not touching me, then maybe this won't be real. Maybe it's just a dream." Tears welled in her eyes and he did groan then, the sound tearing from the deepest depths of him. "I prayed for you to find me, Lyon. I called out to you. And I heard your voice telling me you would find me. But it had to have been a dream. It can't be possible. What if this is just a dream I'm having now because I ... need you so much to be here holding me?"

His body shaking with the control it took to hold back, Lyon slowly pulled her closer, his arms tightening possessively. She was practically in his lap and he shifted her so that her sweet bottom fit directly on top of his hardening erection. Roughly he groaned the words out, "Does *that* feel like a dream, baby?"

She gasped softly, her eyes widening. But she didn't move away, and that acceptance was nearly his undoing. Lyon took in several deep breaths in a heroic effort to calm his raging emotions. It didn't work. "Kitlene, I'm sorry, baby." He had to release her now, or... never. She was too vulnerable right then. He had to be the strong one for both of them. "But if I don't get clothes on right now..."

He abruptly lifted her in his arms and stood up. Then, set her on her feet. Forcing his mind to think clearly, he instantly willed on a pair of jeans. It was a small respite, and he knew it. The scorching waves of hot sexual energy was flying between them, arching, targeting all the most sensitive spots of their bodies with invisible, direct hits of fire. A fire that was threatening to rage out of control at any moment.

Desperate for some sense of that rapidly slipping control, he closed his eyes for a long moment. His whole body shook with the strength of will it took to keep from pulling her back into his arms. "Talk," he spit out hoarsely. "Tell me what happened."

Kitlene sighed and the sound whipped through him like a painful arc of electricity. He made himself listen to her words, not her soft sweet voice. He concentrated on what she was saying but then forced back another groan as lust punched him in the gut once again ignoring his valiant efforts. "I had a headache from the storm," she told him, rubbing at her temples. "Jade was looking for pain meds for me when it suddenly got worse and I nearly blacked out. Then a maid came in—at least I think she was a maid. She gave me something for the pain." She stopped and wrapped her arms around her waist. To keep from touching her, Lyon moved back a step. "Suddenly, I realized that the pill I had taken was actually some kind of strange drug. I could feel myself falling, deep, into this blackness that scared me to death. But I couldn't pull out. When I woke up, I was here. Zachary was with me." She turned wide eyes up to him, fear darkening the depths. "He said he was on his way here, when he saw someone carrying me into the woods."

"If he rescued you then why the hell did he leave you here?" He didn't like the unanswered questions. His instinct was telling him that something more was behind this.

Kitlene shook her head. "He said he followed them—there were three men—here to the cave. Then, he knew he wouldn't be able to fight them so he created some kind of distraction that would take them far away from the cave. He said he would come back for me when it was safe." She frowned at him. "I believed him, Lyon.

Zachary has never lied to me or hurt me in any way in all my entire life."

"Well too bad, sweetheart," Lyon muttered. "I don't believe him. When I get my hands on that old bastard, he's a dead man. I didn't smell anyone else's scent here—or around you—except for Zachary's."

"Why would he do something like this?" Kitlene demanded defensively. "He loves me. He's protected me for years from that darn destiny, kept me from being chosen time and time again. You have to believe me, Lyon. Zachary is innocent."

"We'll talk about this later," Lyon told her. He could see she was shivering, and was just now noticing that her clothes were still wet from the storm. "I want to get you back to the house. I'll find Zachary then."

"I won't let you hurt him," Kitlene stated, anger tingeing her soft voice.

Lyon took her hand in his and started leading her out of the cave. "Sweet baby. Have you forgotten so soon that I told you nothing would stop me from getting what I want? I want you safe, kitten. And I'll kill to make sure you are. So shut your beautiful mouth before I have to do it, and let me get you out of here."

She hurried to keep pace with his long strides. "Did you just threaten me?"

"Hell." Lyon came to a stop so fast she ran into him. "Kitlene, I'm trying to do what needs to be done, and that's getting you back to safety. We'll argue about Zachary later. When I can think straighter."

She stubbornly stood her ground, hands slapping to her hips. "What's there to think about, Lyon? I told you he's innocent. I would know if he meant to hurt me in any way. He's always loved me."

"Yeah, right." He glared at her, pent up anger and burning lust vying for supremacy. "He loves you so much that he still kept you listed as a candidate for some Alpha male to claim. Even knowing that your life would be forfeit with that claiming, he would still eventually choose you to fulfill your destiny. For that alone, Kitlene, I'm going to kill him."

His harsh words echoed in the small confines of the cave. He tried to calm his breathing, tried to get control. She stood there staring him down, defiance and sensual temptation all in one, and he shook with the need to take her right then and there. He balled his hands into tight fists.

"It's not his fault," she said, her voice sad and quiet. It spurred his anger.

"Damn it, it is." He couldn't stop the words and they spilled out of him hard and fast. "A man protects those he loves. He should have kept you away from all this. He shouldn't have chosen Ariel for me, knowing you'd come into my life. He knew, Kitlene. He knew you are my Truemate. And he knew that I would either claim you or I'd move heaven and earth to protect you from myself."

She took the step separating them coming up so close against him he felt her breathing. Slowly, making him hold his breath with the look in her eyes, she reached up and touched his cheek. He felt that soft caress all the way to the hidden part of his soul. "Don't you see, Lyon? You just explained his reasoning. He knew that if I was ever to stay safe, ever again, from the threat of being claimed then I needed to be in the one place, with the one person in the world who could and would protect me. The only man who would do anything in his power to protect me from any other. You."

The groan that tore from him was rough and harsh. He wrapped his arms around her and pulled her tight against him. Burying his face in the curve of her neck he breathed deeply of her sweet scent, shaking with emotions that threatened to unman him.

"Who the hell will protect you from me, baby?" He lifted his head. He stared down into her eyes and felt so lost it scared him to death. "I don't know if I have the strength. The thought of you being out of my sight, of being too far for me to hear you, smell you, or see you, scares the hell out of me. But, baby, what scares me more than anything is the fact that having you near is destroying me. How can I be your hero when I want you more than air to breathe?"

Tears welled in her beautiful eyes and it broke him. Groaning, he pressed his lips to her eyelids. "Don't. Please, Kitlene. Don't cry, baby. You'll kill me."

She leaned back. "I won't cry if you'll promise me something." She was trying, but the tears fell anyway and he couldn't kiss them away fast enough.

"What? Promise you, what? Baby. Anything. I swear I'll do

anything for you."

"Never let me go."

His entire body stiffened in shock. He swallowed hard, his arms automatically tightening around her. He couldn't believe she'd just said those words. It took every ounce of willpower he had left not to break completely.

"Kitlene. I've already promised that. It may be the death of us both, but there's nothing in heaven or hell that could take you away from me." He closed his eyes tight for a long moment. "I'm just not sure how I'm going to do it. How do I keep you with me ... and never touch you?"

She inhaled a shaky breath, the move pushing her breasts harder against his bare chest. His body tightened even more. "I know you will belong to Ariel." Her voice was raspy with unshed tears. "I know that being near you will destroy me. And the thought of going through the rest of my life without ever feeling your touch again..." Her tear filled voice trailed off. She hid her face against his chest and he forced himself to wait for her to finish. Scared to death at what she was about to say. Yet, needing to hear it more than anything. "I want something to hold onto."

The words sucked the air out of him. He placed his hand under her chin and forced her face up. "I won't claim you, Kitlene," he bit out harshly. "I'd die before I selfishly took what I want, no matter how desperately I want it, knowing what the end result would be."

She took him completely by surprise when she lifted up on tiptoes and kissed his mouth. The touch was butterfly soft but it still managed to leave shock waves careening through him. "I don't suppose you have ... um ... protection in those tight jeans, do you?"

He spit out so many expletives he wasn't even sure what he was saying. He finally calmed down. A little. "Are you crazy, woman? Do you realize how stupid it is to tempt a man whose beast nature is strongest when he's aroused? And I'm more than just aroused, baby. I've been on fire with desperate need since the first moment I met you." He made the valiant effort to clamp down on the lust that had flared to life with her words. "And damn it all to hell! No. I don't have protection with me. I can't believe you would even say that to me, after all I've admitted. Are you trying to be cruel, Kitlene? Or just deliberately stupid? I've spent all my energy trying to keep my hands off of you from day one. I've promised myself that I'd do anything I had to, to keep you safe from me. And then you open that beautiful mouth and utter words that nearly take me to my knees and have the nerve to look like it's the most casual request in the world." He growled rough, and shook her a little. "Why don't you just kill me now and get it over with."

"Kiss me. Please. Kiss me one more time, and I'll never ask another thing of you."

"Why are you doing this?" He shook her again. He was so close to the edge. Another moment and he wouldn't have the strength or willpower to resist. "Sweet baby. Don't you realize that if I kiss you I won't stop at just that?" Gods, he wanted her so bad he couldn't even think straight.

She broke the final straw holding him together. She leaned into him and whispered, "Kiss me."

Chapter Sixteen

$\mathcal{S}$he'd lost all her common sense. Any sanity she might have been clinging to. Any self-preservation she'd kept in reserve. And she didn't care. All she knew was that she wasn't going to lose this time, here, now. She wanted one taste of love before the end.

Kitlene hadn't told Lyon the full conversation she'd had with Zachary before he'd disappeared. She couldn't bring herself to. She was afraid of what he'd do.

Zachary had been there to rescue her. He'd known about the kidnapping attempt. He'd hoped to reach her before she was taken from Gwen's home but the storm had slowed his arrival. When he'd returned back to the cave to let her know he needed to lead her kidnappers farther away, he had taken the precious time to tell her the truth.

The kidnapping attempts wouldn't stop. The remaining women carrying the jaguar genes were being sought out. Someone was desperate enough to want to stop at nothing to prevent the women from bearing any more Jaguars Shifters with pure DNA. Zachary wasn't yet sure why someone was intent on eliminating the entire Jaguar people, but targeting the women only proved that the plan was in its desperation stage. And slowly succeeding. Already two of the women had mysteriously disappeared. What Zachary couldn't yet figure out was the explanation behind the fact that once the women were mated, they were no longer targets.

He'd left her with the warning to be alert and careful. And he'd promised her that once the Shifter's Moon Ceremony was over, he'd make sure she was placed in a safe, secure place for the rest of her life.

Waiting for Zachary to return to the cave she had the time to finally search her soul and decide what to do. She didn't want to spend the rest of her life hiding. Always afraid of an unseen enemy lurking. Alone and ... lonely. She knew, deep inside her very soul that if she were destined to die then she wanted it to be because she had given herself, body and soul, to the only man she would ever love.

Lyon.

If he knew the full truth, he'd still do everything in his power to protect her. But she knew that he couldn't. No one could save her from destiny. But, Lyon would die for her, to keep her safe at all costs. She knew that, with everything that was in her, knew it to the depths of her soul. And she couldn't risk his life. Or anyone else's. She would rather die because of his claiming. She wanted, needed to be his. Just once. Nothing else mattered.

Convincing Lyon that it was only once wasn't going to be so easy. She could see it in his dark eyes. His handsome features were flushed with stark desire, his sensuous lips thinned with holding back, and a muscle clenched in his jaw. His grip on her was painful but she didn't care. At least he hadn't pushed her away yet.

Instead, he groaned, the rough sound tortured. Holding her gaze captive with his, he lowered his head to meet her upturned mouth. Against her lips he muttered harshly, "Gods, help me."

He claimed her mouth with a ferocious hunger that stole her breath and sent her senses reeling with overwhelming desire and need.

He kissed her like a man starving, ravaging her mouth like he couldn't get enough. She melted into him, willingly opening her mouth when his rough tongue demanded entrance. He plunged deep, over and over, erotically mimicking the physical act of possession.

One hand clasped her neck beneath her hair to hold her still. His other hand smoothed down her back and cupped one jean-clad cheek. He gripped her tight and pushed her into him. His hard erection strained against his jeans and pressed into her stomach. She wiggled against him, wanting to feel more.

Lyon suddenly broke the kiss. She gasped in much needed air and tried to plead with him not to stop. He didn't give her a chance. Both hands reached down under her butt and lifted her.

"Put your legs around my waist," he demanded. She immediately complied and he lifted her, gripped her securely against him, and started walking back into the cave. With every step, his hard, jean-covered erection rubbed against the vee of her legs, hitting her mound in just the right spot to send electrical currents of hot pulsing need into her.

She was thankful for his preternatural senses right then because he started kissing her again as he walked and she could only hope he didn't trip on anything because his eyes were closed.

He ate at her lips with little stinging bites, and then followed with sensuous licks. She returned kiss for kiss, copying his moves. He growled his approval into her mouth, his voice hoarse and gravelly. "That's it, baby. Kiss me. Eat me. Because I'm sure as hell going to eat you."

He stopped walking. Kitlene felt the world tilt for a moment and then found herself lying on her back on the blanket. Lyon came down on top of her, full length. He was deliciously heavy and she wrapped her arms around his shoulders as he subtly aligned their bodies to a perfect fit. He rested between her legs, his erection pushing hard and thick against her jean-covered center. He stared down at her, his turquoise gaze hot and glittering with fire.

"There are other ways to make love, baby." His voice was hoarse with his need and she shivered at the look in his eyes as they darkened. "I can pull out before I spill inside you. But, sweetheart, you're going to have to help me here. Don't fight me when the time comes. Promise that, Kitlene, or I swear I'll find the damn strength to walk away from you right now."

No way was she going to let him do that. She hoped he would forgive her. "I promise."

After a long moment of searching her gaze, he leaned down and kissed her. This time his lips were gentle, coaxing, promising more heat to come. She moaned into his mouth and he answered back with one of his own. Their breaths mingled, their hearts tuned in to beat in perfect rhythm with each other's. The kiss went on forever.

Until the desperate heat built again. Lyon's hot mouth moved over every inch of her face, kissing and licking, then moved down to her throat and neck. "Your skin is so soft. Like a flower petal. And you taste like you smell—like orange blossoms. Gods, I love your scent, baby."

She wanted to tell him that she loved his too, but every time she opened her mouth to say something he would nip her in a sensitive spot and then lick it with a hot swipe of his rough tongue and her mind would go blank all over again. All she could do was feel.

Lyon moved down her throat, closer and closer to her breasts. The low-cut silk T-shirt she was wearing was still damp from being out in the storm and her bra-less nipples were pushing against the material. He stared down at them and suddenly grinned. Before she fully realized his intent, he leaned down and sucked one cloth covered nipple into his hot mouth. Deep into his mouth with a groan so sexy that it sent shivers of lust streaking through her entire body.

At the same time, he lifted up off her enough to slide both his hands under her T-shirt. He glided up her stomach and straight to her breasts. He released the one from his mouth the same time he cupped both breasts. He moaned and gently squeezed the soft flesh. "You're a perfect handful."

"It's because I'm your Truemate," she murmured with soul-felt certainty. "My body is made for you. Only you."

What made her say that? She felt him suddenly stiffen and she held her breath afraid he would stop. *Please, don't stop. I couldn't bear it.*

"Don't, Kitlene."

"Don't, what?" She knew what he was saying, could see the desperation in his eyes.

"Don't ruin this time for us." He frowned down at her. "If I stop and think, then I'll somehow find the strength to stop completely. And I don't want to stop. I need you, sweetheart. With a need so deep, so hard, so devastating that it's destroying everything decent inside me."

Her heart stuttered, breaking a little. She was going to inevitably destroy his feelings for her just to have this one chance to love him. He would never forgive her. She could hear it in his broken voice, and see it in the agonized depths of his eyes. He trusted her promise. She choked back the words she started to say and clutched him closer. "Then don't think. Just take now, Lyon. I promise it will only be for now."

After a long agonizing moment of indecision, he finally nodded his head. He kissed her briefly, hard, and then whispered huskily, "Let's get you out of these clothes."

"What about you, too?" She couldn't believe she could tease at a time like this. Her heart was racing, she was breathless simply from his look and kisses, and wasn't sure how she'd be able to stand much more stimulation at this rate. She just wanted him to claim her. Completely. Now.

He grinned sexily. "What clothes?"

She gasped. He was naked, again, hot and hard against her. She groaned, desire heating her insides like teasing, licking flames. "How do you do that? I wish I had Shifter talents. I think they would come in handy sometimes. Like now."

"Ah, but then you wouldn't be able to enjoy the sensual thrill of having me get you naked by using my hands instead of my Shifter magic. Trust me, sweetheart. This way is much more … fun."

And he proceeded to prove it. He slowly pulled the T-shirt over her head, his hands caressing every exposed inch. His mouth followed where his hands touched, hot and smooth against her skin. The heat in her body built, making her breath come in catchy gasps. Every time she moaned when he kissed a particularly sensitive spot he would lick the spot with a long, slow swipe of his rough tongue. And he would purr.

That purring against her skin was the most erotic sound, and the most exquisite feeling she'd ever known. She tangled her hand in his long hair and clutched the silky thickness as his purring mouth drifted over her throat then down to her breasts. When he finally took one of her nipples deep into his mouth, his soft purring vibrated erotically against her breast and she uttered a small cry of pure pleasure. "Lyon, oh that feels so good."

She felt his mouth grin against her breast. He rumbled a soft growl of agreement and then moved to give her other breast the same rapt attention. He swirled his hot tongue around the nipple, and then suckled deep, pulling hard enough she could feel the sensuous tug all the way to her womb. An odd restlessness was building deep inside her and she wiggled against him.

He lifted his head and stared down into her eyes. His eyes were turquoise shards of hot fire. Lust and hunger shone in the dark depths, stealing what little breath she had left. He slowly lifted off her enough to move his hands down to her hips. Holding her gaze he slipped his hands under the rim of her waistband and started tugging the jeans, along with her silk panties, down. He had to sit up to finish pulling them off. He threw her shoes, jeans, and panties over his shoulder.

He sat back on his heels to look at her, completely bare now. She had the feminine urge to cover her nakedness, suddenly feeling shy … and a just a little fearful from the look he was spearing her with. He looked like he wanted to eat her.

"Gods, Kitlene." His voice was reverent, hoarse. "You're so damn beautiful."

She took the moment to let her gaze caress over his nakedness too. He was so incredibly virile it took her breath away. Slender but muscled. Wide shoulders. Slim waist. Washboard stomach. Slim hips. And heaven help her … but she couldn't tear her gaze from his erection, thick and pulsing, straining toward her. He was bigger than she had thought possible. A tiny spark of fear streaked through her and she bit down on her bottom lip to keep it from becoming vocal.

Lyon's eyes told her he knew what she was thinking. He growled, a low, soft sound full of heat. "You were right, baby. Earlier. Your body is made to fit mine. You're my Truemate, kitten. I won't hurt you."

Before she could dwell on it any longer, Lyon lowered to cover her body with his again. His heat and hardness settled against her softness, fitting in all the right places. She wrapped her arms around his neck and buried her face against his chest.

But he untangled her arms and shook his head. "As much as I love the feel of your arms clutching me, baby, it will have to wait." He grinned sexily. Kissing her hands, he placed them by her head. "Keep them there for awhile longer." He kissed her lips, a fleeting touch that had her arching for more, but he grinned again and started another slow foray down her body, nipping and licking every inch with a mouth so hot it scorched her.

When he reached the tender, sensitive skin on her lower stomach, Kitlene's entire body stiffened, a gasp of pleasure slipping free from her mouth as she whispered his name, "Lyon."

"I want it all, Kitlene," he murmured hoarsely against her skin there. "I want to love you every way possible. Just this once. I have to. I want to take everything you offer, and more. When this is over, I want to know that there wasn't a spot on you that I didn't claim. Just this once."

She wanted to echo his words, but couldn't speak. Gripping her hips, he moved his mouth lower. Her breath swooshed out of her when she felt the first hot touch of his lips against her bare mound. She cried out, arching up. His hands held her down. "Shh, baby. Damn. You're so soft and silky. I could lick you forever and never get tired of the feel or taste of your skin against my tongue."

For long excruciating, pleasure-filled moments that's all he did. He kissed and licked the top of her quivering mound, over and over, sliding his mouth back and forth. She couldn't get enough air into her lungs, the incredible sensations streaked through her choking every breath she tried to breathe in.

Just when she was about to cry out in pleasure again, Lyon growled low and rough. Then, stealing what little senses and breath she had left, his mouth moved lower. His tongue, hot and rough, suddenly breached her and plunged deep inside.

She screamed then. Her entire body bowed, rockets going off deep in her from where he was devouring her with fast strokes of ravaging, hot, unbearable pleasure.

She twisted her hands in his hair and cried out his name. She couldn't bear the heat, the spiraling sensations eating her up. It was too much, too fast. He was relentless. The harder she tugged his hair, the harder he stabbed his tongue and sucked.

A molten wave of pleasure rose from deep inside her, taking her by surprise. It built in speed, matching the erotic strokes of his tongue, and she cried out again. Seconds later the wave crashed and so did she. Her body shook with the climax, the shivers so hard she felt them from her head to her toes.

She laid there, eyes closed tight as the shivers slowly receded. She felt Lyon move back up her body. His hand caressed across her cheek and his lips touched hers gently. She opened her eyes and met his hungry gaze. She lost her breath all over again.

"I want to taste you more," he gritted out, jaw clenching. "But it will have to wait. I need you now, Kitlene. I need to make you mine. Now."

She said the words then that her heart had known were true from the first moment they met. "I'm already yours, Lyon."

He groaned and laid his forehead against hers. "If I could, I would make you repeat those words forever. Damn it all. Sweet baby, I would beg you to say them forever."

Forever yours, Lyon. But she couldn't say it aloud. Never. After tonight, he would belong to someone else. And she wouldn't have forever, anyway.

She whispered instead, "Love me, Lyon. Please. Now."

"Yes," he choked out, his tone ragged, raging hunger blazing in his eyes. He shifted, grasping her hips tighter, nudging her legs apart with his.

His erection pushed against her center, hot, heavy, hard, and pulsing. She caught her breath, their gazes locking in that suspended moment before he would fully claim her. She saw herself reflected back, and ... saw something deep in his eyes that made her heart stutter and tears threaten.

She loved him. With all her heart and soul.

And she saw his love for her. Saw it as clearly as if he had said the words aloud.

He leaned down and touched his mouth to hers, his lips claiming hers in a kiss that promised forever.

At the exact moment his body claimed hers, their voices echoed in the other's mind and heart, saying the word that could never be spoken aloud again.

"Forever."

In one long thrust, Lyon surged deep into her. Tearing past the thin protective barrier and irrevocably taking them past the point of no return. She cried out against his mouth, tightening her arms around him. He stilled instantly, his mouth still drinking in her soft cries. Barely lifting his lips from hers, he said, "Shh, sweet baby. Relax. Take me in."

He moved, inching in deeper. Kitlene's inner muscles clenched around his shaft, and she gasped at the hard shivers that wracked her in pleasure-pain. The feel of his hardness pulsating inside her was the most erotic, incredible feeling she'd ever had.

"Can you take more?" His voice was hoarse, gruff. "Can you take all of me, baby?"

Yes. More. All. She wasn't sure if she said the words aloud or not, but Lyon moved then, sinking deep with a thrust she felt all the way to her womb. They both cried out, their voices and breaths mingling.

"Kitlene. Baby. Yes, angel, take me all the way. Clench tight, sweetheart. Hard and tight."

He moved his hips, pushing deeper into her. Slowly, he pulled almost all the way out of her and then suddenly lunged back in. Shock waves of pleasure-pain shot through Kitlene, and all she could do was hold on as his thrusts increased in pace, seeming to go deeper each time.

His fingers dug deep into the soft flesh of her hips, holding her and helping her at the same time to arch up and meet his thrusts. Their gazes stayed locked, seeing past all the physical ecstasy straight to the very depths of their souls.

A building force incredibly strong started in the deepest depths of her, stunning her with the ferocity. She couldn't fight the engulfing wave, didn't want to. Her body tightened, her breathing stuttered. Desperate, she reached for something she wasn't even sure of.

And then Lyon stopped. She choked out his name, shocked and aching with a painful need that had her shaking so hard her teeth rattled. He gasped in a deep inhale of air, rested his forehead against hers for a long moment, and then blew his breath out on a harsh exhale.

"No." His growl was rough and drawn out. "Not yet, baby. I can't let go just yet." He kissed her deeply, desperation and hunger in his lips. "Breathe with me, kitten. *Help* me."

Womanly instinct recognized the raging desperation in him. She could feel it in every inch of his hard body pressed so deeply into hers. His whole body shook with the force of willpower he was exerting to keep from moving. Their bodies were covered in a fine sheen of sweat, and a trickle dropped from his forehead onto hers.

She stuck out her tongue and softly licked at a drop of sweat on his upper lip. He groaned, the harsh sound torn from his throat as he took her lips again. He kissed her deeply. "Sweet kitten," he murmured against her lips. "I'll remember your taste forever. Gods help me, but I'll crave it forever."

He lifted slightly, pulling out of her. Kitlene tried to grasp him, her muscles tightening around his pulsing hardness. "Lyon, don't," she begged. "Don't stop."

He leaned down and bit her shoulder, then licked it soothingly. "Stop? Sweet baby, I couldn't stop now even if this cave was about to collapse down on us." He suddenly shoved in her again, deep, hard. She gasped, arching with the rough pleasure. His grin was hard and sexy at the same time as he stated with another growl, "I want this to last. As long as possible." He pulled all the way out again. Another thrust took him deeper than the last time. "But your grip is so tight, baby. So incredibly hot and tight. I can't think straight. All I want to do is bury myself so deep in you and be lost there forever."

"And you need to think about that?" She shook her head. She didn't want him thinking clearly enough to be able to control this moment. She wiggled against him, tightening her inner muscles before he could pull out again. She knew her next words would either stop him or force him to lose control. She was hoping for the latter. "We only have this moment, Lyon. We'll never have it again. Take it all. Take me any way you want, only don't stop."

"Kitlene," he growled, her name sounding like a prayer and a curse in one.

Before she could say anything else, he suddenly sat up and leaned back on his knees. He scooped his hands beneath her lower back and lifted her upper body against his chest. With her legs wrapped around his waist, she straddled him in this sitting position and it opened her even more to him, pushing him even deeper into her.

"Hang on, baby." It was the only warning she got. His strong hands lifted her, helping her arch, as he thrust fast and hard into her. She locked her arms around his neck and held on tight.

The impending orgasm rose up surprisingly fast from the deepest part of her womb, painful in its breath-stealing intensity. She cried out his name. He suddenly took them to the floor again, pinning her there as his thrusts increased. Then, twisting his hips, he touched against the most sensitive spot in her. She exploded, hearing his harsh, hoarse demand ring in her ears, "Give it all to me, Kitlene. All of you. Now, baby. Now."

The climax hit her so hard she screamed.

Wave after ecstatic wave hit her. Taking her under ... and then throwing her adrift into an invisible, undulating sea of white-hot pleasure.

She didn't have time to recover. Couldn't even catch her breath before Lyon was moving again. He groaned, long and rough, as he started his hard, fast thrusts all over. As the waves built again and raced through her, Kitlene rose up to meet his thrusts, tightening around him as hard as she could and crying out his name over and over again. She clung to him, inner muscles as tight as possible so that he wouldn't be able to break free at the last moment.

Another orgasm hit, harder than the last. She screamed, her voice hoarse. But Lyon's roar drowned her out. It echoed off the walls of the cave, loud and harsh. He stiffened, and then with one hard, deep thrust, he exploded in her, his ferocious release shaking her to the very depths of her soul.

He collapsed against her, burying his face in her neck. His harsh breathing was hot against her skin. His body continued to spasm with the lingering waves of his climax. Her arms trembled as she wrapped them around his back. Her own body still shook from their simultaneous release. She was having a hard time trying to calm her breathing. Lyon was still deep in her, and she had a brief moment to pray that he wouldn't move. That he would stay. And take her again. And again.

Heaven help her. He hadn't pulled out at the last moment.

There was every possibility she could get pregnant.

Lyon suddenly stiffened. His head jerked up and he stared down into her face. His eyes were wild. His features were set in rage. He gripped her shoulders with a painful grasp that she knew would leave marks later.

"Damnation! Hellfire!" His whole body shook with his wrath. "Kitlene. Gods!" He cursed, words so foul and full of self-hatred and rage that it shocked her beyond belief. She couldn't get her throat to work, couldn't stop him long enough to try and calm him.

He suddenly released her and lunged to his feet. Right before her eyes he instantly changed into jaguar. Roaring with rage, he raced across the floor of the cave.

And slammed head first into the cave wall.

Kitlene screamed, horrified. "Lyon, stop!"

The big cat backed up and then rammed into the cave wall again. Over and over. Kitlene screamed again and surged to her feet. Shaking harder than she'd ever done in her life, she ran over to jump in front of the cat just as he made another lunge at the wall. "Lyon, stop. Now! Stop, or I swear I'll—"

He skidded to a halt, sides heaving, dangerous, ferocious growls rumbling from his throat. Blood dripped from his face. She could only stare, horrified, as their gazes locked and she saw the depths of his rage and despair shining in his eyes.

Tears blinded her. Choking back a cry, she sank to her knees to the dirt floor. "Oh, God. Lyon. Please. Stop. Don't do this. It was my fault. All my fault." She covered her face with shaky hands, the words spilling out fast. "Forgive me. Please! I ... wanted you to do this. I needed it. More than anything. It was my only chance. Forgive me. Please, Lyon. Don't do this to yourself. I can't bear it."

She felt a stir in the air and then moments later she heard her name whispered brokenly. She lifted her head and saw him standing in front of her, man once again. She wanted to jump up and run into his arms. But the look in his eyes kept her still. Oh God help her, but she couldn't bear his anger...or his hatred. She felt like she was dying inside, it hurt so much.

"It wasn't your fault, Kitlene." His voice was low. Dead almost. It made her shiver and want to start crying all over again. "I knew I was taking a chance in not being able to stop at the last moment." He straightened his shoulders and then exhaled harshly. "I swore I would protect you with my life. And now I've broken that vow."

He slowly walked over to her. Then, bending, he scooped her up into his arms. She automatically wrapped her arms around his neck, but hid her face against his shoulder not wanting to see the look in his eyes.

"I'm taking you to Wren. If there's any chance that you might be pregnant, then he can give you something to ..."

Kitlene's head shot up. "Lyon! No! I couldn't do that. I won't. No matter what."

Lyon walked out of the cave, staring straight ahead, his features set in hard lines. His voice was controlled but tinged with fury. "Yes, you will. I'll see to it. I won't let you take this chance. You can fight me on this, Kitlene, all you want to. I'll tie you down if I have to. You can scream, you can cry. I don't care. I have to fix this before something happens to you." He stared down into her eyes, something dark there she couldn't decipher. "Don't you understand, Kitlene? I can't live with knowing that ..."

"It was my choice," she whispered, tears choking her. She couldn't stand to see the despair and rage emanating from him. It was destroying her.

"I won't lose you, kitten. I don't know how the hell we're going to live together, but it's going to happen. Even if I have to leave you with Gwen and be satisfied to know you're near. I won't let you go, and you will live." He growled, the sound ragged.

"You will live, Kitlene. Because, sweetheart, if you die … then so do I."

Chapter Seventeen

$\mathcal{L}$yon carried his precious burden through the forest back toward the manor. He concentrated on taking one step at a time, careful not to slip on the muddied, rain soaked ground. If he kept his mind on getting Kitlene back to the house as quickly and safely as possible then he wouldn't have time to think about other things.

Like ... how it had felt in that soul-encompassing moment when she had given herself to him completely.

He'd died in her arms, buried so deep in her sweet body, so lost he didn't care if he ever found his way out again.

And then he'd died a thousand deaths again when the realization hit him what he'd done.

He'd sworn to himself, and promised her, that he'd pull out at the last moment. But when that moment came, he was already so lost in her he had no other thought than taking them both to that incredible, heaven-haven where their souls joined.

The rage that had taken over when he realized what he'd done had left him reeling with horror. Pure instinct had him changing to jaguar. Pure self hatred had him slamming himself head first into the cave wall.

But her voice had finally stopped him. Her sweet, soft voice begging him to stop. Defeated, feeling dead inside, he'd changed back to man. Seeing her standing there, frightened, crying, had nearly destroyed him all over again.

She was his Truemate. He was sworn, heart-body-soul to protect her. Cherish her. Love her. And yet it was his love that would now surely kill her ...

No, dammit. She was going to live! He'd move heaven and earth, and fight hell itself if he had to but he was not going to let her die.

He'd take her to Wren. The physician would know what to do to make sure that she couldn't stay pregnant. And it didn't matter how hard she tried to fight him on this. She might not even find it in her heart to forgive him. That thought hurt, but he resolutely shoved it aside.

Then later, he'd make sure she was safely settled with Gwen.

And no matter how much it killed him, he would never touch her again.

•

Lyon heard the sounds of the battle long before they reached the edge of the forest line. He carefully put Kitlene on her feet. "Stay here," he commanded. He hurried forward, keeping close to the thick clump of trees in front of him. When he reached the very edge of the forest he sank to the ground and crawled forward a few more yards.

Despite the hard pouring rain and moonless night, Lyon's cat eyes were able to clearly discern the fight raging across the front lawn of the estate. There had to be at least twenty of his own men fighting as men instead of in their jaguar forms battling against thirty or more other men—humans.

What the hell was going on?

He fought back the immediate urge to charge into the fight. He had to get Kitelne safely into the house first. He turned around and hurried back to where he'd left her. He saw her face turn very pale as soon as she looked at him. He just hoped she wasn't going to fight him about getting her to safety first.

"What is it? I can hear the noise from here."

"A fight," he stated tersely. "I'm going to find a quicker path to the house." He grabbed her hand and pulled her toward a trail that led north of where they'd been walking. His mind raced with questions. Who had attacked, and why? Their smell was obviously human, but that fact only made him more confused.

The rain fell harder, forcing him to slow down so that Kitlene wasn't stumbling on the muddied path. He glanced up at the stormy sky. This storm was nastier than anyone had first realized. He briefly touched on the mental thought that maybe it wasn't entirely a natural storm. He growled under his breath. That thought certainly didn't need dwelling on.

Animal instinct led him in the right direction and within minutes they came out of the forest right into the backyard of the estate. Grasping Kitlene's hand tighter, Lyon broke into a hard run. They reached the back door entrance just as it swung open to admit them. Shoving Kitlene in ahead of him, Lyon swung around and closed the doors.

Gwen, Jade, and Ariel stood just inside the foyer. Ariel rushed to her aunt and wrapped her arms around her, crying. The first words out of his mouth were for Kitlene's welfare. Turning to Jade, he ordered, "Get Wren here. Now. No matter what the hell is going on out there. Tell him I said come in the back way. Do it, now, Jade, dammit."

He swung to face his aunt. "What the hell is going on, Gwen?"

She frowned ferociously at him. "That's Aunt Gwen to you, young kit." She waved her hands, anger apparent in every line of her body. "And it's a damn battle. Right in my front yard! Caleb showed up just ahead of a group of men hot on his tail. He was able to tell us some of what was going on before they arrived. Luckily, Mason had just come in while Caleb was explaining. He called the Club but Beau said there were only a few of your men there. Still, they all hightailed it here and managed to arrive just as those human trespassers were breaking down the gates." She growled. "I don't know what they were up to, but a fight immediately broke out between them and your men."

"Why were they following Caleb? Did he tell you?"

"He didn't have time to explain very much. He and Mason dashed out of here to join the fight. He said something about Zachary and a discovery."

Zachary. Lyon swallowed his growl. That man was just as good as dead when he finally got hold of him. He glanced at Kitlene. Just another reason for her not to forgive me.

He started for the door. He needed to be out there with his men. "Keep the women in here, Aunt Gwen. I'm trusting you to keep them safe."

"Smart-ass cat," his aunt muttered as he stepped out the door. He hid his grin at her words. "Just let someone try to come in here."

Just as he stepped out into the raging storm Kitlene called out his name. He froze. He slowly turned around to look at her, already knowing she would have tears in her beautiful eyes. "Don't, baby. You know your tears can kill me." He hardened his resolve. "I'm not changing my mind. Wren will be here soon and I want you to cooperate with him. It has to be this way, Kitlene. We both know there's no other solution."

He closed the door behind him before she could reply. Damn but that agonized look on her face and the tears in her eyes was almost enough to destroy him. It took a lot of willpower to walk away from her.

He joined the fight, rushing in with the hot rage that was still dwelling, still boiling in the beast inside him. He slammed into the nearest man, taking them both down. They grappled, throwing punches. Lyon had the advantage. He could change his fists into claws, the flesh-tearing nails on his hands causing more damage in mere seconds than a fist ever could. His moment came when he rolled the man under him. One deep swipe across the man's throat was all it took to kill him. Then, he was up and running to the next opponent.

The humans outnumbered his warriors, but they were weakly matched against the ferocity of the Shifters. Another human hit Lyon from behind and he fell to his knees. The man was on him instantly. He was a bigger, tougher opponent. As they fought, each trying to gain the advantage, Lyon realized the man was fighting with an odd kind of manic ferocity. He didn't have time to dwell on it. The two men struggled, unable to get the upper hand on the other.

The man managed to stay on his back despite Lyon's hard maneuvers to dislodge him. One beefy arm wrapped around Lyon's throat and tightened in a deadly grip. His breath left his lungs in a choked swoosh and his vision started to turn grey then black. With supernatural strength fueled by his killing rage, Lyon grabbed the man's arm and snapped it in two.

His opponent bellowed in pain and rage and fell away from him. Lyon swung around, claws extended, and struck. He hit him so hard, the man's head snapped back and blood spurted in gushes everywhere. He fell dead at his feet.

"Lyon! The house!" Mason's hoarse shout penetrated the killing haze swamping his senses and Lyon swung around to look in the direction of the manor. Three men ran, faster than humans should be able, right to the front door. As one unified weapon they hit it with such amazing force it broke, the wood splintering down the middle and leaving a gaping hole. Before he could even move, they were tearing the remaining wood apart with their bare hands and pushing into the interior of the house.

Lyon ran. Faster than he'd ever run in his life. The fear and rage controlling him then was enough to make his feet fly across the ground. He hit the foyer and skidded to a halt so fast his head swam for a brief moment. He heard a scream from the back of the house. Kitlene! He bellowed, his roar shaking the walls. He rushed down the long hall to the back. Jade and Ariel were screaming now, and he hadn't heard any more from Kitlene. His heart threatened to stop. Was she already hurt?

He dove into the room, roaring his rage. He took the closest man down, slicing the back of his head wide open. He jumped to his feet and swung around to a shocking sight. He froze where he stood.

Jade and Ariel had one of the men down on the floor between them. They were ferociously beating him with their fists and landing bone-breaking kicks to every vulnerable part of his body. He was fighting back, but it was already obvious he wasn't going to come out of that battle alive. There was certain death in their yells and punches.

But it was Kitlene he couldn't tear his gaze from. She had her arm locked around the other man's neck, his back to her. Her other arm was clamped around his waist. She was holding a knife across his throat.

Lyon had to blink fast and clear his vision to make sure he was seeing this right. His fragile, sweet, little Truemate was holding an already bloodied knife against her attacker's throat and saying with a voice cold enough to still the bravest heart, "Move and I'll finish slicing your throat open."

Lyon choked as love, pride, and awe swallowed him whole and left him shaking in his boots. Sudden energy-stealing adrenaline swamped his senses, and he slumped back against the wall behind him. Painful nerve tingling relief poured through his veins.

Lyon heard Gwen's words as her voice broke through the haze keeping him stunned. "That's my girls," she stated with obvious pride. "I couldn't be more proud. What do you think, Alpha? Are they as good as any of your warriors, or what?"

He couldn't help it. He laughed. It broke free from him in a startled burst and he doubled over with the force of his relief sounding in his mirth. He laughed until he almost cried. He stopped short of that. After all, Alphas did not cry! But he laughed until his breath was catchy and he had to straighten up and try to breathe again.

Mason and Caleb came running in, and they too skidded to a sudden stop, their faces expressing their shock. Jade and Ariel were standing over one dead man and the other man that Kitlene was holding was looking like he very much wished he were dead, too.

"Gods," Mason breathed out in awe. Caleb slumped against the wall beside Lyon.

"I'm scared, Lyon," Caleb whispered, his tone sounding more reverent than anything else. "I'm not sure I'm ready to see something like this. Who turned our women into killing machines? When did that happen?"

Lyon couldn't answer. He couldn't tear his eyes from Kitlene's. Their gazes were locked with a scorching heat so tangible he could feel it like an invisible thread tying them together across the room. He was torn between stomping over there and killing the man she held captive, or pushing him aside and taking her into his arms to kiss her senseless. He wanted her in his arms so bad at that moment that he had to fight his urge and stand still. He balled his hands into fists.

Instead he looked deep into her eyes and slowly nodded his head, a smile creasing his lips. "Baby, remind me to never make you mad at me."

"Don't worry," his Truemate replied softly albeit a little weakly. "You can count on it."

Beau and several other men came in. "The fight is over, you deserters," he told Lyon, Mason and Caleb. Then his expression sobered. He looked at the man Kitlene still held captive. "He's the only one left alive. Kill him or question him?"

Lyon debated on the merits of just killing the bastard. He'd intended to hurt Kitlene, and that alone was enough to sentence him to death. But he needed answers. First. "If he isn't willing to talk, kill him."

Beau grinned at Kitlene. "You did good, honey. But it's my turn now. Hand the bastard over. Nice and easy. That's it." He grabbed the man by the back of his bloodied neck and escorted—shoved—

him out of the room.

Lyon, so attuned to her, was across the room in a flash as she suddenly slumped and fell forward. He caught her up into his arms. She cried out and his heart stopped, shock stilling him with icy cold fear.

"He cut her before she could take the knife from him," Gwen told him shakily, her fear now evident. "He caught her off guard when he came up behind her. He didn't realize she was hurt because she went into instant fighting mode and took his knife. We were afraid to say anything until you had him in control. If he'd known she was hurt, he might have been able to kill her before any of us could have reached her."

Kitlene hid her face against his neck. "It's just a little cut. I'm fine. And don't tell Beau. He said I did good."

Lyon felt the warmth of her blood coating his arm, near her left shoulder. The damn bastard had struck her in the back! Choking back fear he spit out orders, fast and furious. "Damn it, Kitlene. Caleb, find Wren! He should be on his way. Gwen, get your first aid kit. Jade, help me here."

He carried her over to a long sofa and carefully laid her down. She winced, biting her lip. He cursed again. Careful of her injury he helped her turn over and lie on her stomach. His whole body clenched painfully when he saw the amount of blood soaking her back.

"Lyon," Gwen's voice was firmer now. "It really isn't anything worse than a superficial cut. Calm down, or you're going to upset her. And she's been so brave until now. Stand back and let me clean the wound."

Lyon growled out a wordless threat. Mason stepped forward and laid a hand on his shoulder. "Move back, man. Do it, for Kitlene."

It took every thing he had in him to step away from her when all he wanted to do was take her in his arms and hold her, keep her safe. Damn. He couldn't keep going through this. He was going to break. And then … all hell was going to break loose too.

She was his whole world. The mental litany mocked him, taunted him. He realized he was still growling when Kitlene raised her head and looked up at him. She smiled weakly. "I'm fine. Stop being so dramatic."

Damn if he didn't want her then more than ever before. Her

spunk renewed the fire always simmering in him. He tamped it down; now wasn't the time or place for those kind of thoughts or feelings.

Hell, he thought with a frown, would it ever be again?

He hovered over her as Gwendolyn changed her hands into claws and carefully sliced Kitlene's T-shirt off her back. Jade came rushing back into the room carrying her medical kit in her shaking hands. She pushed Lyon aside with the curt demand, "Move it, cat. Your hovering isn't helping any."

If Lyon hadn't been so worried that hurting Jade might also hurt Kitlene, he'd have willingly choked the smart mouthed woman. Instead, he backed away a few steps and muttered to Mason, "Some one needs to tame that woman."

Mason glared at him with a look so nasty Lyon almost laughed. "Well, don't look at me to volunteer. I'm not stupid."

Kitlene winced when Jade started cleaning the wound. "Be careful," he warned the woman. "Make her cry out again and I'll have your hide."

Jade sent him a glare, managing to smirk at him too. "I keep reminding you, cat, that I don't have a hide. Go threaten someone else."

Mason smartly clamped a hand on his arm and pulled him farther away. "Let's go see if Beau's unique questioning techniques have gotten any answers out of the prisoner."

Lyon caught Kitlene's gaze with his. "I won't be far," he promised softly.

•

The prisoner wasn't talking and no matter what Beau did, he couldn't get even a grunt out of him. Lyon finally gave the order for his execution, thinking the threat might make the man talk. He died with a determined look on his face.

"What the hell was this all about?" He told Beau to go meet Caleb and Wren and make sure they got to the mansion safely. He paced the floor, his thoughts divided by his worry for Kitlene and the possibility of a new, unknown threat. "Those men were completely human."

"Caleb mentioned something about Zachary," Mason told him. "Did you find any signs of him in the forest?"

"Kitlene says he rescued her from her kidnappers." Lyon

frowned, recalling his realization upon entering the cave to find Kitlene alone. "But I didn't smell anyone around her, with the exception of Zachary. I should have been able to scent a human. She also said there were three kidnappers and that Zachary led them away from her. Damn rainstorm washed away any tracks that might have been there earlier. I doubt we'd be able to go back and pick up any kind of trail." He stopped short of slamming his fist into the wall as frustration built inside him. "Zachary disappears for weeks and then suddenly shows up in time to rescue Kitlene. I don't trust that man's motives. He's had an ulterior motive for everything he's done and set in motion lately."

"And you *should* trust your Elder, Alpha Lyon." The voice was deep and tired. Lyon swung around to see Zachary standing a few feet away. He growled and took a step toward him, fists balled. He stopped before he reached him and inhaled a sharp breath. Zachary smelled like death.

"Where the hell have you been and what's going on, old man? And why the hell do you smell like death?"

Zachary sat down in a chair. He sighed heavily. "You're not the only one who must deal out the death punishment to those who deserve it, Alpha Lyon." He looked at Mason. "Find out if Gwendolyn still has that special whiskey in her cabinet in the study. Bring me some."

He turned back to look at Lyon. "She is safe?"

Lyon nodded. "No thanks to you. She would have never been in danger if you hadn't brought her here to L.A. in the first place." His jaguar rage surfaced, slowly boiling to the danger zone. "You knew, didn't you. You knew she was my Truemate. Yet you chose Ariel even knowing it would bring Kitlene into my life." He snarled. "She says you love her. Knowing there was every chance her life would be forfeit you still allowed all this to come into play. I could kill you for that, Elder. Easily."

"I did what I had to," Zachary stated too calmly. His tone made Lyon angrier. "I had to sacrifice the one to save the many. You of all people know what that means, Lyon. Your sacrifice in taking Ariel as Mate instead of anyone else is something you are willing to do to save your Pride."

Lyon bit back all the angry words he wanted to say. Then and there he silently vowed that as soon as he was given full Alpha status he'd ban the damn elder back to South America. Permanently.

Wren came rushing in and Lyon pulled him aside. In a low voice he tersely explained, knowing the doctor would understand what needed to be done for Kitlene. His gut clenched as he told Wren, "Gwen says her injury is superficial. So, take care of the other situation first and foremost, Wren. Don't let her take any chances. Her life depends on it."

Wren nodded in understanding. "I could put her on birth control after," he murmured low.

Lyon could have sworn his heart almost stopped at the words. But he mentally shook himself. "No, Wren. It won't be necessary. I will be officially mated to Ariel soon and I won't make the mistake of ever touching Kitlene again." He bit back an angry, frustrated growl. "Just do what's best for her, and make sure she's safe from—earlier."

And later, when all this was straightened out, he'd make sure she was completely safe from him, too.

No matter how much it killed him inside.

Chapter Eighteen

Kitlene cried herself to sleep after Wren left. He'd given her something for the physical pain but couldn't risk anything for the mental pain.

Her heart was breaking. Deep inside she knew Lyon had made the right decision in forcing her to allow Wren to purge her of any possible pregnancy. But it nearly destroyed her. Even knowing what would happen if she became pregnant and carried the baby full term, she couldn't hold back the odd pain of loss.

When she woke, it was early morning. Yesterday seemed far away. It almost felt like a dream. Ha. Most of it was a nightmare. She'd never forget the fear surging through her when those men had invaded the house and tried to kill her and the other women. All the training Gwen had forced on her came into instant play and she'd somehow managed to fight back when one of the men had attacked her. She was still having a hard time believing she'd got the upper hand with her attacker and had him contained when Lyon had rushed in. But she'd done it. And was very proud of that fact. She could protect herself now.

A dull ache in her chest reminded her that no matter what, she couldn't protect her heart. Tears threatened again when the memory of yesterday came flooding back. Every detail, every moment spent in Lyon's arms for that too precious, too short time, would be forever stamped in her heart and soul.

She looked around the spacious, palatial room. Gwen had told her that she was to stay at the mansion now. Even Jade was going to take up residence. Despite the odd attack yesterday from the humans, Zachary was still insistent that the women would be safer with Gwendolyn than anywhere else on their own. Jade had agreed, but Kitlene was hesitant to make the commitment.

Just the thought of being near Lyon and never being with him again was enough to destroy what sanity she had left. How could she go on, day after day, knowing that he would never hold her in his arms again?

He hadn't even said goodbye when he'd left last night. Wren had given her a sedative and pain pill and yet she'd fought off the drugging effects hoping that she would be able to talk to Lyon one more time. She'd stayed conscious as long as she could. When she finally fell asleep the only person sitting by her side was Ariel.

Kitlene released a sigh. She had learned she was strong enough to protect herself from physical attack. Now, she just had to learn how to fight back the heartache that threatened to become so much a part of her if she let it.

She would be strong again. One day.

•

The closer the night of the Shifter's Moon came, the more anxious Ariel became. She was driving Kitlene, Jade, and even Gwen, crazy. She alternated between tears and temper tantrums. She hated everything and everyone and didn't hesitate to tell them all in loud bursts of crying sprees that lasted for hours. She'd also threatened to run away again, so Lyon left Caleb at the manor to guard her. And the only time Kitlene saw her niece calm was when she was with the handsome Shifter that guarded her with his life.

It didn't take long to realize that Ariel was falling in love with Caleb. Kitlene didn't know how the warrior felt about her niece but it didn't matter. Ariel was destined to marry Lyon.

And it broke her heart knowing that her niece had lost her heart to the wrong man. Just like she had.

Kitlene sat in a lounge chair on the back lawn, along with Jade, and they watched as Caleb walked with Ariel and tried to calm her down after another long temper tantrum earlier.

"Every time I see the two of them together I get angry all over again," Jade muttered. "They belong together. That man worships the ground Ariel walks on. What the hell is going to happen when she's forced to marry Lyon? Damn it all."

Kitlene chuckled softly. "Jade, you're beginning to talk like Mason or Lyon. Watch your language. Ariel is already picking up too many bad habits. Did you hear her growl at Gwen last night when she suggested Ariel try on her wedding gown for fitting? I almost choked, the sound was so real."

"Maybe that's the problem, Kit," Jade answered. "We're too complacent. We've accepted this whole situation without fighting back. When did we willingly give up our independence and our own rights to whatever happiness we want?"

Kitlene shrugged nonchalantly, but didn't feel that way. Jade wasn't saying anything she hadn't already asked herself a thousand times since—

Since she and Lyon had made love ... and she had given him her soul as well as her heart and body.

She thought about it for days after. And the closer the fateful day came for Ariel's wedding, the more she came to realize that her destiny truly did belong to her. She had to be the one who had the final say.

•

Zachary forced Lyon and Bryce to meet in neutral territory. They came, with only their Betas at their sides, angry at being summoned like children. The meeting destination was actually a weapons warehouse that belonged to the Pride. They kept all their cache of weaponry there and both brothers had full access to it.

Lyon looked around the fully stashed warehouse. The Shifter's Moon was only a few days away. He couldn't help but wonder how much of the weapons his men would have to use to wage a battle against his brother and men if the time came and war broke out to prevent the mating ceremony.

Hell. He wished that something would stop the damn ceremony anyway. He'd tried, unsuccessfully, to convince himself that he could go through with it and marry Ariel. He had to remind himself that his people depended on him. He couldn't fail them. If Bryce managed to become Alpha of the full Pride, their future would be uncertain. Lyon knew it was selfish to even think about wanting things to be different. But he couldn't sleep, couldn't even breathe without thinking about Kitlene. And how much he needed her to be his. Forever.

"Sit down," Zachary told them. He was sitting behind a small table with the other two elders. Their expressions were solemn, giving no indication what the meeting was about. Lyon sat, but his body remained tense.

Zachary looked at the brothers, and then waved his hand at the room. "Appropriate place to meet, don't you think?"

Lyon growled under his breath and heard his brother do the same. "Why the meeting, old man?"

"Your respect for your Elders is lacking, Lyon," Zachary stated dangerously. "Do not forget that we have the power to control everything here. Until you or Bryce is finally declared Alpha, we rule." He sat back and let the words sink in. Lyon gritted his jaw closed to keep from saying anything else. For the time being.

"We are here to discuss the threat hanging over the heads of the women." Zachary stated. "When I left here, I traveled to Africa. I had suspicions that needed to be dealt with. Unfortunately what I suspected turned out to be all too real."

"What does this have to do with the women?" Lyon couldn't shake the sudden feeling that what he was about to hear would mean more danger to Kitlene. His jaguar soul stirred to life, ready to protect her.

"In the past, we have kept the women's past, their family lines, secret," Zachary answered. "It was easier to protect them if no one knew about where they originally came from or who their relatives were.

"Kitlene's past, especially, was important to keep hidden." He stared hard at Lyon. Lyon fought back the urge to get up and hit the old man. Zachary continued, "Her father was a famous archaeologist. Her mother was one of the special women who carried the jaguar genes. Even though Adam wasn't jaguar, they met, fell in love, and then married in secret. When Leta died giving birth to Kitlene, Adam left. He disappeared, leaving the baby in his brother's care."

"What happened to him?"

"We thought he later died in a cave-in at a dig in Africa." Zachary shook his head. "Better for everyone if he had died then."

Lyon's patience was almost non-existent. "Explain," he demanded. If there was some kind of new threat to Kitlene he wanted to know what it was and how to fight it. Now.

"Adam was searching for a certain item when the underground cave he was in collapsed, trapping him inside. He didn't die. And he did find what he was looking for. Adam Skye found the elixir're demon."

"What the hell is that?" Lyon felt the cold hands of unease

skitter up his back. He didn't like the look on the Elders faces.

"It is a underworld demon long buried, held prisoner, beneath the grounds of a sacred burial ground in Africa. He can be released only after his 'rescuer' promises a sacrifice worthy of his help.

"It was a sacrifice Adam was willing to promise. His soul. In exchange, he wanted the supernatural powers he thought he needed to wage war against the Jaguar people."

"Hell," Lyon muttered in disbelief. "Why?"

"Because he wanted to prevent any more of the women from being sacrificed as 'breeding tools' for the jaguar. He wanted to protect his daughter.

"Since he didn't know where I had hidden her or Ariel, he began searching out the other women, hoping to be led to her. We thought the women's disappearance meant they were dead. But Adam was kidnapping them, one by one. In his own warped state of mind, he thinks he's saving them. He mistakenly thought that all the women carried the same defective gene Kitlene does, and that he needed to save them from getting pregnant.

"His wife's death broke him. He loved her more than life itself. And although his grief made him abandon Kitlene when she was born, he still felt it was his responsibility to protect her future."

"So," Lyon leaned forward, resting his elbows on his knees as he thought through Zachary's stunning revelation. "The humans who attacked were working for Adam?" The implications scared the hell out of him. It meant that Adam had finally located Kitlene.

Zachary nodded. "And they are only a few of his manic followers. He has amassed a very large cult following. These are men who believe it is their duty to rid the world of anything preternatural. More will come, and the kidnapping attempts won't stop. Adam will never stop until he's 'rescued' every woman. But his priority is Kitlene, and always will be. He'll kill to get her."

"He'll never get close to her," Lyon muttered dangerously. "I'll get to him first."

"Not if you're too busy fighting a battle with your brother."

Lyon growled, and stood. "Damn you, Elder. I'm at the end of my patience with you."

"Too bad. Sit down and listen." Zachary glared at Bryce who was standing too. "Sit, Bryce. Don't make me use my power to control you both."

Try it. Lyon wanted the old man to do something. Anything. He needed an outlet for the rage simmering deep in him, slowly burning its way to the surface. His jaguar soul rumbled restlessly.

"The rumors of war between Shifter races is very much a fact," Zachary stated. "Someone is trying to build an army that will one day strike at the human population and be able to win against them for dominance. Although plans appear to be escalating, in fact they are only now being organized. It will be many more years—decades even before a war of that magnitude can even become possible.

"The Elders and others will work against this ever happening. But we will need the help of the races. We must have unification. If the Shifter races spend all their time, energy, and resources fighting against each other simply because they don't agree on which side to join in this possible future war, then our ranks are already weakened." He gave Lyon and Bryce a long hard look. "As your Elder I am demanding that you two stop this fight between you. Now."

"We're not fighting," Bryce stated sarcastically. "Yet. We're just being vocal about which side to join. And that decision is not yours to make, Elder. Each Shifter has the right to choose. You know that." He snorted. "And you certainly can't go around killing every one of us who disagree with you."

All three Elders stiffened, their expressions darkening. Lyon felt the air in the room change and thicken. Palpable anger, strained tension, and even a touch of power circled like mist around the table where the three men sat.

Lyon stood, Mason following. Bryce and Holden stood then too. "My brother is right, Zachary," Lyon said, making the effort to keep his voice low and calm. He had the feeling that if any of them showed aggression they might not walk out of this meeting unscathed. He didn't know exactly what kind of power the Elders had, but with other priorities on his mind just then, he didn't want to chance finding out the hard way. "Our Pride will be unified once one of us is chosen as reigning Alpha. But, that doesn't mean any of our people will have their free will taken.

"Hell. I don't know what we'll be facing in this possible war," he ground out. "But I'll be damned if I force anyone to choose a side." He straightened to his full height, and pushed back his jaguar trying to emerge. The beast was angry, ready to fight, and he knew this wasn't the time or place. "And once there is a reigning Alpha, your position of power recedes. Your authority in the Pride will be second, not first."

He turned away and started for the door of the warehouse, his strides angry. "I've got priorities right now that have nothing to do with your push to have us do what you want. Go recruit others. I don't want to see your damn face again until I have to at the Mating Ceremony."

He stomped out, and he and Mason got in the jeep. Lyon forced his jaguar back. But what he really wanted to do was release it. He just couldn't decide if he'd go after Zachary first ... or Adam Skye.

Days ago his only fear was keeping Kitlene safe from himself. Now there was a new threat to her and he hated the feeling of not being able to control the situation. His mind was racing. He could put more guards on her, and at the estate. Hell, he could make that place an impenetrable fortress to the maximum if he had to. He grimaced. Yeah, like Gwen or Kitlene would accept that move.

He could put guards on Kitlene twenty-four seven. And she'd come after him with a vengeance. The thought made him grin for the first time in days. His Truemate wasn't going to accept becoming a prisoner, no matter what he said or did in defense of protecting her.

The only solution was to find Adam and eliminate the threat to Kitlene ... permanently.

"Caleb is probably our best bet in back-tracking the trail of those men who attacked the estate," Mason said, breaking into Lyon's dire thoughts. "But that would mean pulling him off guard duty from Ariel. I don't know if that's the best idea." He frowned. "As much as I hate to admit this, Lyon, I have a bad feeling the only thing keeping your intended mate here, and sane, is my nephew."

Yeah, he'd already come to the same conclusion. Lyon didn't know what he was going to do about that situation. But right now it wasn't his main priority. "I have a feeling it won't be necessary, anyway. I think that attack was a test for Adam to see how hard it would be to get past any protection we have on the women. And that means he's closer than we think. He's planning his next move. I can feel it."

And Lyon would be ready for him. He'd kill the bastard before he ever got close enough to even touch Kitlene.

"The Ceremony is two days away," Mason said. "Do you think he'll try and hit before then? Ariel is his niece. And he'd be just as determined to protect Bryce's mate, Niki, considering she's also one of the special women."

Lyon made up his mind. Startling clarity and resolute acceptance settled deep inside him. He pulled out his cell phone and dialed his brother's number. As soon as Bryce answered he stated without preamble, "We need to talk. Meet me at the Club before you go back to the ranch."

It probably wasn't the best idea he'd ever had, but it was the only one he could think of that would save the women and permanently eliminate the threat hanging over Kitlene. The consequences of his decision would inevitably affect his people. It was possible that the change would leave them vulnerable in some ways. But he didn't really believe that would happen. The Jaguar Shifters were strong. They had survived against a world that had tried for centuries to eradicate them one way or another. He knew they would continue to survive.

•

"Zachary was right about one thing," Lyon told his brother as they sat in his office with Mason and Holden. "There is every chance that a war is imminent in the future. I don't like that our people will be indecisive on which side to choose when the time comes simply because they don't know which leader to follow.

"There isn't anything we can do to stop the Prophecy. Zachary was very adamant on the fact that the Alpha son born after the mating ceremony will be the one to lead the Jaguar to fight in the war.

"But it doesn't mean that this Alpha will be the only leader." He met his brother's calculated look. He could tell Bryce already knew what direction he was taking this. "We'll both have Alpha sons, Bryce. That's a given. But only one of them will have the birthmark."

Bryce slowly nodded his head. "And our mates will also bear a daughter each. Daughters that will carry the genetic genes that mark them as special. If we don't eliminate this threat now, our children will be in danger for the rest of their lives. What are you proposing, brother? I'm with you if you're saying let's hunt this Adam-bastard down and kill him." His eyes narrowed. "But that's not all you're suggesting, is it?"

It was now or never. If Bryce balked at the solution, then so be it. Lyon was prepared to fight any way he had to protect those he loved. "Our Pride is already divided," he stated. "I'm proposing that we decide here and now that we remain two separate packs. There's no reason why we can't live peacefully in the same area. We don't have to fight against each other simply because we don't agree on certain things. Maybe we were both meant to reign as Alpha, Bryce. Maybe two Prides are stronger than one. And just maybe it's time to stop those damn Elders from interfering and giving us ultimatums."

Dead silence followed his statement. Lyon kept his gaze locked with his brother's, and waited. Whatever happened here would determine the entire future of the Jaguar Pride. He knew the proposed solution was the only logical one. It was time to give his people the choice of which Alpha to follow.

And when the Alpha son was born with the birthmark, he would one day unite them all as one Pride and lead them into a future that may or might not include a war.

Bryce exhaled. "You're right, brother. I see the logic. We'll give the people the choice." He folded his arms across his chest, suddenly looking more relaxed than Lyon had seen him in a long time. "I'll keep my pack in the ranch area. You can have the city. There's no reason we can't be there for the other, should the need arise."

It took a lot of effort to keep his features neutral, but Lyon managed it. Right up to the last minute, he hadn't been sure Bryce would agree. Why the hell hadn't they done this months ago? "I have to say, brother," he drawled with a smile, "You seem a bit different lately. Don't tell me I was actually wearing you down and you were getting ready to concede until I opened my big mouth?"

Bryce grinned. "In your dreams, cat." He turned serious. "I've had time to think through a lot of things lately," he admitted. "My mate has a very smart head on her pretty shoulders and she's been working on my attitude too."

"Glad to hear it," Lyon said, and meant it. He straightened in his chair and tried to sound a little less Alpha as he said, "Before we go any farther, I think you should tell me about the countless Shifters coming and going at the ranch. What's up with that, Bryce?"

"The war, Lyon. Shifters are starting to hear rumors and it's stirring them up. Most of them are rogues without packs, or prides, or leaders. They're looking for direction. I've met with several different cat breeds who are moving here simply because they've heard rumors that the war will start in California. Some of the Alphas are even sending groups here to get firmly established in case the rumors are true. I thought I'd have a better chance at being on the 'inside' of the grapevine if I made sure it was known what side my loyalties lie."

"What about the African lions? The three I tangled with, and the set Caleb saw?"

"Troublemakers, to say the least," Bryce muttered with a dark frown. "I didn't know they intended to get rid of any opposing forces immediately. You, included."

Lyon swallowed back a growl. "Where are they now? Still at the ranch?"

Bryce grinned again. "On their way back to Africa with their yellow tails tucked between their legs."

Lyon shared his grin. "I think I'm beginning to like Niki very much. She must be an incredible woman to make this kind of change in you. You're the strongest iron-willed Shifter I know, Bryce. So, treat her right. She's obviously very special."

Bryce smiled at the obvious jab. "I already care about her, and despite the fact that she was forced on me, I'm beginning to be glad it happened that way."

Lyon's gut clenched. He was glad that his brother had accepted and now cared for his intended mate, but he couldn't help wishing it had happened that way for him too. He'd give anything and sacrifice everything if only Kitlene could be his, and not Ariel.

"So, that brings us back to Adam Skye," Bryce said. "My trackers aren't as skilled as Caleb is, but I will get them out there now looking for this bastard. Do you want to team up, or do this in groups?"

"I think we'll have better success if we team," Lyon told him. "I need to put more guards at Aunt Gwen's estate first. Maybe we should have Niki stay there too, until the Shifter's Moon Ceremony."

Bryce agreed and got on the phone to call the ranch. Lyon called Beau in and explained what was going on. Within an hour, every warrior available was ready and most of them were thoroughly searching throughout the city of L.A. before darkness fell. Cat Shifters hunted best at night, and this was their territory. If Adam Skye was anywhere in the city or even on the outskirts, he didn't stand a chance at hiding for long.

Chapter Nineteen

*K*itlene stood in the middle of Ariel's bedroom and stared in shock at the clothing shreds scattered across the floor. Ariel had taken scissors to her wedding gown. There was nothing salvageable even if they'd had the time to try and repair it.

Her niece had always been high strung, but Kitlene would have never thought she'd do something this drastic. She was worried about Ariel's state of mind. Quickly she searched the room, and finally spotted the scissors on the bed. *Thank God.*

"Where is she now?" she asked the maid standing at the door. The poor woman looked like she was afraid to come into the room. No doubt Ariel's theatrics had scared everyone.

"Mr. Trent," the woman hurriedly explained, "Caleb, madam, took her out for a walk."

Kitlene released a worried sigh. She no longer had any doubts that Ariel had allowed herself to fall for Caleb. She just didn't know what they were going to do about it. "Will you find Gwen and Jade, please, and ask them to meet me in the den? I think they're in the upstairs library." The women had been studiously searching the Jaguar history for days now after Gwen made the comment that something might be discovered that would help Kitlene's particular health problem.

On her way down the stairs, Kitlene had to pause for a minute and lean against the railing. Not sleeping and barely eating was starting to take its toll on her. She waited until the dizziness passed and then made her way down the stairs to the den. She hadn't been able to concentrate, eat, or even sleep since Lyon had left her after making sure Wren had did what he needed to do. She wanted to hate him for taking the decision from her, but she couldn't. Deep inside her she knew his love for her had left him reeling when he'd realized what might have happened after they had made love. He cared enough about her to want to protect her from the possibility of being pregnant.

She didn't have time to dwell on what might have been. Wren had made sure of that. And she had to concentrate on Ariel for now. If they could just get through the upcoming wedding before any more disasters struck ...

She walked into the den and over to the large picture window. Looking out, she immediately spotted Ariel and Caleb as they walked across the back lawn. Her niece was waving her arms, no doubt shouting at the top of her lungs. Caleb walked beside her, stoic and silent as he let her rant.

He really was the perfect man for Ariel, Kitlene mused, her heart breaking for her niece. He was brave. Strong. And he handled Ariel with infinite care and incredible gentleness. No matter what she did, he handled it. Kitlene wanted to cry at the injustice of it all. She had the feeling that Caleb was in love with Ariel too. And just where did that leave them all?

Thunder suddenly boomed. Kitlene glanced at the sky. How odd. Those storm clouds came up very sudden. Just as she was contemplating going out to meet Ariel and Caleb with umbrellas, the heavy, dark clouds opened and rain poured down in torrents. She started to turn away and grab the umbrellas when something caught her gaze. Shocked, Kitlene stared hard to better make out what she prayed she wasn't really seeing.

A huge, black shadow raced across the wide stretch of lawn. Straight toward Ariel and Caleb.

She gasped, icy cold fear shivering through her as she stared, frozen in place. The shadow was at least seven or eight feet tall, bulky like a man, but yet definitely not a man, or at least any human male. And she'd never seen any man move that fast.

Coming out of her shocked daze, she spun away from the window and ran out of the den. As she ran toward the back door she yelled for Gwen and Jade. "Ariel and Caleb are in danger!" She didn't have time to wait and see if they'd heard. Her gut was telling her to get to her niece as soon as she could. She had no idea what she'd do when she got there and confronted a shadow of all things, but she knew she had to reach them now before the threat did. Kitlene ran faster than she'd ever done in her life. As she ran toward Ariel and Caleb she screamed out a warning to them. But the wind and rain was too fierce and her words were drowned out. Looking to her left she saw the shadow speeding toward them and knew that it would reach them first. "Ariel! Caleb! Look out!"

The huge shadow seemed to thicken and become more of a solid form right before it spun into Caleb and Ariel. Kitlene heard her niece's terror-filled scream and her heart stopped for a moment. *Oh God, save them!*

Just as she was within yards of them she saw the shadow turn into a man. Yet, she wasn't sure he really was a man. He was as tall and as bulky as the shadow had been. He looked like a hulky giant, all lethal muscle. In the space of a heartbeat he swung out his massive arm and struck at Caleb. The Shifter went flying across the ground. When he landed he lay still. Unconscious. Ariel and Kitlene screamed.

Kitlene raced to her niece's side. Shocked and horrified, they faced the giant. His features were oddly human looking, though extremely craggy and harsh. Long blond hair hung below his shoulders, tangled and waving wildly in the roaring wind. And his strange, large eyes held them captive, unable to even blink. His pupils glowed red. Kitlene didn't know how she knew but if there had been any human in this creature at one time or another, there were no traces left now. Those eyes were demon eyes.

She was so terrified, she couldn't think straight. She knew she and Ariel didn't stand a chance of running. And after seeing what he'd done to Caleb, she knew they couldn't try and fight either.

Before she could form a plan, the beast spoke. The deep and raspy words that came out of his mouth shocked them both, horror clutching at their hearts, and they had to cling to each other to keep from falling.

"Kitlene. Ariel. I have found you."

Kitlene had to force the words out of her frozen mouth. "Who are you? How do you know us?" She was shaking so hard she was having a hard time even breathing. But she knew with soul-felt certainty that she didn't dare show her fear to this demon.

The giant made a sound in his throat, something close to a chuckle. His eyes flashed an eerie black for one long moment. Then, he answered, "I am your father, Kitlene. I am Adam Skye."

"No!" Kitlene heard herself scream out the denial. What

horrified her most was that she knew it was true. Somehow, some way, she knew. Her vision blurred, her heart raced, beating so fast and painfully she lost her breath. She fell to her knees, shock reverberating through her entire body. *It can't be true! This is just a nightmare and I'll wake up any moment. This isn't real!*

"Yes," the beast stated. "I have been searching for you for a long time. That old man, Zachary kept you safely hidden from me but even he knew it would be just a matter of time before I finally found you." His voice deepened. "I can sense your emotions and thoughts. I know that Zachary told you a partial truth and now you are realizing that he kept the most important fact from you. But, deep in your soul you know I am your father. Stand up, daughter. Face me now. I am your salvation. I have come to take you and Ariel to a safer place. Away from these soul-damned creatures. Away from the certain death you face in your future."

Kitlene closed her eyes. She pushed back the choking fear threatening to make her sick. She concentrated, hard, bringing up a face in her mind. Reached for the safety of his arms as she mentally whispered his name, *Lyon.*

Instantly, strong and clear, she heard him answer, *I'm coming, kitten. Stay strong, baby. I'll have you in my arms soon.*

She exhaled, suddenly feeling stronger. She knew that no matter what happened, this connection between them would always be there to give her strength when she needed it. She didn't know if they could really communicate like this but she had to say one final thing. Just in case he didn't reach her in time ...

I love you, Lyon.

There was a long silence in her mind as she waited. Had he heard? Was it only her imagination that she was connected to him this way?

Then—

Tell me that again when I get you alone. Sweet baby. Be prepared to repeat it for the rest of our lives.

The maniac giant claiming to be her father suddenly roared. Ariel screamed and fell to her knees beside Kitlene. Mouths open, they stared up at him.

"This can't be! You were communicating with that—that *beast* telepathically. How the hell did this happen? Has he touched you, daughter? Has he mated with you? I'll kill him! He has defiled you.

He has sentenced you to death!"

Kitlene forced herself to stand. She reached down and helped Ariel up. Heart pounding she looked into his glowing eyes and said, her voice oddly calm, "I am his Truemate. You are too late to save me."

"Don't, Aunty," Ariel choked out. "Don't tell him that." She bravely faced him. "She's only saying that to protect me. I'm the one chosen to marry him. Don't hurt her. Please."

The beast shook his head. "Hurting either of you was never my intention. I've come to save you both. I will take you away from here." His head jerked up and he swung around to look behind him. "We will leave now. Come, daughter. Come, Ariel."

Kitlene grabbed Ariel by the hand and they quickly moved back several feet away from his outstretched arm. "No! We're not going anywhere with you." She looked toward the front of the manor. Her heart raced with trepidation and joy. "That sound you hear is Lyon's warriors coming to rescue us. They'll kill anyone standing in their way. You should leave now."

He roared. The sound echoed all around them. For a terrifying moment Kitelne thought he actually grew in stature, his bulky form expanding and becoming more muscled.

She didn't have time to look closer. A ferocious growl, full of rage and death, split the night. She looked up just as Lyon made a running leap into the air and slammed into the beast. The force of their collision shook the ground.

The Shifter and the beast fought to the death. Because death could be the only outcome and they both knew it.

But, despite his horrendous rage allowing his own beast to emerge and fight like a ferocious, indestructible force, Lyon's six-foot build was no match for the giant, muscled man.

Kitlene watched in horror as her father managed to break free from Lyon long enough to raise his huge beefy arm. One hard blow landed across Lyon's chest. He flew through the air. He fell, slamming bone-breaking hard against the trunk of a tree. Then he lay still.

A scream lodged in her throat and Kitlene swore her heart stopped far longer than was safe. She couldn't breathe. Couldn't think. Grief engulfed her. "Oh, God. Lyon! No!"

She watched in horror as her father stomped toward Lyon. In

his hand was a long, gleaming knife. Through her vision-blurring haze she heard him shouting, "I will have his head. It's the only way to kill one such as he."

She didn't think. Didn't hesitate. She was racing across the ground toward them, rage turning her blood to ice and her fear into adrenaline. She made it split seconds before her father reached Lyon.

Lyon was regaining consciousness. Shocked, he looked up and shouted, "Kitlene, gods, no!" just as she threw herself over him ... and between him and the descending blade aiming for his throat. He couldn't shove her away fast enough. Adam's arm arced down, and the knife plunged into her back, near her waist. She screamed with the excruciating pain, blackness instantly swamping through her. She felt herself being thrown from Lyon's side.

The last thing she heard was the deadly, killing rage that came from Lyon's roar.

Chapter Twenty

$\mathcal{V}$oices called her back. Screams and roars echoed all around her. She heard Mason's voice as though from a distance, finally registered his demanding words,

"Lyon, stop, man. There's nothing left of him. Enough! Now! Control your beast! Lyon, don't make me beat the hell out of you..."

She tried to sit up and realized her head was lying in Ariel's lap. Then she looked up and saw Wren bending over her. She couldn't figure out what he was doing there. She couldn't think clearly—her mind was still in shock. Jade was beside him, her face white.

"Don't move, Kitlene. The bleeding has stopped, but I don't want to take any chances."

What was she talking about? Kitlene moved anyway and winced with the dull pain in her lower back. "What happened?" As soon as she asked, she remembered. "Lyon! Where is he?" She tried to rise but Wren pushed her back down. He pointed over his shoulder.

"I don't think you should see him right now. Bryce and Mason haven't got him controlled yet."

"And besides," Jade commented, swallowing hard, "All that blood and gore would make you vomit. I already have."

"Lyon—tore—him—apart. Tore him to shreds," Ariel stuttered, her words jumbling fast together as she glanced over Wren's shoulders. Her face was white too, and she looked like she was trying hard not to be sick. "Lyon sliced his head off. And every limb, too. It was horrifying, Aunty."

Ignoring the mental picture her niece had just painted, Kitlene released a heartfelt sigh. Relief swamped her. Lyon was safe. Thank God. Nothing else mattered now. She felt a warm stickiness coating her lower back. It hit her then; her father had tried to kill Lyon and she'd taken the blow instead. "The pain is dull." She looked at Wren and Jade. Clearing her throat, she asked, "Did the knife hit a vital organ and that's why I'm not feeling much pain?"

Before either of them could answer her, she heard Lyon choke out, "Let me go. Damn it, Bryce. Mason. I'm going to kill you both if you don't release me now. I've got to get to her."

Seconds later he was there by her side. She bit back a horrified gasp. Blood coated him, from head to toes. "Please tell me that isn't your blood," she whispered on a choked plea.

He pushed Wren and Jade aside and gathered her into his arms. "I'm fine, baby. How bad is she hurt, Wren? Gods, Kitlene! I died when I saw you throw yourself in front of me and that knife. If you weren't injured, I swear I'd turn you over my knees."

"She's fine, Lyon. She'll be a little sore for awhile," Wren answered. He grinned. "I think it would be perfectly safe for you to give her that spanking any time you're ready."

"What?" Kitlene and Lyon spoke at the same time. "Hey!" Kitlene frowned at Wren, "That's really mean."

Lyon's expression was shocked as he stared at Wren. "What are you doing here, Wren? How the hell did you know to come? And what are you talking about? She's fine? I saw that damn beast cut her!"

Wren's grin widened. He carefully reached out to untangle Lyon's arms from around Kitlene. "Let me show you." He gently pulled Kitlene forward, and then pulled away her bloodied blouse.

Everyone gasped. The blood from the cut was already drying.

And the wound was already healing.

Wren beamed. "It turns out that your Truemate's body simply needed your blood, Lyon. I suspected it when she had that reaction after we had given her your blood. I was afraid at first that we'd given her too much. It was a dangerous amount for anyone, human or Shifter. But I had to be sure of my suspicions so I took a sample from her when she was injured last time from the cut on her shoulder. I checked and re-checked the tests results. I was coming to get another blood sample from her today so that I could be one hundred percent sure before I said anything. Turns out, I didn't need any more proof than this."

"Proof?" Lyon's tone was low, hoarse. "What are you saying, Wren?"

"Because she's your Truemate, her body completely accepted your blood. And then went to work to destroy the defects in the jaguar genes she carries. Her blood indicates that she's almost as much a Shifter now as you are, Lyon. Her blood matches yours. And she doesn't carry those damn death genes anymore."

Kitlene heard Jade and Ariel crying softly. But all she could concentrate on was Lyon. His dark, hot gaze bore down into hers as he slowly stood up. He reached down and lifted her into his arms. The look that passed between them pierced her to her very soul. "Sorry I'm a mess, baby," he murmured as he cuddled her close against his chest and she wrapped her arms around his neck.

"Mason," Lyon cleared his throat, but his voice was still rough and hoarse. "Make sure there is no trace of that bastard left. Then, get the men out tracking down and destroying the rest of his group."

He turned away from them all and started carrying her back to the manor. Kitlene finally managed to gasp out his name, "Lyon?"

"Yeah, baby?"

"Where are you taking me?"

"To bed."

She gasped again. "But Wren said I was fine. I don't need to be in bed."

"I know, sweetheart. I heard what he said. I'll remember his words for the rest of my life."

"So? Um ... bed?"

He grinned down at her, so sexy, so primal male she lost her breath all over again. "First, I'm going to turn you over my knees and spank you. You killed me with that crazy stunt, baby, and I need restitution. And then, after I get out of these bloodied clothes, I'm going to take you to bed and claim you. Heart, body, and soul, Kitlene."

As much as the words brought indescribable joy to her heart and soul, she was still afraid. "I know it's safe for me now in case I get pregnant, but we can't do this, Lyon. It will only destroy me to have you walk away again."

"I'm never letting you go again," he told her, his voice hard. "I don't care what happens with the results from the Prophecy. If it means that Bryce's mate gives birth to the chosen Alpha, then so be it. You are my Truemate, Kitlene. I won't accept any other mate."

He placed a hard quick kiss on her open mouth. "I was on my way here tonight to tell you that. I was going to tell Wren that he would have to give you some kind of permanent birth control because I was never taking a chance with your life again. It doesn't matter to me that I would never have the promised son. All that matters is you, Kitlene. I can't live without you, baby. I will willingly sacrifice anything to make sure you are mine forever."

"But the Prophecy. Ariel." Kitlene's mind was racing ahead, still trying to sort it all out. So much had happened in so short a time. How could it all turn out so easily? "The Shifter's Moon Ceremony. What's going to happen if you refuse to marry Ariel?"

Lyon grinned down at her. "If I tried to marry Ariel, I'd have to fight again. And I don't want to be fighting on my wedding night."

"Fight? Please stop confusing me. I'm an injured woman, remember. I need comfort."

He growled softly. "Comfort isn't what I have in mind."

"I'm going to hit you," she threatened just as softly.

"Okay, kitten, sheathe the claws." He reached the back door of the house and managed to get it open without having to release her from his arms. "I am going to marry *you*, baby, during the ceremony. You. And I'm sure Caleb will be thanking me for that, right after."

"You know about Ariel and Caleb being in love?"

"Shifters are very sensitive. Haven't I proven that? Ouch. You pack a punch, sweetheart. Okay, stop frowning and I'll explain. I knew the truth when he brought her to the Club that night after tracking her down. His feelings were very visible even though he honorably tried to hide them. It can only mean that she's his Truemate."

He started up the stairs. "What a shame. All this blood on me is now on you too. Looks like we'll have to take a shower first. Together."

Kitlene kissed him. She put all her heart and soul in that kiss. And he gave all his back to her. When she was finally able to talk she whispered, "A shower sounds great. Especially since I'm hoping it will distract you from that promised spanking."

"Not likely, baby. I may be distracted for a long time tonight. But you can count on a spanking. I promised myself I'd do it. Just accept it as warning that I will never allow you to place yourself in harm's way again."

She sighed, her heart nearly bursting with love and joy. "I love you, Lyon."

He smiled down at her, his heart and soul in the words he murmured back to her,

"I love you, Kitlene. I'm never letting you go. You're mine. Forever."

•••

Epilogue

Nine months and various days later ...

$\mathscr{T}$here were four weddings the night of the Shifter's Moon. Then, months later, the two Jaguar Prides were more than a little proud to announce the various births of precious babies into their lives.

Mason and Jade Trent: a baby girl, Krystal.
Caleb and Ariel Trent: a baby girl, Beatrice.
Bryce and Niki Savage: twin boys, Brock and Neal
Lyon and Kitlene Savage: twins—
a girl, Carolene, and a boy, Blade.

Blade Skye Savage was born with the birthmark of the moon-and-jaguar, thus fulfilling the Prophecy of a coming Alpha that would one day rule, surpassing all past Alphas.

His father, although immensely proud, didn't dwell much on the fact that his son was the prophesied ruler.

All Lyon cared about was the fact that his Truemate, Kitlene, was healthy and completely safe after the birth of their twins. Forever safe. And forever his.

Kari Thomas

Kari Thomas has been writing for years. An active member of RWA's Desert Rose and Northern Arizona chapters, this multi-published author is a bookaholic with over 3,000 titles in her collection. She loves to research subjects like history, religions and the supernatural. Raised in Florida, Thomas moved to Arizona in her teen years, and still resides there.

www.AuthorKari.com

Also by this author!

The prophecy said she belonged to a stranger ...

For decades, the Wolf and Cat Shifter Clans of Washington State have been kept in peace by an uneasy truce and a favor owed between their leaders. At last, Damian is calling in that debt, and with it, his natural enemy Logan Cross has just become entrusted with the most precious of tasks: to retrieve the prophesied mate of the Wolf Prince and protect her from all others.

... She had other ideas.

Tara Stuart has always known of the powers that came with her birthright, powers that could either unite or destroy depending on the mate at her side to help wield them. She's been trained in the magick, her skills honed. But she would run far and fast before letting primal, seductive Logan Cross deliver her to a complete stranger. She believes her destiny lies elsewhere, maybe even with Logan.

ISBN: 978-1-934912-03-4
Price: $11.95 paperback

Breinigsville, PA USA
18 January 2010
230929BV00001B/8/P